Re-discover
kind of hu

LOVE and MISS HARRIS

COMPANY OF FOOLS, BOOK 1

PETER MAUGHAN

To the memory of Robin Cook, the Lords Maidstone,
Finch and Elm of that shared other country, the past.

Chapter 1

On a wall in the art deco Burbage Cocktail Bar in Shaftesbury Avenue, a black and white production glossy of John Gielgud stared out from among the other photographs, a prince of Denmark impaled on a throne, his eyes wide with stage horrors.

Jack Savage also saw the dead still, when sleep and his imagination made nightmares of them. And when he hit the man in front of him it carried the force of those who weren't there, who could no longer speak for themselves.

Reuben 'Books' Kramer's dove-grey trilby went flying, his tall, expensively tailored weight hitting the ground with the force of a sack of potatoes.

He was out briefly, and then lifted a hand, as if feeling for his hat, or his head, and struggled to get to his feet, his eyes wondering what had hit him.

It wasn't the first time someone had put him down. But when his eyes focused on the young man waiting for him to get up, on his expression, it was the first time he'd decided to stay down.

The look Jack left him with before walking away added to his humiliation.

'You'll pay for this!' he shouted, the blow mangling his words.

Jack was leaving before he was asked to, walking through a growing audience of the curious, followed by Titus Llewellyn-Gwynne.

'Jack. Jack, love,' Titus said, stopping him outside the bar. 'It doesn't do for an actor to chin angels. Even one who's fallen as low as this one. I didn't get a chance to tell you – he intends putting up the money.'

Jack put together what that meant for him, and waved it away with an abrupt gesture. 'Well, in that case I wouldn't have taken the bloody job anyway.'

'Art must stay aloof, dear boy,' Titus said, as if it were an obligation that he, if not Jack, was burdened with.

He leaned in conspiratorially, black-bearded and piratical looking, his Welsh-dark eyes in the half-light from the Burbage fluid with drama. 'But Jack, Jack, lad, have a care. I'd say Mr Kramer is the sort who keeps his wounds green. And is one for the shadows. Watch where you walk. Dear lad,' he added, lightly touching Jack's cheek like a blessing.

Jack had arrived at the bar, as arranged, after the time Titus was due to meet Books Kramer, to talk up Titus's credentials. He did an actor's job at being pleased to see Titus, and asking, as also arranged, how the filming was going.

Titus then introduced him to Kramer, who, after sizing up Jack's cheap suit, had barely bothered with the introduction.

Reuben, who had been a bookie's runner at the age of thirteen, had got his nickname from his days working as an illegal bookmaker in the back streets of South London. And then war broke out and Reuben, among the first at the table, had grown fat on it. After it, he had branched out into brothels, drinking and gaming clubs, and protection.

His accountant had for some time been suggesting that he diversify his investments, and an ad in the *Standard* offered an opportunity to do just that.

It promised a fair return on his money, and the glamour of the theatre, a chance to meet the right sort of people. It had led him to Titus and the Burbage Cocktail Bar.

Reuben, with a Manhattan garnished with a preserved cherry in his hand, had then given Jack more of his attention, his eyes going over his brown pinstriped suit again like a pawnbroker's, its cut worn like a label saying 'Fifty-Shilling Tailors'.

'The war's been over, chum, for the past six years,' he said.

Jack expressed surprise at the news. 'I thought it had gone quiet.'

Reuben lost some of his complacent smile.

'Well, I mean, still wearing that demob suit after all this time. Like a uniform isn't it for you blokes. Like the geezers you see working in their army and RAF blouses.'

Jack, ignoring Titus's attempt to change the subject, said, 'What were you then? Navy?'

'Now, Jack,' Titus started, and was stopped by Kramer putting up a hand.

Kramer's eyes had become still, as if he were listening, as if he had picked up in this place that was foreign to him a language he understood. He had felt, despite himself, despite his money and the swagger of who he was, a long way from the backstreet pubs of South London in this sort of place, this sort of company. But it was turning out to be just like home.

'I had a certified medical condition, as it happens.'

'Oh, yes,' Jack said. 'How much did that cost you then?'

Reuben tutted and shook his head, as if amused by him, by his cheek, a well-built young man but soft-looking, in his rollneck sweater, his hair untouched by Brylcreem, like some poet or artist.

He put his cocktail down carefully on the bar, without looking at it, his eyes, still amused, on Jack, and then moved. But not fast enough.

Jack was younger and fitter, and he had nightmares to shed.

He said goodbye to Titus and joined the Saturday night bustle on the avenue. The fire of a roast chestnut brazier burned on a cart in the gutter, the vendor's voice hoarse with selling and the weather, the shouts of other street traders, the smell of fish and chips and the sound of a barrel organist busking a theatre queue, the West End lit up again, back in business,

The top billing lights on the front of the theatres spelled out for him his future still, but his present had taken a step back, now he had thrown away his first principal part. He thought of turning off for Soho, for another drink and the company of his fellows in the French House pub or the Act One Club. But after considering what he had left in his pocket, carried on instead for Piccadilly Circus and the Tube home.

Emerging from Earl's Court station, he said hello with a wink to one of the street girls loitering as if waiting for someone at the entrance, and walked down to Prince of Teck Gardens.

The stucco on the porch pillars of his lodging house was peeling and there was a smell in the hall from the food cooked on the landing stoves. And the sound of a violin from the third floor back, where Mr Somovich, a musician in his Saturday night cups, wept over its strings for old Russia, the dirge-like notes speaking of home and exile seeping through the building like a melancholy mist.

Chapter 2

Jack saw Titus again a few days later, when calling at a theatrical agent's near the Windmill Theatre in Soho. He was on his way up to the third-floor office as Titus was leaving.

Before continuing down them, Titus waited for him to climb the narrow flight of stairs, where the glamour of the theatre turned into grubby whitewashed walls and no carpets. He posed on the small stage of a half-landing, leaning on a cane of black malacca as if waiting for a hansom cab.

He was wearing a velveteen Edwardian smoking suit of black and pale green stripes, a silk scarf, threaded under the collar of his shirt and blooming in full colour from his throat, and a wide-brimmed black felt hat which, Jack knew, pinned to the crown and with an ostrich feather added, had served for his Captain of Musketeers in *Soldier of Fortune*. Titus dressed largely from the wardrobe of his theatre.

'Casting another principal, Titus?' he said, putting a smile on it. 'Who's behind the desk today, Bubbles or the Ice-Maiden?'

'The Ice-Maiden. Although I remain convinced that under that chilly exterior is the promise of heat, like a laid fire waiting to be lit. But I'm not here with a job, I'm here looking for one. For me.'

Titus and two dwarfs tipped their hats to each other, the dwarfs on their way up to the variety agency, doing the rounds now the pantomime season was over, dressed like little gangsters in fedoras and sharp suits, and smoking cigars.

Jack smiled at them in a way he knew to be ingratiating. Dwarfs made him feel uneasy, exposed, as if his fly were undone or his shirt tail hanging out. He'd worked with a few of them for a couple of weeks at Pinewood Studios on the set of a circus film, and became convinced that they saw something from their height which was denied him at his, some absurdity of normal-sized humanity which they tried politely not to notice, but which nevertheless kept them secretly amused.

'For you? Why? What happened to the tour?' he asked.

'First you, dear lad, and then I happened to it. After you had left, Mr Books Kramer started pushing his investment in my face, obliging me to make it clear to him that his money entitled him to nothing other than any returns on it. That everything else was the province of art and the business of its servants, the director and actors. Art, sir, art!' Titus exclaimed, as if ready to defend it, his hand clenching on the chased silver top of the cane, an elegant sheath for seventeen inches of finest Sheffield steel.

Musketeer Captain de Granville, Jack thought, and winked at a showgirl edging her scented way between them.

'What happened then?' he asked, watching her legs go up the stairs, seamed stockings and a flash of petticoat lace like a promise.

Titus held out his cane. 'I was driven to this,' he said, as if in soliloquy, as if a dagger he saw before him.

Jack looked startled. Titus was a man of passions that could take off suddenly and in any direction. And one who had also known war, had seen its face close up across the mud of Flanders.

'You didn't – did you…?'

'What? Dispatch him?' Titus laughed. 'No, no, of course not. There was no need. I'd only drawn it halfway when the bounder turned and legged it, scattering drinks and customers. And I,' he added, pausing as if for a curtain to fall on the line, 'was shown the door.'

'This is my fault, Titus. I—'

'Nonsense! Nonsense, my boy,' Titus said briskly, off stage, the curtain down. 'It was bound to have happened sooner or later with a fellow like that. And later may have meant halfway through the tour. So you see, dear lad, you may well have delivered us from all sorts of dreary complications.'

About to continue on his way, Titus hesitated.

He had grown fond of Jack and feared that with nothing to do, nothing to discipline him, he might easily take the wrong road, if only out of boredom. He understood what war could do to people; he'd seen it in his own generation after returning as he had done from France. And Jack, he knew, had spent four years in a commando unit waging its own war, with its own rules, deep behind enemy lines in German-occupied Europe. And there was a part of him, Titus suspected, that had yet to return.

'Tell you what, dear boy,' he said, 'there aren't many hopefuls waiting upstairs. So if you should find yourself outside Lyons in Piccadilly in the next half hour or so, drop in and I'll buy you a bun.'

Chapter 3

Titus was having the tea leaves read by Dolly Burke in the kitchen above his ruined theatre, the Red Lion in London's East End. Dolly, her voluptuous figure clothed in an eau-de-Nil silk evening gown, shook her head regretfully.

'I still can't see a job on the horizon, darling.'

'Oh,' he said.

She grinned mischief at him. 'But don't worry, mate. I mean, it's not as if you believe in it, is it.'

'I don't entirely disbelieve in it either. There are, after all, more things in heaven and earth, Horatio—'

'And anyway, I might be wrong. I've been wrong before, you know.'

'You weren't wrong about Joan,' he said, gloomily accepting his fate.

Dolly blew out smoke from a Woodbine and laughed huskily. 'Darling, Joan chases after so many men she was bound to catch one of that description sooner or later. And every male according to her is the one. So cheer up, cock, the good old sun will shine again as it always does.'

But where Titus was it was raining still. 'First Hitler puts me out of business. And then, after spending money on that damn newspaper advertisement, I lose the only genuine response I had in the entire month. And now I am denied my hour on the stage, denied my art. How many more slings and arrows am I obliged to suffer? Perhaps it's time not to be,' he said, staring off. 'Time to end it. To—'

'Well, have your lunch first.'

'Time to repay God the debt of a spent life, and take a short walk to the river.'

'You'd only end up back where you started in this fog,' Dolly said practically from the kitchen range, feeding its firebox more coal from a scuttle. 'There's only dried eggs left, but we've got enough cheese so I'll scramble them. And there's bacon to go with it. Nice bit of back bacon.'

Titus, diverted, frowned.

'Bacon? I thought we'd had our ration.'

'Mr Fletcher let me have a bit off the book.'

'Did he! Did he indeed! And for what payment, I should like to know?'

Dolly laughed, not displeased. 'Don't be daft. You know perfectly well he used to admire my act. Like you used to. Only I never got half a pound of back bacon out of it.'

Titus ignored it. 'How many rashers?' he asked cautiously.

'Three each.'

Titus wrestled briefly with drama and three rashers of back bacon, before the bacon won.

* * *

The dishes had been washed and they were waiting for the kettle to boil again when there was a knock on the kitchen door.

A head under a hat with a feather in it poked round it at them, and it opened on an elderly woman wearing brogues and a tweed suit under a well-worn riding mac, and carrying a capacious-looking brown leather briefcase with her handbag, and an umbrella with a duck's head handle.

She closed the door and said something, before remembering the college scarf covering her mouth and pulling it down.

'I've heard and read about them, of course, and seen newspaper photographs. But until now had never been in one. A pea-souper, a London particular. What an experience!' she said, her tone suggesting that it was one they were missing, sitting about indoors.

Outside the room, fog with a yellow tinge to it and the stink of sulphur stalked Dean Lane. Tugs on the nearby Thames sounded lost in it, the capital stumbling through its day, blinded and coughing.

'It's this cold snap we're having,' Dolly said, as if apologising for it. 'More people lighting their fires, see, dear. And I only cleaned the windows yesterday,' she added, looking over at them, the fog's breath staining the glass.

'When I left the Tube train station,' the woman said, 'it swallowed me up. I was rescued by a bus conductor leading a double-decker bus like an elephant. He told me where you were and very kindly invited me to walk in front with him until we arrived at your turning. It was magical,' she said, more to herself, her eyes wide with it. 'Like a fantasy. Like a lost world. His flaming torch leading us through caves of ancient air, their walls in its light like gold tarnished by the ages. It was magical!' she cried, and coughed violently as if trying to bring some of that air up.

'Don't just stand there, duck, come in and warm yourself,' Dolly said.

'Thank you. Thank you so much. But I'm forgetting my manners. Do please forgive me for barging in like this. I tried knocking on the street door, but—'

'The knocker's stuck,' Dolly told her. 'Rusted. The river air.'

'And I did try telephoning first of course,' she assured them. 'But the exchange said there was a problem with the line.'

'Yes, it's called not paying the bill,' Dolly said, and laughed, laughter a wellspring in her, finding in the world, its cruelties aside, much to laugh about.

'Ah, that explains it,' the woman said. 'Well, allow me, if I may, to introduce myself. My name is Marjorie Devonaire. But everyone calls me George, always have done. I've no idea why. Nor, it seems, has anyone else.'

She looked diffidently at Titus. 'May I ask if you are Mr Titus Llewellyn-Gwynne?' she said, as if expecting to be refused the request.

Titus, who had stood out of politeness, said solemnly that he was, and eyed the briefcase with suspicion. 'And what can I do for you, madam?'

The woman, about to tell him, was taken with another fit of coughing.

Dolly cleared a chair of a large marmalade cat, which then leapt up onto the table and, fiercely indignant, started cleaning itself. Tilly was not only a cat, she was a theatre cat. She had made several unscripted entrances from the wings, once during Titus's soliloquy as Hamlet. He had simply picked her up and, stroking her reflectively, as if it were part of the act, finished the speech. Tilly was used to star treatment and the sound of applause.

'Come and sit here, George, near the fire,' Dolly said. 'Take your mac off or you won't feel the benefit. And I daresay you wouldn't say no to a cuppa. The kettle's nearly there,' she said, indicating the kitchen range where a large cast iron kettle with a polished brass handle and a spout like a striking snake gently breathed steam. Above the range, up under the ceiling, more steam rose from a hoisted pulley-maid loaded with washing.

'Oh, how kind of you. How very welcoming,' George said, settling herself down in the chair at the mahogany table with her things, glancing about the kitchen: a dresser and cupboards, shelves

11

of books and shelves hung with pots and pans, a workmanlike Belfast sink, a mangle and washtub and dolly, theatrical posters and photographs on the walls, the air smelling of the coal fire that a sulking Tilly, back rigid still with umbrage, now sat in front of, of bread baking, and clothes drying, and fog.

'But if I may say so,' George went on, gloves off and hands held out in the direction of the fire, 'I knew you would be. Yours is not, as some are, a front door that when closed shuts out the rest of the world. And I knew that if, in the excitement of being in a London particular, and in the East End, where, when I was a child, Jack the Ripper was at work on the cobbles, I forgot myself long enough to turn the door knob downstairs and enter without right or invitation, as indeed I—'

Dolly waved it away with a hand. 'Oh, don't worry about all that, George. Liberty hall, this is.'

George smiled on her. 'Thank you...?'

'Dolly, dear.'

'Thank you, Dolly.'

'Dolly Burke. Ever heard of me?'

'Dolly Burke...?' George politely considered the name, and was startled by Dolly leaping to her feet and breaking into song.

'*Has anybody here seen Dolly? D-O-double-L-Y. Has anybody here seen Dolly? Find her if you can. But she won't be on her own-io. For she's not skin and bone-io,*' she sang and, as she did in her act, winked with exaggerated suggestion at the raucous heart of the gods and shook her ample breasts.

'And then I get off with this,' she added, and disappeared to the sound of tearing cloth in a sudden full spilt.

George clapped her hands delightedly. 'Oh, bravo! Bravo! But you've torn your beautiful gown.'

'Oh, I'm always doing that, ripping and stitching. It's from downstairs, from the theatre wardrobe. I use it as a housecoat. Got a good elasticated waist. Titus picked it up second hand with other costumes from up west. It was last on stage in Rattigan's *After the Dance*,' she said, and waltzed a few steps in the arms of an imaginary partner.

'Hey-up! Tea time,' she said then, the kettle busy with steam.

'Rattigan chose entirely the wrong time to attempt a move from comedy to drama,' Titus said. 'The play had a short run at St James's in thirty-nine, and was then packed away. Too dark with war in the wings. People went to be cheered up by another *French Without Tears* and were given moral disintegration and a suicide. It's a good piece and had good notices. But the public of course always has the last word, our art as much a servant of the grubby traffic at the box office as any shop or business.'

'Mr Llewellyn—' George, who'd been listening with interest, started, as if suddenly remembering why she was there.

'Titus, please.'

'Titus. Such a splendid name! It marches with ancient Rome.'

'The tenth emperor,' Titus said. 'It was also the name of the King of the Sabines and is to be found in the New Testament. Shakespeare borrowed it, of course, as did my late da, a Glamorgan draper and haberdasher, when he heard it was a boy. The Bard gave it to a Roman general. My da gave it to me. An outbreak of grandeur in a life that otherwise knew its place. And here I am, in my sere and yellow, in the place life has now put me, among the ruins of his hopes and my vaulting ambition. A name that will die with me, its grandeur unfulfilled. I never married,' he added on a dying fall, answering George's look of appalled sympathy.

'Never say never, cock,' Dolly broke in cheerfully, pouring tea and winking at George. 'Help yourself to sugar, George. We've got plenty.'

'Thank you, Dolly,' George said, dragging her attention away from Titus's performance.

'Like a gasper?' Dolly added, offering the Woodbine packet.

13

George said she wouldn't, thanks, that she used to smoke but had to give it up because she kept setting fire to things.

Dolly lit one and settled in the chair with her tea.

'Oh, yes, dear, I'll get the old chap to the church yet. He's an actor, see, George, got all sorts in there, he has,' she said, indicating Titus's head. 'Get him in the right mood, the right character, and he'd come in on cue. Oh, I'll get him there all right, one of these fine days. On time or not. *So I think I'll get wed in the summer time, I think I'll get wed in July. I think I'll get wed when the roses are red. And the weather is lovely and drrry.* Harry Lauder used to sing that. Sir Harry, as he became. And quite right, too. He was a gentleman, God bless him.'

She leaned forward, sharing sudden delight with George.

'Got a beautiful wedding dress waiting in wardrobe, I have. Needs letting out, but it's only been worn a few times. Nineteen thirties, lace halter and satin gown with a small train, and a dear little hat.'

'Oh, how lovely!' George cried.

'It's white, I know,' Dolly said, winking at her again. 'But, well, it's not every day, is it.'

'What are we thinking of!' Titus said, abruptly changing the subject. 'Poor George here has come all the way from – where have you come from, George?'

'From Suffolk,' George said.

'From Suffolk. To tell us whatever she's come to tell us, and we entirely and with unpardonable rudeness monopolise the conversation,' he said, looking accusingly at Dolly. 'George, dear lady, please,' he added with a sweep of his hand, giving her the floor.

'Well,' George said, looking suddenly bashful. 'Well,' she said again, and, putting the briefcase on her lap, opened it, and clipped a black-ribboned pince-nez onto her nose. 'Well, I have written a play.'

'Oh, how marvellous!' Dolly said, springing up to look over her shoulder. '*Love and Miss Harris*, by Lady Devonaire. Devonaire…? Is that you, George?'

'Well, yes. Yes, it is, rather,' George admitted.

'Lumme,' Dolly said. 'Fancy that…'

'I wouldn't normally use it in such a way, but I thought it might help get it accepted. It hasn't. In fact, to be perfectly frank, I have to tell you that all the principal London theatres turned it down one after the other.'

'Oh, them!' Dolly waved the West End away with a scornful hand. 'All they know is farces and whodunits. Love's out in the blooming cold these days. I'd go and see it on the title alone, George. And look how beautifully bound it is!'

And when Titus saw how beautifully bound it was, it told him all he needed to know about its contents. And, perhaps, in this case, with her ring-less left hand, the author.

That perhaps the child she never had was in there, between expensive-looking cream pasteboard bound in blue silk ribbon ending in a bow, the play lovingly named, painstakingly inscribed in copperplate on the cover. Dreams, yearning, self-delusion, the desperate strivings of strangers, had all come dressed like that when he had a theatre, and he had never seen one that he could use. And for the first time since it had happened he found himself glad of the ruin downstairs.

'George – George, dear lady,' he said on a gentler note. 'It may not look it from outside, but there is no longer a theatre here. Not the parts that matter at any rate. There's no longer a stage or auditorium. A flying bomb one night in forty-four saw to that.'

'Oh!' George's hand flew to her mouth. She had seen newspaper reports, had seen the photographs of what a flying bomb could do to bricks and people.

'There were no casualties, mate,' Dolly told her. 'Even Tilly, the cat there, escaped. We were on rehearsal time for a new production then. Six o'clock finish and off to the pub.'

'And it wasn't as bad as it could have been,' Titus added. 'It was put out of business by one of our RAF fighters and we got what was left. It was an act of war, so no compensation. I used what money I had left from a legacy to put a new roof on and for a new bedroom ceiling and floor. But it was the end of the Red Lion Theatre.'

'Oh, I'm so sorry,' George said.

Titus shrugged. 'Well, as Dolly said, even Tilly kept a life.'

'Yes,' George said. 'And that of course is the main thing. So many lost. So many. Well, on, on noble English, and all that.'

'That's the spirit, George. And there are other theatres outside the West End,' Dolly said. 'And I wouldn't be surprised, now the halls have almost disappeared, if they don't follow the fashion and turn into theatres. This place started as a pub, then when the fashion for music halls grew it turned into one. I should know. I played it.'

'I should have liked to have seen your act,' George said.

'You could have done, almost any night. Played them all, I have. The Queen's, Hoxton Hall, the Palace, Holborn, the Victoria, the London Pavilion. The dear old Paragon in the Mile End Road, the Alexandra, Wilton's, the Shoreditch Empire. *In the gay old days there used to be some doings...* Marie Lloyd used to sing that. And she should know, the naughty girl. And to think she used to live in Little Heaven.'

'Little Heaven?' George said.

'The name of an area in Brixton, George,' Dolly said. 'A lot of the headliners used to live there. Marie had a big house there. Some of the times we had! She did like a party, Marie. Well, she was a Hoxton girl, like me. Anyway, then the talkies came in and the puritans had a go at the licensing laws, and, well, I couldn't get a shop in the end from one week to the next.'

'And when the hall here shut its doors I bought it with the legacy I mentioned,' Titus said. He smiled. 'My da, handing me a second shot at grandeur.'

'I was his cleaner,' Dolly added. 'Then, when he couldn't pay me one week, I was promoted to wardrobe mistress. Live in,' she added, giving George another of her winks.

'But I'm just sorry, George,' Titus told her, 'that you had this journey for nothing.'

'Oh, but, Titus, it's not been for nothing. Far from it. It was worth it simply for the time spent in this kitchen. And a London particular, the sound of the boats on the river and footsteps in the fog…'

She came back from wherever she was about to disappear to and looked at them.

'Titus, you talked of failed grandeur, but you and Dolly have far more than grandeur. You have warmth and kindness, and a welcome for a stranger,' she said, ending on a note that threatened tears, and, tugging her suit jacket to one side, peered at the jewel fob watch on her chest. 'And now I see I must go.'

'Nonsense, woman!' Titus said. 'Not in this. You must stay the night. It'll be clear in the morning. We have a spare bedroom. The replacement for the one Hitler removed, taking my wardrobe, bed, a first edition of *The Pickwick Papers*, and a bottle of ten-year-old single malt with it. The house painter has much to answer for.'

'And there's cow's heels for dinner. We've got a very obliging butcher,' Dolly said, with a swift glance of mischief at Titus. 'Done in onions, with dumplings and homemade bread, and stout to wash it down with.'

George looked swayed for a moment. 'No. No, I really must get back. For one thing there's Augustine,' she said, gathering her things.

'Augustine?' Dolly said.

'My dog. Gus. Named after Saint Augustine.'

'Give me chastity and continence, O Lord, but not yet,' Titus said.

'That's the one.'

'An admirable compromise, I always thought.'

George smiled. 'A saint of more human scale. Well, his namesake is being looked after by a friend. Just for the day. And he's a large and rather unruly animal, so one must not impose.

And my conductor guide informs me that the buses I want for the Tube station regularly pass your turning. So in the interest of not getting lost he suggested I simply wait there for one.'

'Very well, George,' Titus said. 'I'll get my coat.'

'Oh, but there's no need for that, Titus. Thank you, it's most kind of you, but—'

'Don't argue, woman,' Titus said, helping her on with her riding mac.

'You've been told,' Dolly said. 'And I'll see if the bread's ready, cut you something to eat on the journey back.'

'Bless you, Dolly, but I came prepared with sandwiches,' George said, indicating the briefcase.

Dolly gave her a hug and told her not to forget them the next time she was in London, and that she was to come back if the fog didn't cough up another bus, and then handed her the umbrella she was about to leave behind, Titus ready to escort her, his swordstick at her service should footpads lurk.

'There are, as Dolly said, other theatres, and of course the provinces. But I must warn you, George, that these are threadbare times,' he added, wanting to say something that would perhaps steer her away from what was almost certain to be disappointment, or at least prepare her for it. 'When it comes to putting bums on seats managements will not look far from what's playing in the West End. They're unlikely to invest in—'

'Oh, but I have money to invest myself. Something I mentioned to all the managements when I sent the play in. Not that it made the least difference.'

'They've got their own backers,' Titus said. 'Regular investors who expect returns on their money. They're businessmen, George, bean-counting abacists and scriveners. Peddlers of shares, not dreams. A stage should be writ large, a place apart from the small, scurrying world outside. A home for wonder. A place where imagination and truth can slip the surly bonds of...'

He paused, what she had said catching up with him.

'How much money, George, may one ask?'

'Well, whatever, if need be, it costs to stage a play.'

'A full production?'

'Oh, yes. Yes, of course.'

Titus stared at her. 'George,' he said, a man in the grip of a sudden revelation. 'George, it occurs to me that there is another possibility you might like to consider.'

Chapter 4

Reuben 'Books' Kramer was born in a noisome, crowded South London tenement, into a world struggling to keep its feet, to not go under. A world of squalor and despair lashing out at itself in violence, in the rooms they called home, or in the dirt and cobbles of the street, women as well as men tearing drunkenly at each other.

He had thought his life there no different from anyone else's. That that was all there was. Until, at the age of seven, he had climbed the hill that ran from Lewisham to Blackheath like a ladder and found another world waiting.

There were trees and green grass everywhere, like a picture he'd seen in a butcher's shop window, but with no animals on it. And water he thought might be the sea, with sailing boats and birds called ducks and swans, a woman in a uniform with a pram told him. The water was called, she'd said, the Prince of Wales Pond.

And he had come away as if she had told him a story, the big houses he'd stood gawping at after that, unwashed and barefooted, like palaces in his eyes.

He returned to despise the world he'd been born into, as if he'd been told a lie and had found them out.

And in 1941, after driving up there with a blonde in a stolen car, he watched it burn as German bombers targeted the factories south of the Thames, watched as his past went up in flames.

And after a war that had been good to him he had made it to Blackheath, made it up the hill. He had ruthlessly fought his way up there and now, like his neighbours, the professionals and men of business, left it behind each day down there, where London was spread before them like something conquered.

He had bought a large detached house, one of the palaces in the eyes all those years ago of a young Reuben, and furnished it from the best of Liberty's soft furnishings and household accessories, bought greedily, making up for the years when he could only look. And had then married a middle-class secretary to go with it.

But it was still a world in which he had yet to arrive, to be accepted socially. He had thought that it was all about money, and for the first time had found something that it couldn't buy.

Sponsored by a bent Greenwich solicitor he'd used over the years, he'd applied for membership to the Royal Blackheath Golf Club. His application, the rejection letter said, had not on this occasion been successful.

'Try again next year, old boy. You know what club committees are like,' the solicitor had drawled when he'd phoned him, emphasising the difference between them, knowing that Reuben had no idea what club committees were like.

He'd tried rationalising the rejection, putting it down to other than what he knew it to be. And then he overheard one of his neighbours talking to her friends about him, and mimicking the accent he thought he'd got rid of.

And not long after that, another attempt to climb the social ladder had ended up on the carpet of the Burbage Cocktail Bar. And by someone not only doing it in front of the sort of people he aspired to, but beating him at his own game, not even leaving him that.

The rage and humiliation he took away with him was a wound that went deep, a wound he kept picking at. Until Jack, by using the language of a backstreet boozer against him in a West End cocktail bar, had come to take vague perverse shape in his mind as the past following him and reminding him of it, holding him back from his future, putting him in his place.

Jack not only had a lot to answer for. He had everything to answer for.

When Reuben was in this sort of mood his eyes took on a melancholy cast, as if saddened by life, as if at the thought of what it obliged him to do to someone. A look that seemed to invite a shared understanding of the sad inevitability of it.

In this case, it was Jack Savage he felt obliged to do it to. He'd deal with them both given the chance, Titus as well, a man who had pulled a sword on him, who had made him run. But it was Jack, Jack, who, like a lover, was never absent from his thoughts for long.

It was Jack he intended killing. He'd find him, walk up behind him and call his name, quietly. He wanted him to turn, to see who was doing it. Wanted him to understand what he had done, to both of them, before firing into his head.

He'd killed four times. The first before the war, with his hands, a girlfriend called Mary, a loose cannon who knew too much. And three after that with the gun. The first of those had been a man who'd made the mistake of belittling him once too often in public, and who paid for it while following routine and walking his dog when the early morning dew was on the grass in Greenwich Park.

There was no one around to witness that murder. But there were witnesses to the other two, local people, both law-abiding and criminal, shocked into a silence that left both killings on file.

With people ready to swear he was elsewhere, he expected his fourth job with the revolver to end up the same way.

And he was now carrying the gun again, a Colt Cobra .38 with a two-inch barrel, fitting snugly into an inside jacket pocket of his suit, without pulling the tailoring about.

He'd phoned the Burbage Bar a couple of times since that evening, trying to establish if Jack Savage was a regular there. But the bar staff didn't know him. He'd got Titus's Christian name when he introduced himself, but not his surname, which had sounded to him like a mouthful of Welsh. But nobody at the bar knew Titus, either.

And he'd got nowhere when he phoned the principal London theatres, his enquiries about both men meeting enough suspicious reserve to warn him off.

He had then rung again the number in the ad Titus Llewellyn-Gwynne had placed in the *Standard*. It was an answering service, because the client was out of town filming, as they had told him at the time. And no, they had no further details, not even a contact phone number.

He was sitting at his reproduction antique desk in the room he called his study, the shelves along one wall lined with calfskin-bound books, their spines shiny with gold leaf, and oleographs of the old masters in ornate gilt frames on the other walls, and buttoned red leather armchairs.

He'd been going over the accounts, finding particular satisfaction in the profit margin from the newly extended security arm of his business – or protection racket, as the *News of the World* insisted on calling it. He had now branched out into the West End, beginning with the Burbage Bar. Someone had to start paying.

He put the accounts book away and lifted the receiver of his desk telephone, a solid-looking creamy white model of the sort he'd seen in a film years ago, ringing in the impossible elegance of a Mayfair flat. An image that for him came to represent a world that over the years since he had shared with no one, and which had now found an echo in the room he called his study.

One of the theatres he'd phoned had suggested, rather dismissively, that he try Equity, the actors' union. It would be for him the last toss of the dice, and he wanted someone with a better accent, and who was more skilled at what he had in mind than he was.

The phone was answered and, after a few brief exchanges of pleasantries, Reuben said, 'Wally, Nancy – is she still banged up? Only, if she's on the out, and wants to earn a few straight quid, I've got a little job for her.'

Chapter 5

In the large bed-sitting room in Prince of Teck Gardens, the high, ornate ceiling, which once looked down on Victorian opulence, now looked down on sparse deal furniture and a carpet with its pattern walked into it.

Jack Savage sat over a shilling's worth of gas in a fire set into an Adam fireplace of primrose Sienna marble, a refuge from the draughty spaces of the room. The tall casement window was loose in its frame, letting in the fog and the muffled sound of traffic as purblind drivers, their headlights near-quenched in the murk, crawled after each other in the Earl's Court Road.

He had recently returned from the labour exchange called the Green Room by the 'resting' actors of the area, who met there as if at their club, and apart from the latest gossip had come back empty-handed. After phoning his agent again, and checking the *Stage* newspaper, he turned to the jobs columns of the *Standard* for non-acting work, something, even an interview, to chuck to the landlord.

Shortly after Jack had moved in there the landlord, an ex-merchant navy cook, had made a pass at him. Jack hadn't been interested, but now tried, shamelessly, to exploit it by explaining to him with a winsome smile why the rent was late.

But a winsome smile hadn't gone far. If all the landlord was getting was a show of ankle, as it were, then he wanted his money, and by the end of the week. Otherwise Jack and his winsome smile would be out on the street.

After finding an ad for a hod carrier, a job he'd done before, he sorted out coppers for the telephone. If he had to go backwards for a while at least he'd be well paid for it.

He was on his way down to the phone in the hall when it rang. He responded to it with the haste and blind hope of a resting actor. Expecting to find, despite the number of times it was for someone else, that, this time, it was for him. A film job, say, with an advance of money from his agent.

And when he answered it he heard the rotund tones of Titus Llewellyn-Gwynne on the other end. He said that he had got fresh backing, coughed up as it were by a London particular, for a new play, and invited Jack to read for another principal part.

Jack was silent. The offer of another lead part when he could no longer afford to take it. He reluctantly told Titus that. He explained that the money he'd saved had now gone, that he had rent to pay, plus arrears to clear up, and things like food to buy.

He was about to wish him well with the tour, and ask him to keep him in mind in the future, when Titus, who'd been making sounds of impatience while trying to get a word in, said never mind about all that. He could, he went on, pay Jack rehearsal wages in advance. And he could save rent by staying with them in the East End until the play was ready for the road. All that, he added, the tedious details, was merely life, the scurrying world, and that, dear boy, must make way for art. And then he had to ask if Jack was still there.

Jack was silent again. He felt as if he were in a play already, one in which he'd forgotten his lines. And all he could think of to say then, was thank you.

* * *

26

Titus, in the East End flat above his theatre, put down the phone that was on again, now they'd paid the bill, and told Dolly that Jack had agreed.

Dolly was delighted. 'You can't go wrong, mate, with a bit of young love, especially in these dreary days. And especially when it comes wrapped in a couple of lookers like them,' she said, pairing Jack with Lizzie Peters, already cast as the eponymous heroine of the new play, *Love and Miss Harris*.

Lizzie Peters, from the rural heart of the Home Counties, was twenty-two, and hardly ever seemed to stop smiling at life, at its possibilities, and was eager for whatever came next. She had hair the colour of fresh straw, cut short, by her own hand and in her own unfashionable fashion, in a pixie crop. A style that before long would be copied by young women wherever her films were shown.

Titus had first seen her in a small part at the Duchess Theatre. She had recently finished a stint in Stratford as the third witch in *Macbeth*, and had jumped at the chance of a lead part, even if it was only an East End company, and one with a bomb site for a theatre.

Lizzie's acting carried the polish of RADA, getting a place there straight from school. Jack, eight years older, from a small town in County Sligo, with Spanish-dark hair and green, watchful eyes, had found acting while in pursuit of something else.

He had left Ireland and the Great Depression and was labouring on a building site in London when war was declared. After demob, and back in London, he'd joined an amateur dramatic society, simply because a girl he fancied was a member. And surprised himself by liking it, the people, and the feeling of creating something, if only shifting scenery, after the years of destruction.

And he'd surprised himself again then, when he started acting, by being good at it. And he had found in it, in the different parts, the different people and other lives, an escape from his own and a war that had followed him home. And out of the pay he couldn't spend because of that war, he had paid for a year's training at Italia Conti drama school, and left it with a working technique and his accent smoothed out.

Titus saw all the cast now in the play that, with George's enthusiastic approval, he had rewritten, saw them as if on a lighted stage, with his two young principals at its heart.

An earnest young actor called Simon Head, whose last job had been understudy and second assistant stage manager at the Garrick, had also been elevated by Titus, who'd cast him in the supporting role of Rupert Kenton-Browne, Lizzie's fiancé.

Titus was playing the smallest part of the play, and had in mind who he wanted for Lizzie's mother and her uncle. The actress he wanted for her mother had once been a star, of the sort of brightness that never quite goes out, her name carrying the remembered upper-class glamour of the twenties and thirties queued for weekly at local cinemas. A name that Titus guessed would still be a draw if only in provincial theatre.

And sitting above the ruins of his grandeur, above where hope and ambition had turned to rubble, he knew that the provinces were now a last retreat, a last stand against the humdrum, the scurrying world that waited outside the walls of a theatre.

Chapter 6

There was spring in the night air in Dean Lane; even the tired old River Thames after the day's rain smelt fresher, with a tartness to it that hinted at salt and the sea.

Parts of the lane were missing still, the ruins a playground for local children, the pink and white rosettes of London Pride that had persisted after the bombs fell, pushing up through the rubble towards the light, flowering again. The cat-meat dealer's, the saddler's and the printer's, the rag dealer's, the bookbinder, and tailor and cutter on the floor above, and the shoe factory were still there, and the doors of the Salvation Army still open to the destitute, their bright tunes marching on throughout the war, the ruined spaces in between softened by gaslight gathered like a pale green mist around the street lamps.

At one end of the lane was the Biograph Cinema, and at the other the welcoming lights of the Bargee pub on a corner, with a Thames sailing barge in full red sail on a sign that swung in winds from the river.

Inside the pub, the recently formed Red Lion Touring Company sat at two tables in the snug bar. They had just finished the last of the rehearsals in the room upstairs, all their moves in place and without the book, needing only the odd nudge now and then from Dolly as prompt.

The play, much rewritten by Titus, but still with its original title, was ready to go on the road.

On Monday morning the company would set out for their first venue, in a small market town in Kent, and Titus was debating with Hector, the Red Lion Theatre's factotum from its early days, the best route to get there. Hector's expression suggested he expected disaster whatever route they took, but he was happy, in his own lugubrious, Hectorish way, to be back in his old job – even if it did mean spending time in the alien green of the countryside, a place which, for Hector, who had only left the East End for any length of time once, in 1914, was another sort of abroad.

For Dolly, as a child, it had meant escape, if only for the picking season. And she added the route they used to travel to the discussion. A route she'd had a good view of, perched with the rest of the children, and adults and babies and family livestock on household goods bundled in tablecloths, ancient trunks and suitcases closed with string, bedding and collapsible prams, on the open back of a horse-drawn lorry.

Singing their way out of their crowded lives, taking off like migrating birds each year for the hop gardens of Kent.

George, sitting at their table with a glass of the stout she'd taken a fancy to over the weeks, also added her bit, contributing the way her chauffeur used to go when she visited a distant cousin of hers, Lord Maidstone. 'We were once very close. Then we sort of lost contact, the war and that, you know. We could drop in to see him!' it occurred to her. 'It's on the way.'

George had come up to town for every rehearsal, sitting, as she put it, at Titus's feet, and there had from the start been no question of her not accompanying them on tour. Titus had approached the idea of taking her play on the road cautiously, obliquely, in the kitchen that day, like a salesman creeping up on expected resistance.

But when he'd finally said it, George had clapped her hands with delight, her eyes wide at the thought. It was for her the circus she had never run away to.

Simon Head was sitting with the last two members of the company cast, Daphne Langan and Wellington 'Wells' Cheslyn, and was still somewhat in awe, while still trying not to show it, of Daphne, whose face, before first meeting her at the read-through, he had only seen on the screen, as had countless other cinemagoers over the years. Something Titus had made sure was carried on the advanced publicity and fed to the local press.

Daphne Langan, who was playing Lizzie's mother, was born Doris Lumsden in Nottingham, the daughter of a railway porter and an ambitious mother. Elocution lessons and a scholarship to the Guildhall School gave her an accent to go with her dewy English rose looks, an adornment in the drawing rooms of weekly rep. Then the West End and offers from the studios followed.

And it was films that turned Doris Lumsden into Daphne Langan, darling of the Bright Young Things, adored by the camera and her public in picture after picture. Until the drink she found helped her confidence finally made her a liability, and cost her three marriages along the way and the closeness of her children.

She bore her wounds in the breezy persona of Daphne Langan, in public and in private, when alone with herself, keeping her pecker up, darling, as she'd have advised others to do. But there were times, in the stark, unforgiving lights of a dressing-room make-up mirror, her face stripped and defenceless, when it wasn't socialite Daphne Langan sitting there, but Doris Lumsden from Nottingham, sitting there as if abandoned.

She was drinking soda water now, as she'd promised Titus she would for the entire tour, talking about a scene with Simon and Wells Cheslyn, the oldest member of the company. Wells, who'd worked for Titus before, had been cast as Lizzie's Uncle Jasper.

Wells also had a story of drink to tell, one he never spoke of, holding in it as it did another story, one that, for him, was the bigger disgrace.

Born in Boston, Wells was touring in vaudeville with his parents and older sister at the age of ten. The children sang and danced and his mother played straight man to his father, a ventriloquist, until she ran off with a travelling salesman in Utah. Sometime after that, his sister married and settled down, reducing the act to father and his straight man, the young Wells.

They played the vaudeville circuits, until the work dried up because of his father's drinking. And it was drink that carried them to England, on what savings they had left, the wild optimism his father found in enough bourbon. Drink that built in his words a shining future there, a new land in which to build again, sharing it with his son like a revelation.

And it was drink that abandoned him when they reached that future, in the London workhouse where he died, at the end of a road littered with the ruins of all he'd promised his son, and himself.

And in Wells's fastidious heart, where a yearning to be socially what he was not, but had always felt he should be, the irredeemably common workhouse was a shame far worse than drink.

He took to the road after the funeral, a pauper's grave, a life tidied away under the Poor Law, and in Brighton joined a Pierrot troupe with an act on the beach, doing four shows a day, tides permitting, and under the pier when wet.

He had gone on to play concert parties and music halls, in double acts and solo, and straight parts on stage and film that called for aloof superiority, such as butlers, and in the hard times between survived on non-theatrical jobs and post-dated cheques. He was now nearly seventy, with aggrieved eyes, the look life had given him, and a long narrow face.

He had dyed his hair recently, an uncompromising black, a helmet of it, brushed straight back in a style from the 1920s and polished with Brilliantine, his thread veins touched up with rouge, his nose discreetly powdered. A last stand against the years that had ended up in a bedsit and shared landing bathroom in Streatham.

* * *

Not long after that they moved round to the lounge, where an East End Saturday night was underway. Wells sat at the piano and Dolly sang. It wasn't the sort of song she had the voice for. It wasn't Ivor Novello and a baby grand at the Ritz, and at times sounded more like a threat than a loving promise. But her audience knew what she meant. They spoke the same language.

Even those who had never seen an English lane, let alone walked down one, joined in with a feeling that went beyond the song, the words. It spoke of the war, of fortitude and a defiance, of the nights when the East End and its docks burned, of the ruined streets and the lives lost, and of those who would never come home again.

Chapter 7

Nancy Dunn's downfall had not this time been a man, but the green fire of emeralds set with brilliant-cut diamonds in a Victorian ring.

It was nestling in ivory velvet behind glass in the museum quiet of Garrard & Co, the Mayfair jeweller's, and when she was told it was called a Princess Catherine ring she knew that she had to have it.

In a short career on the fringes of London crime, passing cheques for amounts that wouldn't attract the attention of Scotland Yard's Fraud Squad, this was by far her most ambitious job.

But she felt ready for it, in Hardy Amies tweed and with a chequebook encased in the reassuring claret leather of an inherited Coutts bank holder, signing its elegant paper with the flourish of a double-barrelled name, using a black and gold Montblanc fountain pen. It all went with the accent she'd learned like another language from the BBC's Third Programme, and now spoke fluently, a member of the county set, in town with the forthcoming birthday of a favourite aunt in mind.

Nancy had a natural flair for mimicry, and when she went to work she did so with the dedication and skill of an actress, one fully in character. It was for her a starring role at last.

She was twenty-seven years of age, with five years behind her in the trade, started off by her mentor, Alice Monroe. Alice was now doing time in Strangeways, after travelling north to 'kite up Manchester', as she'd put it. Nancy had also done time, not long after starting out, six months with good behaviour, when she had picked up more tips on cheque flying on the landings of Holloway Prison.

Her mistake in a job otherwise perfectly executed was holding on to the ring. She'd lodged the incriminating Coutts chequebook with a friend, as she usually did, to join the other chequebooks from her Deptford supplier. But had held on to the ring. She wanted it, what it meant to her, in her life a little longer.

Passing it on would have been much safer. And even with her pawnbroker fence stripping as much as he could get away with off it, it would have left her with enough to buy a flat, or even a house, and kept her out of prison for a few years.

But it had touched in her a much deeper need than money, a yearning more like love, and like love it made her vulnerable.

It held for her in its jewelled glitter the glamour and romance of another world, a refuge from the one outside her Catford lodgings. A world covered regularly by *Vogue* of high society and the London season, of long white ball gowns and tiaras on the Mall, when Buckingham Palace was lit like a wedding cake. A world of afternoon teas, dance cards, and chaperones and suitable young men, and smart weddings in Hanover Square under a shower of confetti and a shining arch of swords.

It was a little tight, but otherwise fitted her ring finger, and she admired it constantly, holding out her hand with a sort of surprised remembered delight, as if it had been a gift, as if it had been given to her only yesterday in the drawing room of a town house, by a suitable young man on one knee.

But it was her world that had the last word, when two local CID officers on a routine visit following a crime sheet circulated from Scotland Yard spotted the item on her finger.

'Where've you hid the chequebook you used, Nancy?' the senior detective, a sergeant, said, after they'd turned her bedsit over. 'Not that it matters. We've got you bang to rights. And the staff who served you fingering you in an ID parade will do the rest. But it will go a bit easier for you when you go up the steps if you give us the lot, tell us where you've stashed them. Then we can speak for you.'

'I don't know what you're talking about! I told you, I bought it in a pub. All right, I guessed it was hooky. I'll cough for that, for receiving stolen property, but not—'

'Get your coat, love,' the sergeant said, amused by it.

'I don't know, gal, I'd have expected you to have turned it into wages by now, a nice few quid like this,' he said chattily on their way to the car, cheerful not only with the ease of the arrest, but with keeping it in the family, making it before Scotland Yard.

And it continued to be kept in the family when she was tried at Croydon Assizes, instead of the Old Bailey, where, despite the efforts of the dock brief assigned to her, she was handed a three-year prison sentence.

It had been reduced to two for good behaviour, and not long out, she was in need of the fifty pounds Reuben had offered her to make a few phone calls, using his house phone. Reuben, she knew, trusted no one.

She had taken the bus up to Blackheath and the house on the hill, and when she arrived was shown in by a uniformed maid of the sort she'd seen on the pictures, and introduced to Reuben's wife, Cornelia.

It surprised her how Reuben, a man feared throughout South London, deferred to her. Even when saying her name he did so with a peculiar careful emphasis, as if he had just learned how to say it, or as if it were something special.

Not, instinct told her, out of love. There wasn't, she felt, that between them, only mutual need. Her gain was obvious. And his, she decided, was that Cornelia, with her middle-class name and accent, simply went with the rest of the house.

It was raining, so she was spared Cornelia insisting in a middle-class way on a tour of the garden. But she had to trail over the house after her, admiring the furniture.

Reuben offered no explanation for her being there, and Cornelia showed no curiosity. They had cocktails in the sitting room after the tour, mixed and shaken by Reuben behind the American chrome and smoked glass cocktail bar, and then Cornelia, with wifely discretion, excused herself and withdrew.

She had stopped her ears to what her family and others had said about her husband's business, and to her own thoughts, and woke each day to her reward. Not that of diamonds and furs, and a walk-in wardrobe of haute couture and shoes, but a house smelling of Liberty's soft furnishing department.

While she was in her kitchen, consulting with the cook about lunch, Nancy was on the desk phone in Reuben's study, breathing life into an idea that Reuben, schooled in deviousness, had come up with.

She had got through to Equity, purporting to be an accounts clerk in the rebates section of the Inland Revenue seeking the current home address of a Jack Savage, listed on his file as an actor. An overworked clerk, she had decided, going through the motions, not caring particularly whether Mr Savage was paid the rebate he was due or not.

She shook her head then at Reuben. 'I understand,' she said into the phone. 'Thank you for... Oh, yes, thank you. That would be a great help. We don't have that contact for him on file. Just a home address which we've discovered he's since left.'

She wrote down a telephone number on a page from Reuben's exercise book, thanked the person on the other end, and, putting down the receiver, said briefly, 'His agent.'

She rang the number, and went through it again.

'Well, that's kind of you, but I'm afraid we can't, unfortunately,' she said chattily, sensing that it might pay. 'Red tape. It would make our job in rebates a lot easier if we could, I don't mind telling you. But we're legally restricted to sending communications to the home address only of the person named. Not just tax rebates, but all communications... means work piling up sometimes. As I say, red tape. As if we don't have enough of it already. Oh – oh, thank you. That would be marvellous, be one less file to deal with,' she said then, and putting her hand over the mouthpiece mouthed at Reuben, 'His address...'

She wrote it down, thanked the person again on the other end, and handed the page to Reuben.

'Hello, son,' he said softly, looking at it.

Chapter 8

Dolly travelled with Titus and George in the back of George's vintage black and yellow Rolls-Royce Phantom, watching her childhood going by in a different season, the fields of Kent painted with early summer, with meadow flowers, and the shining emerald of pasture grazed by the cattle and sheep she'd had no words for as a child, until her mother named them for her.

Jack Savage was in the front with George's dog. Augustine, Gus to his friends, a Great Dane-boxer cross, his white patched with brown the colour of mud that had still to fully dry, was sitting upright on the passenger seat, his great head constantly moving as he looked out of the side window, as if wondering where the world kept disappearing to.

Jack was acting as the chauffeur George could no longer afford. A chauffeur, along with much else, including the car, that belonged to younger days. She had always meant to learn to drive but had never got round to it, and had held on to the Rolls simply because it did belong to those days, because it was the last of that time.

The house she was born in, the only child of an earl, had, to her relief, since been acquired by the National Trust, its upkeep now their responsibility. She had never married, and lived now with a widowed friend of the same age. The money for the tour had come from a trust fund set up by her late father, before heavy stock market investments and the Great Depression drove him to the wall.

The rest of the cast were following behind the car, taking in the views from the top deck of a London bus driven by Hector. In its London Transport days the bus, mostly red with a white roof and trim, had been a number 9, running between Aldwych and Mortlake. It was put out to grass and ended up in a dealer's yard in Stepney, which is where Titus had found it and bought it out of the investment money the week before. The seats had been removed downstairs and it was loaded now with scenery flats, props and luggage, and a suitcase of playbills, flyers and programmes, the ads in them for Bell's whisky and Benson & Hedges cigarettes secured by Titus.

When the bus had last carried a banner along its sides it had been for the *Daily Sketch* newspaper. Now it advertised the Red Lion Theatre Company's touring production of *Love and Miss Harris*.

George leaned forward and blew a couple of times down the speaking tube. 'The next turning on the right, Jack,' she said, and Jack raised his hand with a touch of deference, an actor playing a chauffeur.

'It always meant such fun,' she told Dolly, 'turning off here. What fun,' she said a few moments later to herself, distant with memory. 'That used to be his favourite expression,' she said. 'What fun.'

* * *

Lord Robin Arthur Finch-Elm, 15th Earl of Maidstone, shield of arms supported by a stag and Pegasus rampant, family motto *Sit dominus liberabit nos*. 'May the Lord deliver us' – please! he always added as a young pilot during the worst of the dog fights over the Western Front, making the sort of jokey face at the idea of God he made while on the ground, while up there in his frail craft, the air loud and dreadful with death, never believing in him more.

He had returned unscathed, and out of guilt perhaps because of it, or a realised and driven sense of the real worth of things, set about spending his inheritance, chasing after life as if discovering it for the first time. He gave freely to charities and to any hard luck story on his doorstep, and went through several marriages and costly divorces along the way.

His estate was now reduced to not much more than the grounds of the house and a fringe of ancient woodland which he shot for the pot. He'd sold everything else, and would have sold the manor as well, had not the aristocratic tradition of the house not belonging to the owner but the owner to the house, obliged him to hold on to it for his eldest son.

The suit he was wearing to greet his guests was made over thirty years ago by Henry Poole & Co of Savile Row. His shoes, from around the same period, were by Lobb of St James's and needed repair. He had worn his Old Etonian tie out of a vague sense of occasion, his linen washed and pressed, threadbare but unafraid, as he put it, a white handkerchief flying like a flag from his suit breast pocket, but not that of surrender.

'What fun!' He'd beamed, finding a London double-decker bus on his doorstep.

'My dear George,' he said. 'It's been far too long.'

'Yes, I know,' George said, and sniffed, as if tearfully. 'The war, and all that, you know, Robin.'

'Yes, the war and all that,' he said, and both looked embarrassed for a moment, as if at some shared unseemly upheaval in their lives. Before George rescued them by remembering her manners.

After the introductions had been made, Robin saw Gus sitting in the Rolls.

'And what is that?' he asked, with a sort of amused interest, as if in this company almost anything might be possible.

'Of course, you haven't actually met him. Although I think I mentioned him in a letter. That's Gus. Augustine to you, as you haven't been properly introduced.' George opened the car door. 'Augustine, meet Lord Maidstone.'

And Gus, spotting someone new to greet, bounded over to him to do so.

'There's a good chap,' Robin said doubtfully, waving a vague hand at him.

Gus reared up, his paws on Robin's chest to get a better look at him, while Robin held onto his legs, dog and elderly earl doing a sort of tottering dance.

'Down, Gus!' George said, having long learned that the most useful command with Gus was the down one. 'I'll put him back in the car. He's had a run on the way here.'

'No, no, bring him into the house. He can say hello to Shoveler. Come in, come in,' he added, waving the others to follow.

'Shoveler?' George said. 'Not the Shoveler?'

'Yes, the Shoveler. Ancient now, of course. But still with us. And still goes out with the gun. But now, if I do bag something, she pretends she hasn't seen me do it, dear old thing.'

They trooped through rooms where the past was shrouded in dustsheets, and there were marks on the William Morris wallpaper where the last of the Stubbs had been.

'I was sorry to hear, by the way,' George said, 'that you and Della had – er—'

'Oh, these things happen, you know.'

'And how are the boys?' she asked. 'Robin has two sons from his last marriage,' she told the others.

'I never seemed to get the hang of it, marriage, you know,' Robin added, sharing that with them. 'Yes, they're fine, George, fine. I see William fairly regularly. Measuring up for curtains, as it were. He's got plans for the old place when I leave it for good. He's something in Whitehall now. No idea where he gets it from. Turned up the other week in a bowler hat.'

'How is Arthur? He was my favourite.'

'He's living in Chelsea. Writing a novel about the state of things,' Robin said vaguely.

'He always did have an active imagination. To Arthur there were elephants in the sky, not clouds. Look, he'd say, look, elephants.'

'No idea where he got that from either,' Robin said, leading them into the kitchen, its past of bustle, steam and gossip, of generations of cooks, kitchen and scullery maids in that large, flagged room, echoing now with their entrance.

'Something smells good,' Dolly said.

'It's rabbit, Dolly,' Robin told her. 'Bagged it myself. So watch out for shot. Can't always be sure of a head shot these days, I'm afraid. She remembers you,' he said to George, Shoveler's tail busy in her basket in front of a cooking range, gazing up at the visitor, her eyes an offering of melting dark chocolate.

Then Shoveler saw Gus and she shed years, standing abruptly upright and barking at him, while Gus, put in his place, lowered his great head. She left her basket then for a walk round the kitchen, her domain, sniffing at the guests, Gus following her as if told to.

'That got her moving. Good man, Gus. But please, sit down, sit down,' Robin said, and indicated a tapped wooden barrel on the big pine table. 'I can offer cider, a good local brew. Foxwhelp, from Sam Battens's orchards,' he added to George. 'Another body still with us. And tea of course. I'm afraid there's nothing in the cellar these days but coal.'

George smiled. 'I was just remembering, Robin. The last time I sat in this kitchen was before the war,' she said, meaning the First World War, 'having a dawn fry-up.'

'Sneaking in a bit of cooking while Mrs McBride was still in bed,' Robin said.

'I wouldn't have dared otherwise. Mrs McBride was the cook, and this was her domain,' George told the others. 'It was at one of Robin's house parties. It was such a lovely autumn. Such *colours*,' she said, seeing them again. 'A last, glorious flowering. Anyway, I remarked on it to Robin, and the next day, a Sunday, he woke me when it was still dark and told me to dress for a country walk. And after our fry-up I walked outside into a dawn morning, to find a hot air balloon coloured like seaside rock waiting to be inflated on the lawns. He wanted to show me autumn from the air,' she said, looking at Robin. 'What fun... What fun.'

Chapter 9

Earlier that morning in London, a dark-blue Ford turned in to Prince of Teck Gardens in Earl's Court, and parked a couple of houses down and across from the one the men inside it wanted.

Reuben 'Books' Kramer was sitting on his own in the back of the car, with the Colt Cobra revolver, retrieved from its hiding place in his bedroom, in an inside jacket pocket of his Savile Row suit.

Edwin Myers and Frank Collins were in front, Edwin at the wheel. Two nights ago, Edwin had stolen the Ford from a cinema car park in Islington, and driven back across the river with it to Frank Collins's used car lot in Peckham, for a change of number plates.

They were waiting for Jack Savage to appear. Reuben was going to do it there, in the Gardens, before he reached the busy Earl's Court or Cromwell Road. The two men were with him to ensure that no have-a-go heroes got in the way.

Afterwards, the Ford would be taken to the Catford scrapyard owned by Wally, Nancy Dunn's uncle, and broken up. And the Colt, with the history of four murders written into its rifled barrel, 'retired', slung on an ebb tide into the Thames.

They had arrived at eight o'clock and it was now nearly ten, the air inside the Ford misted with cigarette smoke.

Frank, who needed a pee, said, 'Like I said, perhaps he's not there. He's an actor. Perhaps he's gone away somewhere, working, you know? Or moved. He could have moved.'

Reuben thought about it, looking with a doleful expression at the house through the side window of the Ford, as if remembering past miseries behind its walls.

'Ed, get over there,' he said then, 'and ask if they've got a vacant room. Say a bloke you met in a pub said it was a good gaff. Say his name's Jack Savage. Say it was in the Pembroke Arms, that local we passed. OK?'

'OK, boss,' Edwin said.

'No, wait. Say you met a mate of one of his tenants there, a Jack Savage, who said it was a good gaff. Throw a bit of dust up, just in case. And then casual, like, as if for something to say, ask if this Jack still lives there. All right? Got that?'

'Yeah, right.'

'But casual, like – does he still live here, by the way? That sort of thing. Like you talk about the weather. Not drawing attention to yourself. OK?'

'Yeah, I got ya.'

Edwin, about to get out, then said, 'What if they've got a room? They might have a room going. What—'

'Have I got to do all your thinking for you? What do I pay you for? You look at it, don't you.'

'Say you'll think about it. Say you've got another couple of rooms to look at first,' Frank put in, trying to hurry things along, his mind on the Pembroke Arms and a lavatory. 'Go on, son, off you go.'

'Then we wait, yeh? If we know it's his gaff? Wait for him?'

Edwin's voice was charged with what that would mean. And that the target was an actor added to it, gave it a glamour. Like something on the films or in a *True Detective* magazine.

'No,' Reuben said. 'We come back another day and do it.'

'That makes sense,' Frank immediately agreed.

'Put a bit of distance between you asking about him and the job. OK?'

'Yeah, right, boss,' Edwin said flatly. This would be his first involvement in a murder and for him the morning had gone suddenly quiet. The excitement that had followed him there like discordant music, getting louder the nearer they got to it, suddenly switched off.

Frank Collins, an ex-light-heavyweight professional boxer, who oversaw the doormen at Reuben's four drinking clubs, was a man for whom violence was simply work, as it was in the ring. Something which had to be done and for which he got paid, and which he had no feelings about one way or the other. Violence for Edwin was both a pleasure and a release.

Taller, and younger than Frank, and with a body built by Charles Atlas and his bodybuilding course, Edwin liked hurting people. He worked in his mother's florist shop in Greenwich, making deliveries and using his natural skill as a flower arranger. A skill he saw as a weakness in him, as he saw other things in him as weaknesses.

Weaknesses he was paid to take out on other people. Work he would have done for nothing.

The porch pillars of the house across the street were peeling, the front door dirty with the city.

The door was shut, but not locked.

Edwin pulled at the brim of his snap-brim fedora and walked in.

He looked with distaste at where an actor lived, the dinginess of a hall with its stained, threadbare carpet and the stale lingering smell of cooking. There were a few letters on a small, varnished deal hall table against one of the walls, none for a Jack Savage.

He regarded himself in the fan-shaped mirror above it, hunching his shoulders, and touching at the knot of a silk tie with a blonde on it in a bikini holding up a beach ball. As a gangster, Edwin took his look from American noir films and pulp fiction. In his violence he was utterly authentic.

He was about to start knocking on doors, when a late middle-aged man came out of the nearest one, in shirt sleeves and carpet slippers, his grey flannels, like his shirt, in need of an iron. He looked as if he too had once known Charles Atlas and his course, the muscle now turned to fat, what was left of his hair plastered in greased, greying strands across his scalp.

And when he saw Edwin, another dangerous-looking young man under his roof, his pale moon face was immediately and unguardedly open to hope again. All the lessons he'd told himself that, this time, he'd learned, forgotten. The casual cruelties, and sometimes violence, his clumsy need for affection and their indifference, the lies he'd bought and longed to believe, the thefts of cash and small treasured things, and the gas meter jemmied again.

Then he looked at Edwin's eyes, and the bright side he always tried to look on went dark.

He put a hand to his chest. 'Oh, I thought it was Elsie, my cleaning lady, coming in,' he said on a breathy note of fear. 'She's due any minute now,' he thought to add, and wondered if anybody else was in the house, if anyone would hear him scream.

Edwin smiled at him. 'You the landlord?'

The other man nodded, trying to smile back.

'I thought you was. Well, I'm looking for a room, see. A single room. Have you got one? Got a room going? A single?'

Relief that that was all he wanted made the landlord voluble, made him almost offer the smiling visitor one of the three he had vacant.

But the eyes that went with the smile did it for him, and he said, 'Ah, sorry, son, no. I did have, but I'm full up now. You could try a few houses along, number fourteen, Mrs Donnelly's.

If you don't mind cats,' he couldn't resist adding. 'Or down on the Cromwell Road,' he suggested, sending him further away. 'They always seem to have vacancy notices in the windows along there. Come to think of it, I saw a couple only the other day. Along on the left there,' he burbled on, in the face of the young man's silence and his smile.

'See, the reason I thought I'd try here was that the mate of one of your tenants, a bloke I met in the Pembroke Arms, said it's a good gaff. Respectable and clean, and all that.'

'Well, that's nice of him, I must say.'

'Yeah, he said to give his mate, this tenant of yours, his regards. If he still lives here, like. He hadn't seen him he said for a couple of months. Does he still live here, by the way? For when I see his mate again?' Edwin asked casually. 'Jack, the tenant's name is, Jack Savage.'

The landlord was having trouble answering, Jack's name like a sudden blow to the chest, winding him.

'No,' he got out, 'no, doesn't live here any more. He left.'

'Oh, he left, did he?'

The landlord nodded. 'Yes.'

'That's a pity. This geezer was looking forward to having a pint with him again. Has he moved locally, this Jack, then?'

'I don't know. I don't know where he's gone.'

'What – didn't leave a forwarding address for any mail?'

The landlord shook his head. 'No.'

Edwin, who had picked up his fear like a scent, moved closer.

'I know this is called bedsitter land, but that's a bit strange, isn't it? Eh? That's a bit on the unusual side of things, even for this manor. Hey, he didn't do a runner, did he? Didn't do a moonlight? Tiptoe through the tulips with his suitcase without saying a dickybird?' he said, as if teasing him. 'Honestly. Some people, eh?'

The landlord wanted to tell him, wanted to please him, to stop him hurting him, as he was sure he was going to. The way he was smiling at him, like all bullies do when they're building up to it, as if they can taste it already.

He thought of fending him off with the list Jack had left with him of all the venues on the tour, to forward any mail.

When Jack had got the acting job he'd paid his rent arrears in cash, money he hadn't wanted to take from him, hadn't wanted to ask him for, doing so only to get at him. He'd have given him money, if only he had asked. Given him whatever he had to give, to have kept him there. He had got nowhere with him. Not even a parting hug, touching only his hand when he'd shook it, the brief warmth of his hand, and had watched love leaving, watched love walking out of the door.

He didn't for a moment believe the Pembroke Arms story, and whatever it was about, he had no doubt that this young man, this spiv, meant Jack harm. And when he thought of that, saw his face again, saw it this time turned to ugliness, opened with a cut-throat razor, he found it in himself to be strong, to be strong for Jack.

'Yes, if you must know, he left owing rent,' he said, haughty with a sudden courage that put Edwin and all the other dangerous-looking young men in their place. 'Took advantage of my kindness, as others have done. And I have no idea where he might be living now, and frankly, don't care. And now, if you don't mind, I've got things to do,' he added, indicating the door with a hand that shook slightly.

Edwin hesitated, reluctant to leave it. He was aroused. Fear in other people did that to him. It's where his reputation for violence came from. He punished them for it, punished them and himself. And in the landlord he saw himself twice reflected.

But he knew he couldn't afford it, not when remembering what they were there for.

He smiled again, and shook his head, as if at how close the other man had come to it.

As soon as the door had closed on him, the landlord shot the latch and hurried back into his rooms.

He peered carefully round the floral curtain one side of the window overlooking the street, and watched Edwin getting into a car.

And now he must tell Jack. Now he must warn Jack, he told himself, fluttering and almost breathless at the thought of speaking to him again, sharing this business, whatever it was about.

At whatever distance, and however briefly, part of Jack's life again.

Chapter 10

When they arrived at the venue in Collington, the Palace Theatre, there was room to park in front for the Phantom, but not the bus, which had to go round again.

And when there was a space, Titus kept it clear as if ready to defend it with his swordstick if necessary. A startling figure in the high street of that small market town, dressed from the ages in his musketeer's hat, dove-grey Edwardian frock coat, a Victorian silk crimson ascot tied extravagantly at the throat, and the polished Hessian boots of a Regency buck.

He was something to look at, along with the London bus, by the growing number of the curious, their first audience. And Titus worked it, handing out copies of the smaller playbills, casually throwing in the name of Daphne Langan, suggesting that the play was touring the provinces before a West End premiere – 'Well, you never know,' he said afterwards, when Jack brought it up.

'Look, George,' Dolly said, nudging her on the pavement and pointing to a board in the theatre entrance advertising the play and the name of the author, George Devonaire.

'My word!' George said.

There had been no room for her name on the bus banner and now, suddenly, there it was. She had seen it on the publicity material and programmes from the printers in Dean Lane, but that was in the privacy of the East End kitchen. This was in public, for anyone to see.

'My word!' she said again, glancing furtively up and down the street, before taking a proper look, peering at it through her pince-nez.

Then she shook herself delightedly, like a chicken puffing up its feathers, quite shameless with a sudden pride that didn't care who saw it, that even had her moving brazenly to one side so that people could see it.

When most of his audience had carried on about their business, Titus, who had not played the Palace before, got a good look at it, and was not impressed,

'More like the local fleapit than a palace,' he said, taking in the state of the paintwork and the grime on the glass of the entrance doors.

The doors were locked.

'The stage door's down there,' Daphne said, standing with the others on the pavement, their luggage still on board, waiting for Hector to take them and it round to the digs the theatre manager had arranged.

'That'll be fun, if we have to take the flats in that way,' Simon Head said, speaking from experience as a second assistant stage manager, and looking at the narrow blind alley Daphne had pointed out. 'Is there an ASM here?'

'You're looking at her, darling,' Dolly said. 'And wardrobe, and company manager, and prompt.'

The theatre and alley sat between Hobson's, a tobacconist's, and the shop of ironmonger S. Roberts. There was a bill advertising the play in Mr Hobson's window but not in that of Mr Roberts, the window Hector was now peering in, lost to a shining world of brand-new spanners. A whole window display of spanners tied to a white cardboard backdrop, whole families of spanners, from baby spanners to those big enough to take on the Forth Bridge, with charts and illustrations of things such as socket sizes and thread pitches, hub nuts and ball joints.

When Jack had visited the town's shops over a week before, arriving by train with a suitcase of playbills, offering two free passes for poster space in their windows, the ironmonger had politely turned the offer down. He'd assured Jack that he had nothing against the play or the theatre as such, and he wasn't going to go into details, he'd leave that sort of thing to others. But he would no longer assist, or be associated with in any way, shape or form, the theatre manager, Mr Smedley.

'I'm a man of principle, me,' the shopkeeper had added, tapping it out with a blunt finger on his counter. 'And in my book a principle's a principle. No matter how many gas mantles he buys.'

Jack tried the stage door and found that locked as well.

'What's up?' Hector said, dragging himself away from the spanners.

'We can't get in,' Dolly told him.

Hector shook his head, as if he'd warned them that this might happen. 'It's closed down, mate. Happens all over the country. Be turned into a picture house.'

'He's just delayed, Hector,' Lizzie said.

'He's legged it with the till,' Wells said. 'He's on the Cote d'Azur as we speak, taking afternoon tea at Lah-grond-oh-tell.'

'Does he have far to come, do we know?' George asked.

'I've no idea,' Titus said.

'What was the arrangement?' Jack asked.

'I told him we were aiming for a two o'clock get-in,' Titus said. 'And he said that if he wasn't here his doorkeeper would be sitting on the stage door from two onwards. And we can't ring him. I've only got his office number.'

'It's nearly ten to three,' Daphne said, as if she'd just been asked the time, her wristwatch an elegant rose gold Rolex, something salvaged from another life.

'And we've got to have a run-through yet for lights and that,' Hector said. 'And sort out the furniture. It's not blinking good enough.'

'Hold on,' Titus said, and strode decisively off to the tobacconist's, Purveyors and Specialists of the Finest Cigars, Loose and Whole Leaf Pipe Tobacco, Cigarettes and Snuff.

A brass bell on top of the door rang him into a den dedicated to their pleasures, the tobacco-scented air added to by the richness from Mr Hobson's pipe. The shopkeeper, pink bow-tied and mutton-chop-whiskered, was smoking an ornately carved meerschaum on a stool behind his counter, head back contemplatively, man and pipe as one, as if each were smoking the other.

Titus bought a cigar and, after lighting it from a counter gas lighter in the form of Mr Punch, said he was looking for the Palace manager.

The shopkeeper twinkled a smile at him. 'I thought you might be something to do with the theatre. Well, he was in earlier, before lunch. For his snuff. He takes Seeger's mentholated and can only get it here. Unless he chooses to drive to Dover. It's your play is it, next door? We're looking forward to it, me and the wife.'

'It will be if we can get in there.'

'Is there nobody there at all? Well, staff do come and go,' the shopkeeper said, when Titus told him all the doors were locked. 'He's not, I imagine, the easiest man to work for, our Mr Smedley,' he added, looking at Titus as if he had more to say, but was wondering if he ought to say it about a regular customer.

'I see,' was all Titus said. 'Does he have far to come, do you know?'

'About five or six miles. He lives in a hamlet called Thornlee. In a house called the Grange,' the tobacconist added, his expression a comment on the size the name suggested.

'Well, we'll drive out there if necessary. Thank you. But meanwhile, have you got a telephone directory I can look at? I've only got his office number.'

The tobacconist smiled and shook his head. 'He went ex-directory some time back. As he made a point of telling me. There's only his address listed. Some people only subscribe to this ex-directory thing to get one up on other people. Some people would have to pay other people to phone them. Some people would have to pay other people to speak to them at all, outside of taking their money,' he added with a chuckle, his pipe sending up smoke again from his world before Titus was out of the shop.

'Trouble at mill?' Simon asked, exaggerating his slight Northern vowels.

'Yes, I think so,' Titus said, 'and I suspect it's our Mr Smedley who's causing it.'

An hour after that, the cast back on the bus, Jack, who'd had a late night, nodding behind the wheel of the Rolls, and Titus about to get him to drive to Thornlee, Mr Smedley pulled up behind the two vehicles in a Ford Prefect that looked recently washed and polished.

After getting out, the manager ran a suspicious eye over it, as if someone might somehow have done something to it on the way there.

'Mr Smedley?' Titus asked.

'I don't know. Can't park outside my own theatre now,' the manager said by way of an answer.

Mr Smedley had tried for a jocular note, but his eyes had spite in them, the sourness of ambition that had ended up at the Palace in Collington. He was wearing a black Homburg hat and coat, with a Rotarian badge in the lapel, a wing collar, and what Titus thought of as banker's pants, pinstripes. The other lapel of his coat, Titus noticed, had traces of snuff on it.

'We were here at two o'clock – as we arranged,' he said pointedly.

The manager looked surprised. 'Two o'clock? I could have sworn we'd agreed four,' he said unconvincingly, and Titus wondered if he'd started as an actor, which would explain why he'd gone into management. Either that or he didn't care whether he was believed or not.

'Still, I'm here now,' he added, dismissing it. 'And you can have the spare key for the rest of the week. Previously,' he went on, 'for a get-in, I'd have left it with one of the two shops here just in case, but...'

Mr Smedley's expression said the rest, spoke of the sort of people he had to put up with. And his sideways glance he sneaked at them as he unlocked one of the entrance doors suggested that he wouldn't be at all surprised if they didn't end up joining them.

Chapter 11

Lizzie Peters was sharing the female dressing-room with Daphne, a bleak room smelling of greasepaint and the hiss of gas from the incandescent light of wall mantles above the make-up tables. And the feel of something like a chill in the air, the feel of a past that had once been cheerfully alive, but which had long grown silent.

A few opening-night cards were lodged in the wooden frame of Lizzie's mirror and on her table, and she had the art nouveau jewellery box given to her by her mother for luck, her make-up sticks and grease-cloths packed neatly away in it.

The premiere of *Love and Miss Harris*, she told herself, seeing it in lights, seeing a red carpet, the admiring faces of fans and the flash bulbs of the press, and was then brought back to a bleak dressing room in the Palace Theatre, when Dolly called for beginners.

Daphne smiled at her, and at her own memories of first nights. 'Off you go then, dear,' she said. 'Break a leg,'

Lizzie walked down the dressing-room corridor with the other beginner, Simon Head, neither of them speaking, their thoughts jumping nervously ahead of them to where the sound of an audience waited.

A plaster mask of Genesius of Rome, patron saint of actors, of fools, clowns and other strays gathered to his protection, looked out from the top of the proscenium arch at an auditorium that had known better days, and fuller houses, the plump cheeks of the nymphs and cupids capering below it grubby with age, their pinks and sky blues peeling here and there.

And then the house lights dimmed like a kindness, and the curtain rose on the bright, redeeming heart of the building, on the lights of the stage, and *Love and Miss Harris*.

George had written a simple tale of love, simply told. The tale of a young girl having to decide between two suitors, a distant echo from her own life – except that then only one of the two men had asked for her hand. The other had been married. And it was because of the married one, because of love, that she had stayed single. The tale was George retelling her youth and giving it, this time, a happy ending. And for her it was enough.

But not, Titus knew, for an audience. It needed something to lift it over the footlights, if it wasn't going to stay that side of them, talking to itself while the audience coughed and fidgeted.

He had updated it and replaced George's rather pale, young upper-class suitor, with Jack's lusty Tom Yardley, man of the people, and turned her other, perfectly blameless, suitor into Simon Head's Rupert Kenton-Browne, a scheming solicitor after Lucinda for the fortune she was unaware she'd been left by her late father (her parents are divorced, acrimoniously, and she lives with her mother, played by Daphne Langan). Titus had then thrown in a wicked uncle and a lost will, that of Lucinda's father. The wicked uncle is Lucinda's Uncle Jasper, Wells Cheslyn, next in line for his brother's wealth, and intent on murdering her to get it. Titus had also added himself to the cast in the role of Edmund Brownlow, a neighbour and father figure to Lucinda. A Titus much restrained in costume in a gent's grey pin-striped suit from a fifty-bob tailor's.

The play opens with Rupert Kenton-Browne calling on Lucinda, establishing for the audience that they are engaged. She then meets odd-job Tom Yardley for the first time when he's fixing a light fitting. He then returns to work on a sticking sash window, and before leaving he tells Lucinda he has done so. A scene they'd had trouble with in rehearsal, Jack managing to turn his description of how he'd unstuck the window into something that would have had the local watch committee closing them down, and which, when he'd tried to make it sound less suggestive, had still turned the two players speechless with laughter.

Titus had had to rewrite it, cutting Jack's inflammatory talk of banging away and where he'd put his chisel. But still feared that first-night nerves might leave them at the mercy of memory and that rehearsal.

In the rewrite Titus had cut the hammer and chisel bit and gone straight to Tom chatting up Lucinda, with Lucinda affronted at his forwardness with an engaged woman – or rather the sort of engaged woman she saw herself to be. She had never been in love, yearned to be, and had told herself that she was, with Rupert Kenton-Browne. And when he had asked for her hand she had said yes, solemnly, in its name, entering into it as if taking holy orders, renouncing in her mind the frivolous life of a single young woman for one dedicated to her future husband and the father of their children.

And then along came Tom Yardley, with green eyes, and laughter, who did something to her that had nothing to do with holy orders, leaving her fighting herself as well as him, before curtly dismissing him, Tom the odd job man.

Titus, watching from the wings, relaxed as the scene moved on past the danger of corpsing. And from the seat she'd opted for in the front row of the dress circle, George, with Gus at her feet, watched contentedly the start of something she knew the end of, while sucking on a pear drop from a quarter-pound bag of them. A surprise present from Robin Finch-Elm before leaving, given to her almost shyly on the doorstep.

The play may now be largely Titus's work but in Lucinda and Tom she still had her happy ending. And like a bridesmaid looking on at a wedding, she could only approve that love had found a home, even if it was in the arms of someone else.

* * *

The next morning Titus was cleaning the ornate woodwork and glass of the Palace's box office, where Mr Smedley had sat last night selling tickets. He was doing so, he'd told Titus, because he could no longer afford to pay someone else to do it. Titus thought it more likely that he was doing so because it gave him a chance to fiddle, to weigh the agreed split of receipts in his favour, using a second roll of tickets.

And he didn't see that there was a lot he could do about it, perhaps even should do about it, if he wanted a return date. Unless the manager got too greedy.

But there was something they could do about the unwelcoming appearance of the theatre entrance and foyer, and they were busy doing it.

Using materials languishing in the cleaning cupboard, they worked under the gaze of players from the Palace's past, tragedians, heroic in tights, Brilliantined leading men, sultry Jean Harlow blondes, and ingénues, still young, their smiles still hopeful, behind the newly cleaned glass.

'We had scrambled eggs for ours,' Lizzie said, answering a remark of Simon's about breakfast. 'Real eggs.'

'From their own chickens,' Dolly added.

'It's because she's got a film star under her roof,' Lizzie said.

She said it lightly, and as if proud of the association. But Daphne knew envy when she heard it, envy of who she had once been. And that suggestion of scorn she'd heard in Lizzie's remarks before, scorn at her fall from that place that she, Lizzie, so hungered to be.

Dumping swept-up litter into a dustbin with a hand-shovel, Daphne blew hair away from her face. 'Nothing of the sort,' she said, just as lightly. 'She keeps a good clean house. With beds that haven't had anyone die in them recently and not changed since. And no bugs in them. Crawling with them, they are, some of the places.'

Dolly immediately endorsed that. 'You can smell 'em soon as you walk in the house. That mouldy smell.'

'And biting at you all night,' Wells put in, and shuddered fastidiously.

George, while not altogether sure what they were talking about, made a sympathetic face at him out of relief that, whatever it was about, she had on this occasion been spared it.

'And we've got a nice fire in the lounge to sit in front of,' Dolly went on.

'And no charge for the coal,' Daphne added.

'No,' Dolly said. 'None of this two-bob-a-scuttle swindle, with half of it dust.'

Dolly and George had opted to share the one double bedroom going, and Daphne and Lizzie had a single each. The landlady, her arms crossed at the front door, had made it clear that she'd take actresses but not actors – not after the last time. So the males of the company, including Hector, innocent of the charge of actor, were spread between two other lodgings, Titus ending up with a room of his own.

'Yeah, well,' Simon said. 'We had no fire and fishcakes. Served cold.'

'Left over from last night's dinner,' Jack said. 'And possibly from the dinner before that, or even older. They had not aged well.'

'There's a rumour going round that we won the war,' Wells put in.

'Better than nothing, mate,' Hector said. 'And there was plenty of bread and butter. And a nice strong cuppa.'

'Some people, Hector,' Titus said, 'don't know they're born.'

Titus had had kippers for breakfast, fat, succulent kippers running with butter, with a couple of eggs poached in the same water, and a plateful of brown bread and butter with the crusts cut genteelly off.

His landlady, a widow of middle years, preferred the pictures to the theatre. And when she answered the door yesterday and found Titus on her doorstep, it was as if the pictures had come to her, stepping out of the silver screen and the world she half lived in. His manly, commanding voice like that of Sir Phillip Steele in the main feature at the Astoria on Friday. Sweeping off his hat in her hall, running a finger under black moustaches, and looking at her the way Sir Phillip had looked at Lady Bellingham, before scooping her up with insolent ease, and carrying her kicking and screaming upstairs.

She'd given him beef stew and dumplings for dinner, followed by marmalade pudding, served, as were his morning kippers, in his room, aloof from her 'commercials', as she dismissively called them, the travellers in trade who, he had learned, whatever they'd had for dinner, had had porridge for breakfast, without the jam.

Wells Cheslyn, who was cleaning the two entrance doors with Jack, said, 'Stale fishcakes. For breakfast! I arst ya, Ada!' he screeched suddenly, a catchphrase from an old charlady drag act of his, the failure of which had added to his long-held conviction that life had turned its back on him.

The charlady act should have been a success, and he hadn't realised just how much he expected it to be until it wasn't. It should have been taken to the hearts of those whose lives it was about. Its catchphrase should have gone from the halls and into the streets, to be heard at work and in Saturday night pubs and shouted, for no particular reason, by errand boys on bikes.

'I arst ya!' he screeched again, a wounded cry of rage at his life. At moonlight flits and pawn shops, and theatrical digs smelling of bedbugs and failure, at putting a brave face on things, slapping on a bit more Leichner and a cheery smile, because the show must go on. At foolish hopes and cruel lovers, and stale fishcakes for breakfast, and tears.

Yes, tears, my dear, and at his age, on his knees like Cinder-bleedin'-ella, head turned away from the others to hide them, furiously polishing the kick-plates on the entrance doors.

After they had finished cleaning, they turned back into actors and took a performance out into the streets, a promotional walk around the town, the cast of *Love and Miss Harris* in the flesh, handing out handbills and courting the citizenry like politicians.

Titus, knowing the English and their dogs, had suggested to George that she bring Gus with her. Gus had slept overnight in the Phantom, on a bed made up for him and with a venison marrow bone for his supper. Titus introduced his owner as the author, while George protested that Titus was the real author, as if shifting blame onto him.

Wells, wearing an end of the pier boater and a blazer striped like a deckchair, with a colourful bow tie of the sort that might light up, or spin round like a propeller, and a daisy buttonhole that might, when one was invited to smell it, squirt water, elegantly waving his long cigarette holder in acknowledgement of his public, whether they knew him or not.

Lizzie Peters in wide-leg trousers, Katherine Hepburn style, and a bright yellow beret, effortlessly beguiling the males on the High Street, while Jack wooed the girls in Woolworth's, his smouldering green gaze leaving them sighing and customers waiting to be served as he moved from counter to counter.

But it was Daphne, Daphne Langan, film star, who drew the bigger audience. In Hollywood-style large, white-framed dark glasses, and a mink coat, something else salvaged from another life, a reminder of who she had once been, or a refuge against who she now was. Signing autographs and answering questions about her life and career, and what she had done since her last film, her public smile increasingly at bay until rescued by Titus.

Chapter 12

Titus had organised complimentary review tickets for the two local newspapers and interviews for Daphne. The first with the Wednesday edition of the *East Kent Observer*, and the second, the most important of the two, for Saturday, the last day of their one-week run, with the more local newspaper, the *Collington Gazette and Advertiser*.

Both papers had reviewed it favourably, and the *Gazette*, which came out midday, had given the interview a two-page spread, with photographs, two of them of George, Lady Devonaire, Titus had let it be known. One posed with the Rolls, the other with Gus at heel, not thinking about anything very much and looking snootily aloof about it, his great head lifted imperiously.

They took bookings in the afternoon and in the evening began selling tickets almost as soon as the box office opened.

Titus heard them coming in when backstage, heard promise in the air, like the discordant notes of an orchestra warming up. The sound of people taking their seats, chatting, laughing, shouting a greeting to a friend or neighbour, boisterous with the freedom of a weekend and a Saturday night's entertainment waiting.

And shortly after the curtain went up on their last performance there, Hector retrieved the House Full board from the props store.

That they were sold out was known backstage and on it before the end of the first act. Dolly told Jack when a move took him near the prompt corner, and in a whisper the audience took to be an endearment after their first kiss, Jack told Lizzie.

After the curtain call, the applause from a full house like an extra brightness under the house lights, the company met to be paid their share of the ticket and programme sales.

They gathered, as they had done at the end of every performance, in the corridor outside the male dressing room, talking and laughing, loud with the night's box office and the thought of extra wages, and with the feeling also of it being an omen for the rest of the tour.

When Titus was separating the key on his key ring, Daphne noticed that the door was slightly ajar. She gave it a slight push with a finger and looked at Titus.

'I locked it. I know I did,' he said, walking in, the others coming to a halt behind him when he stopped and stood looking at his make-up table.

The paperwork, as he called it, was there as usual, the manager's calculations of the split of ticket and programme sales, but not what they added up to, not their share waiting in a green-cloth cash bag.

'Where's our money?' Lizzie said wonderingly.

'It's gone,' Wells told her, as if he for one had expected nothing less, simply adding it to the other things life did to him, his lips wringing sour amusement out of it.

'Somebody's nicked it,' Hector said, as if it were somehow inevitable.

'That door was locked!' Titus said, stabbing at a finger at it. 'I locked it.'

'It doesn't look forced,' Jack said. 'Who else had a key?'

'Just me and Smedley. He let us have just the three. One to Daphne for their room, one for here, and a key for the front door. That's all. He's got a thing about keys.'

'Are we sure it's not here?' George said.

By way of an answer, Titus indicated the sparse furnishing: make-up table, chairs, and the deal wardrobe Dolly was hopefully peering in.

'Hold on,' he said then, turning abruptly.

Mr Smedley would usually by then have left for the day. But he checked first that he still wasn't in the box office, and found it locked. As was the manager's office.

'He's locked up, bar as well,' he said, reporting back. 'I told Gilbert about it,' he went on, referring to the stage-door keeper. 'He hadn't seen anyone going in or out who shouldn't be doing so.'

'That doesn't tell us a lot,' Jack said. 'Every time I've signed in he's had his nose in the racing pages.'

'He hasn't had a lot of luck either lately, he told me,' Hector said. 'So perhaps he took it, to make up.'

'I wouldn't be surprised,' Daphne added. 'He's got that look about him.'

'The haunted look of a man who keeps backing losers,' Jack said.

'If he did take it,' Titus said, 'he's a damn good actor. A performance, when I sprung it on him with that in mind, Stanislavski would have applauded. Besides, he doesn't have a key. Or he shouldn't have.'

'He could have had a copy made,' George, a regular visitor to the whodunit shelves of her local lending library, suggested. 'Got hold of the master key somehow and made an impression of it by pressing it into a bar of soap. And then used his underworld connections to get a copy made.'

'Does he have underworld connections, George?' Lizzie asked, her expression suggesting she was perfectly prepared to believe that he had.

'I don't know,' George admitted. 'But it is possible.'

'Are you sure you locked it, darling?' Dolly said, more prosaically. 'I mean, we can all—'

'I locked it, I tell you! I remember clearly doing so. And as far as I know Smedley's the only other one with a key.'

'Then he's had it,' Hector said. 'Wouldn't surprise me.'

'Nor me. I wouldn't trust him further than I could throw him,' Daphne said.

'He's a creep,' Lizzie said, and shuddered.

'Those accidently-on-purpose hands,' Daphne agreed.

'He's taken advantage of tonight's box office and filled his boots,' Hector said. 'Going by the state of the Full House board, the last time they had a house like tonight Queen Vic was on the throne.'

'He's run off with a trollop,' Wells snarled. 'Left his wife after milking the poor old cow dry, and run off with the young usherette here, the one who needs her roots doing. As common as muck and legs open all hours—'

'Wells!' Titus said sharply, glancing at George, who was listening with interest.

'Well, if he has legged it,' Simon said, 'it must have been a spur of the moment thing, seeing that the paperwork's there. You know, overcome with greed.'

George smiled at his naivety. 'The paperwork is a red herring, Simon. As is the door. We were meant to think that an opportunistic sneak thief, entering when Gilbert was engaged in picking tomorrow's runners, found it left carelessly unlocked by Titus.'

'He's on the boat to Calais with his tart as we speak,' Wells said. 'Opening a bottle of Dom Pérignon to toast all the bums we put on seats for him. The goddamn bloody bastard!' he snarled.

'Haven't they got a concert party coming in next week?' Dolly said, referring to the town council, the owners of the theatre.

Wells sniffed. 'The Twinklies,' he said with great disdain. 'At least the town's been spared that bleeding lot shrieking at them.'

Titus shook his head. 'They come in the week after. Next week's dark. But we don't know yet that he has bolted.' He shook his head. 'I don't know, as far as I can see, it's a damn good job our week's digs includes Sunday night. Because unless it's sorted out before then I can't see there's anything much we can do about it until Monday morning.'

Chapter 13

Titus had looked in on the theatre several times the following day, just in case. He even checked the dressing room, peering in as if in this place that nightly made its own reality, and with an imagination that hadn't been left entirely behind in the shadows of a Welsh childhood, he might surprise a different ending.

But it was as it had been, just another room now their run was finished, like the auditorium, empty and silent, its Saturday night litter waiting for the cleaners.

His last visit there had been just before bed, convinced now that Smedley had taken the money, letting himself in quietly as if hoping to catch him skulking in the dark.

They were all glad to see the back of the day. It had rained for most of it, blown in on winds from the Channel, falling from a slate-blue sky heavy with more of it on a town shut for Sunday, leaving them sitting about waiting for life to start again on Monday.

And Titus woke on that morning with a determination that whatever the story involving Smedley was about, it was not going to end with their night's wages in his pocket.

But he hadn't a lot of time to do it in. In a few hours they had to cross the border into Surrey for their next venue, with three hours and more driving to get there.

On his way out of the digs he met one of his landlady's 'commercials' in the hall loaded with various items, Titus recognising a film reel canister among them.

'Thanks, old boy,' the young salesman said, when Titus opened the front door for him, the accent going with the Brylcreemed hair and RAF tie.

'I do sales presentations using a film projector,' he explained on the way out. 'Get all the bods in the area I want to see under one roof and treat 'em to a film show. Need all the help I can get these days. What with a growing family to support and the cost of living.'

He grinned, a look Titus had seen before. A look that went with high spirits and rowdiness in the mess, and gallantry, duty turned into a youthful sport and met with dauntless courage. A look that would stay young no matter how old the man might get.

'Besides,' he added, 'it livens things up a bit.'

Titus gave him a hand to his car, a low-slung cherry-red Triumph Roadster, not the latest model, but obviously well kept, its bodywork gleaming with attention.

His equipment loaded, the salesman patted the canvas roof affectionately. 'One-seven-seven-six cc, four cylinder engine. I can push eighty out of the old girl on a good road.'

Titus watched him pull away and turn off for the high street, heard the racing changes as he roared up it, and thought that it was perhaps the nearest he could get now to danger and the freedom of the skies, and youth. Leaving briefly behind with his foot down, a life with a growing family and the cost of living in it.

On his way to the Palace, hoping to find Smedley there, before reporting the theft at the local police station, Titus met Jack, out for cigarettes and a morning paper, and they walked up to the theatre together.

There was still no manager there, the sound of voices in the empty theatre coming from the auditorium, from the two cleaners he used, talking to each other across the seats as they worked.

When they were told about the missing money, the elder of the two, wearing a battered-looking trilby over a hairnet, and with an accent with the sound of Bow Bells in it, said, 'You're sure are you, mate, that it was there in the first place? I wouldn't put anything past him. He can't bear to part with money, our Mr Smedley. Keeps us waiting for our few coppers for as long as blooming possible. And then it's a wrench parting with them. Pitiful to see, it is.'

'He's a mean bugger. That's why we're working today, cleaning on a Monday for Saturday,' the other said, 'instead of the morning after like we normally do. He won't pay us extra for working on a Sunday.'

'He's so tight his bum squeaks when he walks,' the older one got out, laughing and coughing over one of the Player's cigarettes Jack had passed around. 'We've only got the auditorium here, while at the Astoria we do everywhere.'

'Auditorium, front of house, front steps, offices,' the other put in, 'projection room, storerooms, the his and hers, the lot. And paid at a higher rate and at a regular time.'

They didn't know his telephone number nor where he lived, except that it was out of town somewhere.

They thanked the women, and were walking away when the younger cleaner said suddenly, 'I saw him earlier, come to think of it. About half hour ago, on my way here. I take a short cut through the square and he was going into the town hall there.'

Following directions, the two men entered the small square at the end of the high street, the town's marketplace and its civic heart. The clock tower of the town hall standing over the blue lamp of a police station, the half-timbers and lattice windows of a library that was once judges' lodging, a museum, and the assize court, the worn, pale Kentish stone steps leading up to it as steep as those to the scaffold.

On a plinth in the centre of the square, the statue of a British naval officer in tricorn hat and breeches sighted a telescope in the direction of the English Channel, waiting for the French to come.

They saw that the Palace manager was still in the town hall, his Ford Prefect parked on the slight cobbled incline in front of the entrance. Titus saw that this was also the venue for the young salesman's presentation, his red Roadster a dashing addition to the few other cars there.

'Collington Town Hall was built in 1725 and is considered to be an outstanding example of early Georgian elegance and decoration,' Jack told Titus, reading off a framed notice inside the hall, something to do while waiting at the reception desk, the patterned tiled floor echoing now and then with people busily crossing it. Portraits in oils of past mayors in full robes and regalia were lined up along one wall, their gaze stern with civic duty.

'The clock tower,' Jack went on, 'was added in 1837 in celebration of Queen Victoria's ascension to the throne.'

'Just don't set your watch by it. It's losing anything up to twenty minutes in twenty-four hours,' the porter said, returning to his desk as if just back from chiding it.

'I'd consider myself lucky,' Titus said, 'if that's all I've lost at that age.'

The porter ignored it. He took in Titus's appearance and pointed to a modern wall clock, a timepiece that could be relied on. 'You're late,' he said, smiling through his disapproval.

His soldierly smartness was a rebuke to Titus's flamboyance. Light swam in the brass buttons on his suit of municipal green serge, the toecaps of his boots black mirrors, and not a hair of his oiled short back and sides out of place.

'It started about thirty minutes ago,' he went on, and when Titus looked blank said with a touch of impatience, 'I assume you're here for that, the sports, recreations and entertainments meeting. Chaired by his worship the mayor.'

'Mr Smedley…' Titus said, trying the name out on him.

'He's already up there. As I say, you're late. Still, you're here now. I'll give them a ring, tell them—'

'No, no. No need for that, thank you. We'll just slip in. Don't want to cause a disruption. Where—?'

'It's being held in the parlour, the Mayor's Parlour. Second floor. On the left. It's on the door.'

As they were walking away the porter surprised them by saying, 'By the way, we enjoyed the show the other night, me and the missus. Nice effort all round. And that Miss Harris is a poppet. You're a lucky man, lad.'

Jack agreed that he was, and said he'd pass the compliment on.

And it was the way Jack agreed that prompted Titus, as they started up the stairs, to say, 'I hope, incidentally, dear boy, that when it comes to Lizzie you're leaving it on the stage. On the stage and in your trousers.'

It was too late for that. He had scaled cliffs on ropes, their heights towering above him into darkness and the machine guns of an enemy. A drainpipe leading to the second floor of her digs, and Lizzie waiting like Juliet, was to him as obliging as a carpeted flight of stairs.

He was wondering what business it was of Titus's, when Titus went on, 'You've never toured before, so you won't have experienced the demented power of local watch committees, the lambs of the elect, a last refuge of the Puritan conscience of England. They are untutored zealots, seeking out iniquity and sexual immorality lurking behind the furniture and between the lines. They are armoured with righteousness and the unassailable conviction that they know best. So no curtain goes up on a town's pleasure without them saying it does. Their remit is censorship and the regulation of places of entertainment, and the regulation part of that, dear lad, covers the activities of randy young actors off the stage, as well as on it. You see why I mentioned it?'

Jack did see. 'Well, yes of course, boss—'

He was saved from having to lie, or confess, by Titus coming to a halt. 'Ah, here we are.'

It was as the porter had said on the door, Mayor's Parlour, written across it in gold leaf on the polished oak, a sign hanging from the brass doorknob adding that the mayor was in conference.

Jack put an ear to the door. 'They're being very quiet about it. Do we knock and wait, knock and walk in, or just walk in?'

'We just walk in. I want to see his face when we do so,' Titus said, and turned the doorknob. The door was locked. He knocked on it, then knocked again.

'Can't you read?' somebody the other side of it said.

'Urgent message for the mayor,' Titus said, feeling as if he'd just come on with the one line to say.

The door was unlocked and opened a few inches.

'What is—?' the voice started, its owner disappearing behind it as Titus shoved it open and they walked into a room in near darkness, curtains that had been lined for war and the blackout, drawn on a large window overlooking the square, tobacco smoke moving lazily in the beam of light from a film projector.

Jack turned on the lights and got the attention of the dozen or so men sitting one side of a long conference table, blinking in the sudden light as if waking from their thoughts in the dark. Behind them, the projector was running in the silence with a sound like a busy toy train set, and Jack watched with interest a scene captioned 'The Artist's Model', showing a pert nude on a chaise longue offering more than a life-drawing exercise, before the projectionist turned off the machine.

The projectionist, Titus noted, was the young salesman from his digs. And he also saw then the man he was looking for, Smedley, sitting at the far end of the table.

Titus took the dramatic route. Using a vacant chair his end to mount it, he strode the table in his hessian boots like a stage, to an audience of councillors along it gaping up at him, past coffee cups and ashtrays, his drawn sword a bright flash of menace under the ceiling lights.

'Titus!' Jack said warningly, keeping pace with him, not at all sure what he intended doing. There were times when he was given to wondering if Titus was altogether sane.

'I didn't take the money!' Smedley cried, and knocked his chair over in panic as Titus, Captain of Musketeers, dropped nimbly to the floor.

He made the air sing with a few swipes at it with the blade, before advancing on the manager.

Smedley backed away until he could go no further, coming up against the mayor's white stone fireplace, the large enamel town crest on the wall above it proclaiming Industry, Virtue, Service.

The tip of Titus's sword touched the area of the manager's heart as if establishing the target, and Smedley squealed.

'And how, sirrah,' Titus said, 'did you know the money was missing?'

He prodded a silent Smedley with the blade. 'Speak, Ghost!'

The manager tried to, his mouth opening and closing on nothing. 'Somebody must have told me,' he got out then. 'Gilbert, maybe. Yes, that's it, Gilbert! He told me. It was Gilbert. I don't know. I can't remember!' he wailed, Titus shaking his head at the wrong answer. 'All I know is that the door was unlocked when I delivered it with the figures. And I left it unlocked because I thought someone had just nipped out, you know… I intended contacting you about it today, of course, after we'd…' he said, indicating the projector, before realising and running out of words.

Mr Smedley groaned among the ruins of his morning, his head moving as if seeking escape, or the next lie.

'I didn't take it. I didn't take the money,' he said on a louder, shrill note, aware that he was now the main feature, someone with a bigger problem than his audience of councillors, and tried a laugh at the absurdity of the idea, the sound coming out like a sob.

The mayor thought it was time to assert authority in his own parlour.

He stood, hands on his suit lapels, his usual pose when speaking officially, and addressed Titus. 'I don't know who you are, sir. But I am the mayor of—'

'Not for much longer you're not, if this gets out,' Titus said. 'Out there the roads are potholed, half the street lights don't work and dustbins go unemptied,' he went on with extra heat, offloading some of the complaints he'd had to listen to from his landlady, the price he'd paid for special treatment at the table. 'While the town's leading citizen, and its representatives,' he said, looking down the table and wondering if that included members of the watch committee, 'are sitting in your parlour having erections on the rates.'

Mr Smedley, taking advantage of the digression, started to edge round the sword, until Titus held him there with it. 'Stay, sirrah,' he growled.

The manager tried for indignation. 'I don't have to stand here listening to—' he started, and squeaked when Titus jabbed him with it.

'You, sirrah, will stand where I tell you to stand. You are a liar and a thief. A scoundrel who sought to drag my name into it by suggesting that I might have taken the money—'

'No! No, I—'

'Quiet! Money that you stole. Money you took from the mouths of artists. And by God, sir, by God, there's a price to pay for that, and I'm here to extract it!' Titus snarled, drawing back his sword arm, eyes rolling in a sudden rage, a man going over the edge.

And Jack, about to step in, was reassured. He'd seen this performance before, Titus chewing the scenery as the mad squire in *The Secret of Haddingtom Grange*.

'No! No – don't! You can have the money,' Smedley cried, fear wrenching the offer out of him. He sweated fear, his face clammy with it and drained to paper. 'You can have it, you can have all you were due, every penny. I didn't take it, but you can have it, of course. Of course you can, the insurance will cover it, I was going to tell you about that,' he burbled, the words falling over each other in their haste to get out, and then he stopped to catch his breath as if he'd been running.

Titus appeared to be thinking about it, which Smedley found only slightly more reassuring. The expression Titus was pulling, with one eye cocked at the ceiling, as if shrewdly listening to advice from there, suggested that his considerations were no less unhinged.

'Today,' Titus said then, as if passing it on. 'It must be today.'

'Yes, yes, of course, today,' Smedley gushed with relief.

Titus lowered the sword. 'Very well.'

Smedley smiled shakily. 'A misunderstanding, that's all. A misunderstanding,' he said, dabbing at his face with a pressed white pocket handkerchief. 'It was obviously some sneak thief off the street, not unknown in theatres,' he went on, sharing it with the rest of the room. 'And you may be sure I shall be having words with my doorkeeper concerning that. Meanwhile, I apologise to his worship and councillors for the disruption it caused. And of course to you, Mr Llewellyn-Gwynne, for the inconvenience. As I intimated, the company accepts full responsibility and restitution will be paid to the penny and without quibble.'

This was Smedley reasserting himself, in the eyes of the rest of the room, and in his own. This was local worthy Clarence Smedley, theatre manager and Rotarian, with friends in the town hall, returning like the blood to his face. And with it, a suggestion of sly calculation.

'There is of course, regarding restitution, proper procedure to follow, but if you put the claim in writing it will be dealt with expeditiously. Most expeditiously, I assure you. I myself will...'

He dried as the tip of Titus's sword found his heart again, and gently prodded it a couple of times.

'You mistook me, sirrah,' Titus said almost gently, as if with regret for what that might mean. 'It is for me a question of honour.

79

We leave your town this morning, and we leave with what you stole from us or it ends here for you. And for me eventually. You skewered on my blade and I in the hanging shed in Maidstone Prison. Honour demands it, boyo,' he added, as if both explaining it to him and apologising for it.

Jack started urgently forward, 'Mr Smedley – Mr Smedley, be advised, sir, that he means it,' he said, dread in his eyes, as if remembering another time Titus had meant it.

Mr Smedley found his voice. 'Yes, yes, well, I must confess that I had quite forgotten you leave today for your next venue,' he said, looking away from the sword, as if whatever he had to say was not influenced by it. 'Well, as the company accepts responsibility, I'm sure I could issue—'

The manager caught his breath as the sword point nudged him.

'Cash, Mr Smedley. In cash.'

'Cash. Yes, well, I suppose that can be done. I haven't banked yet. And if you signed for it. Yes, I don't see—'

'Then, sir,' Titus said, lowering the sword, 'after you.'

Mr Smedley went ahead, his face alive with small, fleeting movements, as if he were seeking an expression, an attitude, to get him past the long table.

'I suggest,' Titus said to the councillors in passing, 'that if we don't want our activities here to end up on the front page of the *Gazette*, we keep quiet about them.'

A mumble of hurried agreement followed them on their way to the door. The young RAF pilot was perched on the table at that end, smoking and idly swinging a leg.

'What about me, old man?' he said to Titus. 'What—'

'You, boy?' Titus laughed. 'You should be given a bloody gong, you should. For initiative in the face of the cost of living and a growing family. And another one to go with it for bare-faced bloody cheek!'

* * *

Mr Smedley, arriving at the Palace with his escort, found that the morning hadn't quite finished with him.

The two cleaners, their morning's work done, were leaving the theatre as the men entered it, and Titus invited them to tag along.

The four of them stood in the manager's office while Smedley, stooping to the large green floor safe, opened it as if at gunpoint.

Chapter 14

Not long after that, the tour bus, loaded again, left Collington and turned towards the Surrey Hills. On the top deck the talk was of their unexpected windfall.

'So who did dunit?' Wells asked, and giggled.

'Who cares,' Simon said. 'Hats off to the guv'nor for getting it back.'

Lizzie laughed. 'Jack said that at one point he thought the old man was actually going to run Smedley through.'

'Titus is a sweetie, an absolute lamb,' Daphne said. 'But he is a Celt. My second husband was. Of the Irish family. They can go off like fireworks. No telling with them.'

Wells flicked the end of the cigarette from his holder out of the window, a Dunhill, in this time of sudden windfall, holding their own in his silver-plated case, instead of his usual small Woodbines, which always looked a bit intimidated by it.

'Well thank gawd for Celts, I say, m'dears,' he drawled.

'Not half,' Simon added.

'Which just goes to show, darlings, you never know what's round the corner,' Daphne said, a woman who'd been round a few such corners in her life.

Wells couldn't agree with her more, and after saying so, vehemently, startled them by sweeping off his boater and breaking into song.

Wells, who'd said often enough that he didn't ask much of life, just a little happiness now and then, and someone to share it with, someone to love, was happy. A happiness that at times came near to tears of gratitude.

He had in his mind been given far more than his Saturday night wages. He saw it as an omen. He saw it as life looking his way for once, a sign that he hadn't been left behind after all, hadn't been forgotten. Another new beginning, one he saw at times like this as an ending, a call after the curtain. As if he were gazing out into the shining dark of an auditorium, stunned by a standing ovation, utterly, *incredibly*, unexpected, a full house on its feet, and his at long last. Wells was on one of his ups, dizzily high on optimism and hope.

And so he sang, camping it up a little to show it shouldn't be taken too seriously, his end of the pier boater clamped to his yearning heart, sang a song about love, because you never know what's round the corner.

The others joined in after that with 'You Are My Sunshine', singing on their way with their vagabond world, the story they peddled dressed in rags and sticks, in costumes and make-up, painted scenery and a few coloured lights, and a red curtain, in case it was needed, the entrance to that world.

A world in which they lived as if a tribe cut off from the wider one, a world for them that was far more intense, far more real than real life, that boring, seemingly aimless business outside the walls of a theatre.

While in his cab, Hector whistled along with the singing, in a tuneless, desultory sort of way, a man short of diversions, with nothing to do but drive and whistle.

He was following the Phantom, the route Jack had found when returning on Saturday after papering Godshall-on-the-Water, their next venue, with playbills. It had hardly any traffic on it and nothing to look at but countryside. That's all there was, countryside, miles and blooming miles of it. No houses, no streets, no pubs, no cinemas, no pie and mash shops, or jellied eel stalls, or street markets, no people.

Just ruddy countryside everywhere, and more of it after the next crossroads and around the next ruddy bend.

And this was the sort of thing his son said refreshed his soul and all that, he told himself again, incredulously, taking another look now and then at all that green, and shaking his head over it, something to do between whistling.

His married son, the manager of the Crouch End Co-op, was an enthusiastic member of the local rambling club. He'd been born in 1914, shortly before Hector, a Thames mudlark and son of a lighterman, went off to war in the Royal Navy.

Serving as a gunner's mate, he had come through the fire and shell of the Battle of Jutland without a scratch, and on unexpected home leave afterwards, had arrived to the news that his young wife was dead, the result of a misstep the day before on a short flight of cellar stairs.

His son was an only child, his relationship with him a perfectly amiable, loving one. A relationship that could accommodate differing views on all sorts of subjects, even the support of different football teams, without raised voices.

But after an exchange between them a few years back, the countryside was one subject that was never mentioned again.

His son had gone on again about it refreshing his soul again, after a summer weekend walking about in it, and Hector had said that he just found it boring.

'Boring…?' his son had said, and laughed. 'My father finds England's jewel boring,' he'd said, as incredulous in its favour as Hector had been against it.

'Yes, boring,' Hector had said, stung. 'Boring. Nothing in it but… but blinking countryside.'

His son had smirked. 'I think you'll find that that is why, Father, it's called the countryside,' he informed him in his manager's voice, as if getting the upper hand with a customer, and things had gone rapidly and loudly downhill after that.

The English countryside, that other garden, that Eden, that place of peace and serenity in so many hearts, had brought a loving father and son almost to blows.

* * *

After lunch at a roadhouse, they journeyed on through a late spring turning to summer, to where the chalk heights of the North Downs ran down to the lowlands of the Thames, up to the Surrey Hills with their spires and blue distances. Down through river valleys and climbing again, to where the afternoon shadows grew longer under the trees.

And then a sight to lift Hector's heart, a roadside fingerpost telling him that Godshall-on-the-Water was a mere two miles ahead of them. A mere two miles and he'd have something to look at again.

'Oh, how nice,' Daphne said a short while later, on the hill down to it, the town suddenly there around a dogleg bend, the cross of St George flying like a battle standard from the pinnacled Norman tower of its church.

A Monday afternoon high street, black and white Elizabethan buildings, teashops, and flower baskets outside pubs, and overhanging ornate Tudor gables, the herringbone brick between the half timbers baked to a pale pink in the suns of four centuries.

Lizzie leaned across to Wells on the seat opposite. 'We're here, Wells!' she said, waking him.

'They'll take *The Times* and listen to the Third Programme,' Daphne said. 'We should do well here.'

'Because it's a play, because it's thee-taar,' Wells said, his up turned into a down after a nap. 'Pierrots and a comedian would be very below the salt. Well, I'm sticking to summer

85

season and pantomime after this, darlings. Walking through the same front door for a few months, even if the digs aren't like Mother used to make. And your day off is your day off. Not spent travelling halfway across the bleeding country,' he snarled, talking to himself while despising Godshall-on-the-Water out of the window.

'Jack's been busy,' Simon said, peering down at another shop window with one of their playbills in it.

They turned off the high street, following the Rolls down a narrow side road to the venue, the Little Theatre, halfway along it.

The Rolls pulled in behind a line of beer barrels reserving a space for them on the road outside, while the tour bus waited with its engine idling holding up a post van.

Jack gave a couple of sharp blasts on the car's horn and got out, followed by Titus.

A tall, stringy young man in a diamond-patterned pullover, creased flannels and a tweed cap, joined them from the theatre and helped stack the empty barrels on the pavement.

Jack introduced him to Titus as Norman, the stage manager, as Hector pulled into the vacant space, sounding a note of thanks on the horn as the post van and two other vehicles it had collected went on past.

'What's that?' Norman said then, pointing at Gus on his lead with George and Dolly.

'That's Gus,' Jack told him, and introduced the two women.

George pulled Gus away when he stopped at one of the barrels, and led him to a lamp post further down.

'Is Mr Prosser inside?' Titus asked Norman.

He was told he was, and when Titus and Dolly headed for the theatre entrance, Norman looked at Jack and added in a low voice. 'So's Alma.'

'Ah,' Jack said.

'I've got nowhere with her, but you—'

'Ah, and that's the trouble, Norman,' Jack said, glancing at Lizzie leaving the bus with the others.

'She really fancies you, mate,' said Norman. 'She's made that obvious.'

'She's certainly a looker,' Jack said, as if admitting the strength of an opponent, and sounding not altogether sure how long he could hold out.

Titus and Dolly came out with Reg Prosser, the owner of the Little Theatre, and Norman's assistant, Alma Cooper, a young brunette. Reg Prosser and Titus were both puffing away at cheroots.

Reg was a short, round, almost spherical figure dressed like an on-course bookmaker or comedian in loud checks, and a grey, curly-brimmed bowler hat and two-tone shoes.

He came to a halt on the steps of the theatre and stood beaming delight at the company and then at the bus.

'Like a show on its own,' he said, and beamed again when he saw Gus. 'With a pony to go with it.'

There was lots of beaming in Reg's world, his plump cheeks squeezing out merriment, turning his eyes into small, shining blue pebbles.

Alma had eyes only for Jack, gazing at him from some unfathomable distance of her own.

Not that Lizzie found it in the least unfathomable. She took it in at a glance, along with the recent make-up job, the tight sweater and bullet bra, and the flow of her long shining hair, washed that morning, the small tosses of her head moving it like Veronica Lake's.

'Mr Prosser here—' Titus started.

Reg waved it away with his cigar. 'Reg, Titus. Reg.'

'Reg here, a man of generous instinct, and a friend to strolling players, has kindly offered us, the entire company, full board in an hotel he owns in the town. And—'

'Now, it's not the Savoy,' Reg put in. 'And most of you will have to share, I'm afraid. But it's clean.'

'And, ladies and gentlemen, he will not accept a penny in payment from us. Not a penny!'

Reg waved that away as well with his cigar, and the applause from the company which followed.

'Well,' he said, looking embarrassed, 'the rooms are empty for now, and the kitchen has to cook for the other guests anyway, so…'

'I have already pointed out to our generous friend here,' Titus said, 'that someone else would have let those empty rooms to a company he knew was on their way here, and charged that company, quite legitimately, for the meals on top. I will not have you sell your generosity short, sir.'

Reg had readily agreed that the bus should stay parked up outside the theatre for the publicity value, and now said that the Rolls could use the hotel's car park.

'Add a bit of class to it. But we'll have a drink first, to wet the new play's head,' he said, beaming it at them, a man who delighted in hospitality. He'd sold the country-wide haulage business he'd started with one lorry, and bought a hotel, a pub and a theatre. All places of hospitality, all speaking of the Reg he could now afford to be.

He indicated the cheerful, red-painted front of the Cock and Bottle pub on the other side of the stage door, with its hanging baskets, window boxes and carriage lamps, and laughed when Titus looked dubiously at his watch.

'There's none of that nonsense about licensing laws there, Titus. Long as we don't start breaking the place up and get the local bobby on the doorstep. I own that as well.'

Chapter 15

In his more heated moments, when there was no room for reason, or anything else, only rage and resentment, Reuben believed, or chose to believe, that Jack was part of some sort of conspiracy against him. A conspiracy behind which he was hiding, hiding and laughing at him.

He was always ready to indulge a plot, life waiting for him in the shadows, and an anger that went back to that seven-year-old returning from Blackheath to the lie, as he saw it, that life as he knew it was all there was. A lie that everyone knew about except him.

It was an anger in which Reuben had found himself, found who he was. The Reuben that years later would learn with indifference that half his family had perished in the rubble the bombers had left behind that night. Indifference, and a feeling that it had somehow served them right.

He was staying most nights in the West End now, sleeping over in the house of a madam running a brothel in Soho's Duck Lane. They'd been lovers, of a sort, once, when both were much younger. She was starting up in a small flat in Dulwich, and he was running his book, and looking after her, as he'd called it, in the evenings, for a percentage of her earnings.

Money she'd handed over willingly, because she'd been smitten by him, finding shelter in his size and maleness. Something he played on to take more of her money, talking of marriage and a need to save, while meaning of course none of it. He wanted a better class of wife to go with the future he had in mind.

She had learned in time the real nature of Reuben, learned and came to know enough about him not to deny him favours when he had use for her again.

He spent those evenings looking for Jack in the West End clubs and pubs he was told actors use, the loaded Colt in his inside pocket. He had no clear plan, except that of following him out of wherever and doing it then, the risk of neon-lit streets lost in the heat of finding him.

Following him and calling his name, softly, only the two of them then, no matter how busy the street. The knowledge of what he had come to do, shared without speaking, without needing to speak, a moment's intimacy between them. Before he ended it, before he had the last word.

The shots like fireworks going off, like a bit of Saturday night idiocy. Shots that turned him into a spectator when alarm set in, and spread, wondering with everyone else what had happened, before slipping away in the confusion.

He had haunted the West End looking for Jack, and then one night he found him. Or someone who knew where he could be found. Where both could be found. Jack and the Welshman.

He was in Ward's Irish House, a subterranean pub in the bowels of Piccadilly Circus, reached down two steep flights of stone steps, its walls tiled like a public lavatory in cream and pale green. It was a licensed, unofficial bomb shelter during the war, the working girls following the uniforms of nations down there when the sirens went, turning the place into a party while the bombs fell.

It was used by actors, journalists, writers and others who had wandered down from Soho, and Irish labourers, still pulling down what the bombers had left behind to build again, patriotically smoking Carroll's cigarettes and drinking the best-kept draught

Guinness in London, the air scented with the smell of malt and disinfectant, and something else, some note that spoke only of Ward's.

Reuben was standing at the bar, next to a middle-aged man with a sort of flamboyance about him that suggested the West End.

Reuben made a show of looking around, and then, opening the conversation, said that he was London born and bred, but had never known, or heard of, a pub under Piccadilly Circus.

And nor had he. A man drawn to darkened doorways, he'd spotted the unlit entrance when walking past it in Shaftsbury Avenue, an invitation calling from the neon shadows.

The man opened up like someone in need of company, or another drink, clutching the remains of one on the bar as if holding on.

'And you are not, by any means, my dear sir, alone in that. Not many people in this town do know about it. It's a sort of club, if you like. A club for the un-clubbable, some might put it. It's said to have been a public lavatory once. And unkind tongues might contend that it still is. You may have noticed that the air is not of the most fragrant. What is that smell? a visitor once asked. Failure, he was told. Anyway, the theory was that it was once part of the Underground system. A lavatory, or lavatories, left luggage lockers, and perhaps a ticket office, that sort of thing. But I must confess that I cannot see that myself. Not that what I can or cannot see has any bearing on it, carries any weight or sheds light one way or the other. Not being a civic engineer or architect, or planner, or whatever anyone involved in the design and construction of such a thing might be called,' he said, and as if it had taken it out of him, touched his brow a couple of times delicately with a hand that fluttered, and trembled briefly.

'Yeah, well, it's certainly interesting,' Reuben said, making a contribution.

'You get all sorts in here,' the man said then, in a sudden, low confiding voice. 'All sorts. Scribblers, painters, film people, working girls of both sexes off the Dilly, refugees from Soho, navvies bringing London's ruin in on their boots, scriptwriters looking for contacts, or seeking solace in its wares. And last, but I hope not least, practitioners of my own trade,' the man added, placing a hand with a flourish to his chest and bowing slightly, 'ac-tors.'

Reuben, who had regular manicures, noticed that he had dirt under his fingernails.

He told him that he thought he looked familiar, and invited him to join him in a drink, picking up his glass when the man appeared to hesitate.

'Well, there's nothing glamorous about my job,' he said, while waiting for their order. 'I'm a businessman. Import and export.'

'Not glamorous, perhaps. But necessary. A far more important qualification, I would submit. I would even go as far as to say vital – yes, sir, I will not quibble. It is vital. Absolutely vital!' the man insisted, slapping the zinc-topped bar in emphasis, charged with the sight of his glass milking the gin optic. 'Trade, commerce, is what gets a country out of bed in the morning. It's nothing short of its lifeblood. Moving its limbs, feeding its beating heart. Without it we die. There's glamour for you, sir, if glamour you must have. Your health,' he added, a double Beefeater secured in his hand.

'Funnily enough, you know, I almost invested in the theatre, in a play, once,' Reuben said, after a brief excursion into the latest export figures, briefing himself on them in the *Financial Times* that morning.

'Ah. An angel at my shoulder. Or almost an angel. A backer, an investor,' he translated.

'Yes, that's right. But nothing came of it.'

'Get a copy of the *Stage* newspaper, my dear chap, if you fancy a punt. They often carry that sort of thing in the back pages.'

'Thanks, I will. Yes, this was an ad in a newspaper, come to think of it. The *Standard*, I think it was. Bloke called Titus – something or other, advertised for investors. But as I say, nothing came of it.'

'Titus…?' The man considered. 'Wayward eyebrows and a black beard?'

'Yes. Yes, a beard.'

'Welsh?'

'Yes. Yes, he was Welsh.'

'Carries a swordstick?'

'Yes, now you mention it, he did,' Reuben said, the memory of it going home again.

'Titus Llewellyn-Gwynne, actor-manager. I know him well, know him well, Horatio. He's drawn that sword at least once to my knowledge, enlivening a summer's evening in Chelsea in the giddy twenties, when we were all young, by chasing some fella up the King's Road with it. It's said to have belonged to Edmund Kean, the Shakespearean actor. One is always supposed to preface that with the word great. But his was a limited range, the quieter reach of the emotions quite beyond him. He needed battle and storm, scenes with lots of noise and shouting in them. Coleridge the poet said it was then like reading Shakespeare by flashes of lightning. Neatly put, and all very well, but—'

'Are we still talking about this Titus bloke?'

'Hmm? No, no, no. Edmund Kean, my dear fella. Long dead. His revels long ended. And, like this insubstantial pageant faded, left not a rack behind. We are such stuff as dreams are made on, and our little life—'

'So this – er – so, you think that this Titus is the bloke I was talking about. Is that right?' Reuben said, bringing him back, while trying to strike a casual note.

The man frowned at the interruption, before registering his patron, his angel of the optics.

'Without doubt, without doubt, sir,' he assured him. 'As I say, I know him well. Worked with him several times. Film and the other. With him and for him. He gave me Iago once to his Othello, when he put the Moor on at the Red Lion, his shop in the East End. A more wordy and far more difficult part than the lead. One must give the paying seats their ticket's worth, while keeping a firm grip on artistic integrity and the iambic line. One must give them the meaning as well as the music. Cast enough light on Iago's darkness to show them the wantonness, the sheer wantonness of his evil. I will wear my heart upon my sleeve for daws to peck at. I am not what I am.'

'Yeah, well,' Reuben said, hiding a growing excitement, and indicated to the barman that he wanted to buy another round, investing in another large gin.

'The esteemed critic of the *Daily Telegraph*, venturing east out of the West End, with, no doubt, native porters and a map, described me in an otherwise indifferent review as an actor at the height of his powers,' the man said, his eyes elsewhere, a place much visited, and sounding resentful, as if it were a verdict that had blighted his life since. 'Of course, all that was when Titus still had a theatre,' he added, a throwaway line, his triumph as Iago and his life perhaps since.

'When he still had a theatre?' Reuben frowned.

'Well, it was bombed out, during the war. I worked there in the late thirties. He still lives over it, I believe, but the theatre itself is a ruin, its own tragedy.'

'How can he do a play without a theatre?' Reuben wanted to know, wondering if he'd been lined up for a con job.

'He takes them on the road, my dear chap. Tours them. Once he gets the money and the venues. And a working play – most are only that, fodder for the gods. But no matter the quality of the words, they must be said by the right actor. The right casting is essential – absolutely essential,' he said, slapping the bar again.

'The times they've got the leads wrong, film as well as the other.' The times he hadn't got those parts he could have made his. 'And of course,' he added, 'somewhere to rehearse. Which these days for Titus is a room upstairs in his local, the Bargee, Jack tells me. A pub that in my time there was our green room. We – my dear sir!' he said, looking at the fresh glass in front of him as if it were the last thing he expected to see. 'It's most kind of you, most kind indeed. But, really, it was my shout,' he said, patting his pockets, as if in search of a wallet.

Reuben wasn't listening. 'Jack? Not Jack Hart?' he said, looking star-struck.

The man laughed at the idea. 'No, no. No, he couldn't afford him. Even if for some peculiar reason Johnnie wanted to do it. No, a young green actor. An acquaintance of mine from the bars of this parish, Jack Savage.'

Reuben felt unsteady, unbalanced, for a moment, as if a door he'd been putting his shoulder to had suddenly opened.

But he said simply, 'Oh,' as if losing interest, as it wasn't Jack Hart.

'He's got a principal part in Titus's latest production. Whether he's ready for it or not is quite another matter. Still, they won't notice the difference out in the sticks. As long as they can hear him at the back they'll be happy. And Jack does, it must be said, have a certain presence. And an easy Irish way with a line, inflating to some degree even the flattest of them.'

Reuben took that in, filed it away. It hadn't registered at the time that he was Irish. 'Well,' he said briskly, looking at his watch, and then seeing off his drink. 'Been interesting talking to you, but I've gotta go. Got things to do.'

He wanted to be alone with what he'd been given, wanted to think.

'And promises to keep.'

'Yeah,' Reuben said vaguely. 'Don't do anything I wouldn't do.'

Set an actor to catch an actor, he thought cheerfully, going back up the stone steps.

Won't be long now, Jack, he promised him, ignoring the sense of unease at the thought. Unease that touched him briefly, lightly, falling like a shadow as he passed through the darkened doorway, out again into the Saturday night lights and bustle of the avenue.

Reuben's anger had long strides. It had taken him far, and now his recklessness over Jack risked sending him back there, risked taking all of it off him, including the house on the hill. And in some part of him that was still listening, he knew it.

Chapter 16

They'd had a good week in Godshall-on-the-Water, the days warmed with a summer that seemed to have arrived early, and full houses nearly every night, as if both had been arranged by Reg.

Lizzie and Jack had swum in the river, and had explored it in a hired mahogany rowing boat, the Thames, as if retired from a busy working life in London, dawdling, as rivers should, round the meanders, and between the grazing fields and water meadows fringed with the first flowers. And they had tied up in caves of overhanging willow fronds, their voices soft murmurings among the sweet grass and budding water lilies.

Jack had basked throughout that week in the summer blue of her eyes. Until yesterday, Saturday, when they had turned to storm and she'd slammed doors, after he'd declined to accompany her to a modern art exhibition in nearby Chertsey. To spend an hour or two solemnly pretending along with everyone else, as he'd put it, including Lizzie in it, to find meaning in walls of meaningless, pretentious bloody daubs at daft bloody prices.

He'd said more than that, to her, and himself, at what he saw as his own ignorance. Snarling at things he didn't understand and thought perhaps he should, guilt at his own boorishness adding fuel to his words.

And it wasn't made up by the next day, by Sunday. It wasn't Lizzie he was murmuring softly to then, parting the dark curtain of hair let down for love, quoting Shakespeare into the heated scent of her neck. 'Poor Romeo, stabbed with a white wench's black eye, shot through the ear with a love song.'

And the love song that had brought him to her bed wasn't Lizzie's either, nor even Alma Cooper's. The only encounter he'd had with Alma was when, after a week of smouldering glances from her, she'd rushed him suddenly backstage, before the curtain on Saturday, and kissed him full on the lips. A kiss more like a blow, or the blow she'd have liked to have given him, before glaring red-faced at him, as if whatever it was about, it was his fault, and then fleeing. Adding absolutely nothing at all to what he was still learning about women, after his years away, and before that the callow engagements of his youth.

The bed he was sharing was that of Abelie Borghese-Parma, a woman he'd met only hours earlier, her love song heated murmurings in two languages.

Abelia in Italian, she'd told him, means 'honeysuckle'. Which hadn't surprised him in the least, breathing in her warm, olive sweetness, tasting it again and again on her lips, her skin, adding his song to hers.

He had met her when strolling back to the hotel after winning four frames and twelve pounds at bar billiards in a pub, using a skill picked up on the snooker tables of his youth. A young woman in a yellow polka-dot dress, her dark, almost black, hair piled up, the sun adding silver highlights. She was standing in front of a green Austin Seven at the side of the road, trying to crank life into it with the starting handle.

She'd blown away an escaped strand of hair, and smiled a little in greeting when he walked past, another human in a street, a town, emptied by Sunday.

'Do you want a hand?' he'd offered.

Her shoulders slumped and she sighed. 'It keeps stopping – when I can get it going, that is!' she said, shaking two hands at it as if to strangle it.

She had the suggestion of an accent he couldn't place. He would learn later that it was Italian, and come to consider then that dark eyes had more to say than blue, holding in them not only summer and winter, but all the shifting weather in between.

'Would you like me to take a look?'

'Oh, would you?'

'Yes, of course. I'm not a mechanic, but I know a bit.'

He opened the bonnet, poked about and tried the connections.

'I can't find anything obvious. It could be the electrics, or ignition system. Or something as simple as the battery having run down.'

'The battery. It's the battery. Always the battery we have trouble with.'

'Then that's probably what it is. Do you live in town?'

'About three or four miles outside, maybe a little longer. Any other day I can get a bus!' she said, shaking her hands again at the car.

'Is there anyone there who could pick you up?'

She shrugged. 'Only my brother, and he's away until tomorrow.'

'Ah, I see.'

'We live on a small farm near Chafford. Just the two of us. Our parents are dead.'

'Oh, I'm sorry.'

'Yes. They were very much in love always. They died in a plane crash. Died together,' she added, telling it him with her eyes as well, a story of a love holding hands on to death. It was, he would come to suspect, another of her lies.

'They left us the restaurant we had in Guildford, and as we wanted to be near nature, we sold it and came here.'

'Right. Well, look, let's see if I can get her running, shall we? And then drive you home, make sure it keeps on running till you get there. Do you have a charger there, something to charge the battery with?'

'Yes, yes. But it takes a long time, a very long time,' she said, as if appalled at how long it took. 'How will you get back?'

'Walk. It's only a few miles. It's a nice day, and I've nothing else to do. There's no Sunday roast or wife waiting.'

'Well, it is most kind of you,' she said on a softer, more personal note.

When she told him her name, she made a small drama out of the Borghese-Parma part, delivering it with a small proud lift of her head. And when he, feeling it somewhat of an anti-climax, said his name was Jack Savage, she smiled at him with great sweetness, as if forgiving him for it.

He bent to the engine, which fired after several tries, as he was determined it should, with those eyes on him, even were he to die in the attempt. The small car rocked, as if petulantly from its rest, before they quickly settled themselves in it, Jack at the wheel, encouraging it as he urged it up the high street like a horse.

When she learned he was an actor she said she had wanted to see the play, but her brother had cut a hand and got blood poisoning, the doctor they'd called in said.

'I couldn't leave him, you understand,' she said, carrying in her voice fevered hours of devotion.

'No, of course not. He's all right now, is he?'

'Oh, yes,' she said, waving it away with a hand.

They made slow progress, crawling along, leaving the town across the bridge over the river that Jack had rowed under with Lizzie. Along lanes where summer gathered in the hedgerows, and in the fields and woods, and Jack glanced at Abelie, his thoughts turning to love.

'Nice day for a drive,' she said, looking brightly about her, then turned to him with a quick, eager movement. 'Tell me about the play, please, Jack.'

'Well, it's about—'

'No, no. Show me, show me. Act for me.'

So he gave her a condensed performance. Abelie scowling at the wicked Uncle Jasper and scheming solicitor, Rupert Kenton-Browne, nudging Jack with a suggestive elbow when Tom Yardley sweet-talked Lucinda Harris, nodding solemn agreement at the wise words of neighbour Edmund Brownlow. And then sighing and applauding happily when it ended as it should, with Tom and Lucinda in each other's arms.

Chapter 17

Jack went even slower, when turning in to the long track leading to the farm, nursing the Austin over large potholes patched with hardcore, into a cobbled yard at the end of it, the car scattering chickens and rushed by a couple of collies, barking and jumping up at it.

The farmhouse and a barn were of Surrey red brick, a few quarried stone outbuildings roofed with corrugated-iron sheets orange with rust, a parked Fordson workhorse, its age in its iron tractor wheels, and the odd bits of abandoned farm machinery sitting about.

Jack removed the battery from the Austin and put it on charge on a work bench in one of the outbuildings. She fed the dogs while he washed his hands, and then invited him to have a drink before setting back.

'We make cider. We have an apple orchard and sell it with the fruit. And we sell milk from our dairy cows. We grow vegetables, and I make jams and marmalade, when I can get the oranges, for the market and shops. And we have some sheep, goats, as well as the cows, that have to be milked two times a day. It is hard work here.'

'I bet.'

'For me sometimes too near nature. I am a woman of education and refinement, now reduced. My brother is a cafone, you understand. Of the soil. We have no help. My brother holds the purse. He adds up our lives each week in pennies, sitting with his little schoolbook in his muddy wellington boots, muttering over it like an old *avaro*, an old miser. While I yearn for culture and intellectual discourse. Please be seated,' she said, after leading him into the sitting room. 'I will attend to the drinks.'

'Well, perhaps just the one,' Jack said politely, looking around.

A pleasant room, lived in, if only by a family of two. It was a home, and he missed that. He had never known it, not a proper home. But he knew what he meant by it, and he missed it. Or told himself he did.

There were many things about himself that he was unsure of. War had asked for only a small part of him, and he had given it willingly, and with distinction. Leaving the rest of him, the part that peace during those years would have tutored, to catch up afterwards. Something it had still fully to do.

He had been away, bedded in behind enemy lines, when his mother died – glad to be out of it, had been his first thought, when the news finally reached him. He had last seen her after another battering from his father, with the usual chorus of weeping and fear from the rest of the family. And he had last seen his father before leaving home for good, and then it was his father's turn to be hurt. Jack, with the strength of shouldering a bricklayer's hod up a ladder all day, and with the anger of years in his fists, leaving him unconscious and bloodied on the dirt of the back yard.

He told Abelie this, told her of his life, or an edited version of it, with another glass of cider in his hand, the golden heat of last summer in it. Sitting with her on the sofa, after she had told him how her parents, who had often and publicly condemned Mussolini, came to England, fleeing when he decided he was another Hitler.

'That fat pig! *Quel maiale grasso!* The local Fascists, *filistei*, beat my papa and plundered our *casa grande* in the golden hills of

Tuscany. French furniture of the Second Empire and the art of Florence on its walls. And they torched our *vigneto*, our lovely vineyard, the mother slopes of Masseto, Biondi Santa Brunello, and Castello Vicchiomaggio, the finest wines in all of Italy. Our beautiful home in the hills, where the air caresses like silk and carries on it the scent of roses.'

She leaned forward as if she could see it, had conjured it up out of the air, and putting her fingers to her lips lightly kissed what had been left behind.

He would later come to suspect that there had been turbulence and hurt in her past, of her own making perhaps, the refusing of one of life's rebels. Which for him meant one of life's adornments.

But wherever that past had been, he also came to suspect it was not in the scented hills of Tuscany, with or without French Empire furniture and the art of Florence on its walls.

'So they came to Guildford,' she went on prosaically, 'and opened a restaurant that served chips. And then they died.'

She followed Jack's story of his childhood closely, searching his face with her eyes as he spoke as if for scars, every recounted blow, or tear, a drama in them, holding his hand through it, and stroking his arm, and then his cheek.

And when they kissed, it seemed as if as well as passion they were sharing what life had done to them, the things they hadn't talked about, consoling each other.

A kiss that became one of many, stopping and starting again on their way upstairs, where Jack told himself that this time he had found love.

And when they were still, when her head was on his chest and he was gazing up at the ceiling, he saw himself returning there after the tour had finished. Saw himself married to her, sharing the work with Ernesto, his brother-in-law, their children, dark, fierce little things, boisterous with the blood of Italy and the west of Ireland, playing in the fields and in the apple orchard, saw the full, loud and happy kitchen table at mealtimes.

Abelie heard it first, and he felt her move suddenly beside him. The sound of a heavy motor on the still air.

She sat up. 'It's the lorry,' she told herself. 'He is back early. To spy on me. To discover me in bed!' she said on a rising, operatic note. 'The Fascist pig! *Il porco!* One day I swear I will kill him. I will kill him! *Un coltello!*' she growled, thrusting as if with a knife in her clenched fist.

'Who – your brother?' Jack said, confused. 'Ernesto…?'

She looked at him, nothing but truth in her eyes now, the dull, commonplace truth of lives added up each week in a school exercise book.

'No, *amato, prezioso, tesoro*. No, *cuore mio*, not Ernesto. He is English. Born here. In this place, this house. It is Ernest. Ernie, my husband.'

She said she was sorry, so sorry, her eyes pleading with him to understand, in them a story of lost dreams and the need to survive, the roads that had led her there.

But Jack wasn't listening. He was busy pulling on his trousers.

Then something occurred to him. 'Will he hurt you?'

She was immediately scornful. 'Him? No! He's *solo bocca*,' she said, miming with her fingers a mouth flapping. 'I hurt him!' she added, proudly indignant.

He sat on the bed to tie his shoelaces, while she stroked his hair and his back, saying goodbye. Outside the dogs started barking, the lorry lumbering into the yard over the cobbles.

He pulled on his jacket and kissed her. And then hesitated, lost for the words he wanted to say.

She held her hands out towards the door, as if encouraging him to go, as if releasing him from them, like a bird, with the wistful expression when he went through it of the one left behind.

'And don't worry about the gun, *bambino*,' she called after him, like a fretful mother remembering a last detail. 'He always misses.'

He went straight to what he knew was a lavatory, almost directly across from the bedroom. He threw up the sash window and saw with relief that a downpipe was within reach. Relief and a passing twinge of guilt when he thought of Lizzie and another downpipe, climbing it like Juliet's balcony. Tomorrow, he would make amends.

He reached out, grabbed it, and swung himself over to it, giving thanks that it stayed where it was.

He didn't believe Abelie would identify him, if only out of perversity. And that, apart from an improvement in Ernie's aim, was his concern – Titus knowing about it.

Titus had added Alma Cooper to his suspicions of Jack's philandering. He'd done so in a jokey sort of way, telling him that any suggestion of sexual shenanigans on the part of a visiting company would get out, and travel ahead of them, carried on legs of scandal, gossiped about in shops and the pub, the subject of the rural lasciviously mirthful and laborious jokes about odd-job men and their tool kits.

But he hadn't been in the least jokey when he added that none of which, of course, would escape the attention of the local watch committees.

And all that, Jack thought now, was before Abelie Borghese-Parma, or whatever her name was, a married woman of this parish. It could scupper the entire tour.

He found himself in a backyard with a washing line and dustbins in it. It was enclosed by stone walls, with a door leading back into the house and one in the direction of the front yard. From the house, he heard what sounded like heavy footsteps pounding up the stairs, and shouting, Abelie's voice an opera in Italian and English. Then the crash of china landing to another chorus from Abelie, and he thought of the rather pretty chamber pot on the dressing table in the bedroom.

Footsteps pounded again on the stairs, in retreat, perhaps, from what might have been the matching floral washing bowl and pitcher on the nightstand.

He took the wall facing away from the house, scrabbling over it from the top of a dustbin, and dropping onto a well-churned tractor path between the farmhouse and the fields.

He was relieved to see a few yards up a five-bar field gate, rather than have to go over the hedge, a hawthorn bristling still with winter.

He clambered over the gate and took off across the field, scattering grazing cows, rearing, wide-eyed, away from him, udders swinging.

He was running straight for the far hedge, and believed he was getting away with it, when he heard shouting behind him and a shot fired. It went wild, but it wasn't a farmer's shotgun, but the crack of a handgun, easier to aim while running.

Ernie shot again, and Jack glanced back at him, a large, lumbering figure in wellington boots and a leather jerkin, shouting and lifting his hand again.

The field gate that end opened onto a road. He went over it with the speed of a hurdler, almost running into a delivery van, the driver swerving away at his sudden appearance.

He looked back, at Ernie, saving his shots and breath, but still coming on, plodding with a sort of grim determination, as if this, after marriage to Abelie, was something he did understand. Jack began to wonder how it would end.

He went up the road, in the direction the van had come. He had no plan except to hope that he was fitter than Ernie, to hope that he would keep on missing with the gun, and eventually run out of bullets and breath.

The road started to rise, to twist and turn its way uphill. Round the first bend, out of sight of Ernie, were what looked like the gates of a factory, tall, solid wooden ones, shut and padlocked.

He climbed them, using the supporting cross timbers like a ladder, and looking down on a deserted yard, paused to give thanks for Sunday, before dangling from them and then dropping.

The small factory looked Victorian, Surrey red brick with arched windows, and a landing of offices up an iron staircase one side of it.

Three Bedford lorries sat in the yard with loads under ropes and tarpaulin, waiting for Monday morning.

Guessing that the factory and offices would be locked, he ran for one of the lorries. They were flatbeds, and he was able to push up a section of the tarpaulin between ropes to make enough room for his head and shoulders, and then haul the rest of him in.

The load was three large wooden crates, engine parts perhaps, in a line in the centre, secured with more ropes.

He sat against the backboard, with room to spread his legs, and waited, listening and waiting.

He didn't know how long he'd been asleep, no food, the rounds in the pub and farmhouse scrumpy catching up on him. But when he woke the lorry was on the move.

* * *

That morning, shortly after opening time at noon, a young Welsh woman had diffidently entered the Bargee pub in Dean Lane. Her face, under a plain cotton headscarf, was innocent of make-up, an overcoat with the look of Sunday best about it buttoned up modestly, and a black handbag that might have been a Christmas present.

Nancy Dunn had no idea how a simple Welsh girl would dress. But then, she'd thought, neither would the landlord of an East End pub.

But it was a woman, not a man, running the place. A landlady with a face that had heard every hard luck story that Cockney wit, and a thirst but no money, could come up with, and who looked as if she did her own chucking out.

Nancy immediately forgot about the prepared little-girl-lost act and the doe eyes, and gave her a straightforward young Welsh woman in the big city story trying to contact her uncle, Titus Llewellyn-Gwynne. She had phoned and tried the theatre, but to no avail. She was in London for the weekend visiting a friend, a sick friend, she remembered to add, but had to be back for work tomorrow in a match factory.

The landlady's expression softened, an East End matriarch as well as a pub landlady, with children and grandchildren and, sitting Nancy down at a table, she told her about the tour, and before she left gave her a programme of *Love and Miss Harris*.

Afterwards, on her way to the house on the hill, Nancy looked at the programme again, at the cast photograph of Jack Savage, and wondered briefly what he had done.

Before telling herself that whatever it was about it was nothing to do with her.

Chapter 18

Jack had given thanks for Ernie's marksmanship not having improved, and for finding his wallet still with him, along with cigarettes and matches.

His watch told him that it was nearly seven o'clock. The Bedford sped on, piling up the miles under him, while he hoped for a halt, in a bit of traffic or at the lights. But it was Sunday and the driver had a clear run, only slowing a few times briefly, and if there had been traffic lights then they had been on green.

He had no idea in what direction they were heading, or where they were. The couple of times he'd poked his head out from under the tarpaulin, all he'd seen was anonymous countryside, and once a village, left behind without stopping.

He lit another of his Player's, leaning back with it for the ride, wherever it was taking him.

He slept again, woke and slept again, lulled by the movement of the lorry, and able to sleep almost anywhere, in almost any position, after his war years. And when he came awake again he did so suddenly, with the cautious alertness of those years. The lorry was no longer moving.

He scrambled to the tarpaulin flap and peered out. It was dark, and raining steadily on what looked like a high street.

The driver had stopped for traffic lights, a wash of red in a shop window opposite turning to green by the time he'd pushed himself out from under the tarpaulin, the Bedford pulling away again, its rear lights leaving him behind.

There was no other traffic, and no lights showing anywhere, apart from the odd display one in shop windows.

Somewhere a clock struck the hour, struck two o'clock, the town wrapped in it, in silence and darkness and the rain.

He found shelter in the deep recessed doorway of a grocer's, and a bed in flattened piles of empty cardboard boxes waiting for collection.

He wasn't at all sure where he was. Either Land's End or John O'Groats, judging by the hours spent getting there. The shop windows merely told him that he was still in Britain. But there was something about the town that reminded him of Scotland, that feel of rain on granite.

And he found now, after Abelie, a sort of comfort in remembering that time, a time when life, if far more perilous, was also far less complicated. When the army did whatever living needed to be done for him. He thought of the comradeship forged between men training together in the forests and mountains of Lochaber, for a war they would take to the enemy across occupied Europe, and sealed in the release of riotous evenings in the pubs, and sometimes overnight police cells, of Fort William.

And when he drifted off again, his dreams threw up another memory, from another time and another country. A memory of blows from an enemy rifle butt, his hands moving vaguely in his sleep to grab it, and he opened his eyes to a large, cheerful-looking man in brown overalls and a donkey jacket nudging him with a boot.

The man indicated the boxes and said something, and although Jack didn't catch what it was, the accent confirmed that he was in Scotland. On the street, the day was waking to the sound of a dustcart and more men at work, collecting rubbish and emptying dustbins.

Jack rose from his bed of cardboard and made a drinking motion.

'Too much last night,' he said, and the other man grinned instant understanding.

The rain had stopped, and it was starting to get light, a slow, grudging dawn.

While Jack gave the man a hand putting the boxes out for collection, he learned the name of the town that had given him shelter and that the nearest railway station was in Glasgow. And was then relieved to hear that Glasgow was a mere seven odd miles away, and that a town bus went there regularly.

He found the café the man had directed him to, an oasis of light in the damp gloom of the town's square, its double windows steamed with breakfast.

The place was busy already, the entrance of a stranger a small sideshow of polite interest. Jack nodded his way cheerfully to the counter, and ordered with relish a full fry-up off a blackboard menu on the wall behind it.

The bouncy, chatty young redhead, serving him with a grin ready for mischief, gave him his change as if teasing him with it, counting it out, slowly, into his hand, while her eyes were saying something else.

But Jack wasn't listening. He wouldn't have listened had even Lana Turner been behind the counter. All he wanted, after Abelie, was his breakfast.

At Buchanan Street station in Glasgow, he bought his ticket for the long journey back. Nine hours altogether, but he would still get there in good time for the curtain at the new venue.

Something he'd emphasise when he rang Titus at the hotel, hoping that the rest of it hadn't reached his ears. The bit that was like something out of the *News of the World*, a young touring actor and a married local woman, and an escape down a drainpipe pursued by her husband with a gun.

Then all he had to do, he told himself, smoking and pacing up and down in front of a vacant telephone box, was to explain the delay getting there. To tell him that he was ringing from Glasgow, that Glasgow, in Scotland.

* * *

Their next date was at the Alhambra Theatre in Bishop's Alton, also in Surrey, a town Jack had visited on Saturday with playbills.

When he had phoned Titus from Glasgow, he'd been relieved to find that he obviously did not know about Abelie. But he was not short of something to say, words delivered with Welsh fervour concerning the responsibility to the company and the play of a principal player – especially a company that didn't have a principal understudy. And before ringing off warned Jack that he had better make the curtain.

He didn't add 'or else' – he didn't need to. A reputation for the sort of irresponsibility that had derailed a tour had stalled the careers of actors of far more weight than Jack.

The story Jack had given him on the phone, told with intentional vagueness, a man with half his memory lost to the night before, was of a wild party and plans to take a train to another party, and then waking up on his own in Glasgow.

Titus's reaction suggested that he didn't believe a word of it, but couldn't prove otherwise. He told Jack that he'd pack his suitcase for him at the hotel, and deposit it in his new digs in Bishop's Alton. Jack, he said, was to go straight to the theatre when he arrived.

Which Jack did, with an hour to spare, taking a taxi from the railway station with money from a much reduced wallet.

And standing at the entrance doors of the Alhambra he found that life had another surprise for him.

The doors were chained shut and padlocked and had insolvency notices posted on them. And along the top of one of them someone had scrawled his name, and said there was a letter waiting for him at the address of the solicitor's on the notice.

Jack, wandering off to find it, found something to smile at. At least Hector would be happy. He'd been warning them something like this would happen.

Chapter 19

Along with the play's programme, Nancy Dunn had passed on what little the landlady of the Bargee pub knew about the tour, which amounted to the name of the first venue. And late in the afternoon of the next day, Tuesday, the blue Ford, with Edwin and Frank Collins again in the front, was parked outside the Palace Theatre in Collington, waiting for Reuben.

'Piece of cake,' he said, getting back into the car.

He had checked out the stage door and had been pleased to find that it was down a blind alley, which meant that Jack, when leaving, would have to come out into the high street. It would be dark by then, and the plan was that Reuben would follow Jack, and the other two would then follow on in the car to wherever Jack went, to a pub first, or straight to his lodgings.

Either way, it would be done as he was about to go into his digs, with Reuben telling him, just between them, why. And then shouting something about Jack sleeping with his wife, firing at him and fleeing the scene in the Ford.

If he had been sleeping with someone's wife, then hard luck on the husband. If not, it didn't matter. He was an actor. It would be readily believed that he had.

That was the plan. But then Frank Collins remarked on the lack of advertising outside the theatre.

'I mean, they have posters and that up, don't they? Something with the name of the play on it? What is it again?'

'*Love and Miss Harris*,' Reuben said, quoting it as if amused at the distance between love and what he had in mind.

'Yeah, that's right,' Edwin said. 'Like they do at the pictures.'

Frank shook his head. 'Don't look right to me. You sure you've got the right place, Books?'

'Well, that's what the pub landlady told Nancy,' Reuben said. 'And this is Collington in Kent, and that's the Palace Theatre.'

'Yeah, well,' Frank said doubtfully, staring out at the entrance.

Reuben also stared out, thinking about it.

'Perhaps they do it later,' Edwin said doubtfully. 'You know, put it out then.'

'Nah. That don't make sense,' Frank said. 'What time is it supposed to start?'

'Eight o'clock, the programme says. Finishes around nine forty,' Reuben said.

Frank looked round at him. 'Eight o'clock? Why are we here this early then?'

'Because I don't want to be pissing about trying to case the place in the bleeding dark, that's why!' Reuben snarled. 'Ed, go and ask at that shop there.' Reuben pointed at Hobson's tobacconist's. 'Say you're on holiday, and you thought there was a play on that you and your wife could watch.'

'Being regular theatre goers. Say you and your wife are regular theatre goers,' Frank added, having read about a couple who were described as such in last week's *Standard*.

'Yeah, say that,' Reuben said. 'And that you wondered if they knew anything about it.'

When Edwin came out of Hobson's he was smoking a cigar.

'They've gone,' he said, getting into the car. 'Moved on.'

He turned in the seat and grinned at Reuben.

'And I know where they've moved on to. Mind you, guv'nor, it's a bit of a trot. It's in Surrey. In a place called Godshall-on-the-Water. The Little Theatre, Godshall-on-the-Water, Surrey,' quoting it as if he'd been practising. 'The geezer what's in charge of the play told him that, so it's kosher.'

'Leave it to tomorrow, Books?' Frank suggested.

Reuben, his finger tracing a route on his road atlas, wasn't listening. 'Take us not much more than a couple of hours, that's all. Off you go, Frank.'

'Yeah, but like I say, why don't we—'

'Off you go, Frank,' Reuben said quietly, and Frank switched on the ignition.

* * *

They found Godshall-on-the-Water, as Hector had, there suddenly, round the dogleg bend on the hill down to it, the Norman tower of its parish church standing above it.

'Ah, that's nice,' Frank said. 'Real sort of, you know…'

'Yeah,' Edwin agreed vaguely.

'Like something on the pictures. Know what I mean?' Frank added.

'We want the Little Theatre,' Reuben said as if to himself, looking out as the high street went past.

'Proper teashop there as well,' Frank said. 'I like a nice teashop. With a nice white tablecloth and serviettes, and cakes and paper doilies on one of them stands, and waitresses in—'

Reuben leaned forward. 'Pull over and ask somebody. That old geezer there, with the shopping bag. He'll do.'

Following the directions they were given, the Ford took the turning off the high street into the side road further down it, as the Rolls and the bus had done, and pulled up a discreet distance from the theatre.

117

'The stage door's there, just beyond the entrance,' Reuben said quietly, as if he could be overheard, a finger going between the two others, pointing out the sign sticking out over the pavement. 'It's not as handy as Kent, so we'll just have to play it as it comes. But we need to check there's been no changes to the finishing time. We need to check that. We've gotta be sure about it. Ed, get in and ask them what time the play finishes.'

'Say you've got tickets, in case they try to sell you them,' Frank added. 'You just wanna know what time it ends.'

'Yeah, right,' Edwin said.

They watched as he walked up to the theatre entrance, and then stopped and stood looking at something one side of it.

'What's he looking at?' Reuben said.

'Search me,' Frank said, and they watched as Edwin walked back.

'Now what?' Reuben muttered, and wound down the window. 'What!' he snapped.

'Er,' Edwin said. 'What's the play called again, boss, the one this geezer's in?'

'*Love and Miss Harris*. Why?'

'Well, only that the board on the steps says *Murder Cashes a Cheque*,' Edwin said, and took a small step back from the look on Reuben's face. 'Well, that's what a poster on the board there says.'

'Perhaps that's about something else,' Frank suggested. 'Forthcoming attraction, or something. Like at the pictures.'

'Yeah. Yeah, could be that, Frank,' Reuben said hopefully.

'There must be another poster there about our play,' Frank said. 'Did you look for one?'

'Well, no, I—'

Reuben thrust his face out. 'Well, go and bleedin' look then!'

'I'm beginning to wonder what I'm paying him for,' he added, as Edwin walked off again.

'He's handy for other things,' Frank said.

'Just as well. That doesn't look good,' Reuben said then, Edwin looking their way from the entrance, hands out, showing them empty. 'That does not look good.'

Frank opened the car door. 'I'll take a look,' he said, glad to be out of the car, with Reuben in another one of his moods.

Edwin and Frank wordlessly passed each other, and Frank, after looking over the entrances, disappeared into the theatre.

When he came out again he shrugged on his way back and stood at Reuben's open window.

'They've moved again, Books.'

Reuben nodded. 'Yeah, right,' he said, deflated, a man who knew he should have expected nothing else.

'I said there was nothing about them there,' Edwin said.

'Last night here on Saturday. They just did a week,' Frank went on, getting into the driving seat, Reuben saying nothing, just staring ahead.

'They've gone?'

'Yeah, a town called Bishop's Alton. The Alhambra Theatre there. They do get about a bit, this lot, don't they. Gawd knows where they'll end up at this rate.'

'What's the name of the town again?' Reuben said, slyly alert, as if the name rang a bell that gave him some sort of advantage.

'Bishop's Alton.' Frank looked round at him, sitting intently over his road atlas. 'But we've got plenty of time, boss. They only opened there last night. Why don't we—'

'Sixty miles, give or take,' Reuben said, tapping the atlas with a finger. 'Do it in no time. Should still be light when we get there. I'll direct you.'

'It's a good job petrol's no longer on ration,' Frank said.

The way Reuben had been lately, and the way he was looking now, it was the nearest he cared to get to a protest.

* * *

119

When they arrived at the Alhambra Theatre they found what Jack had found yesterday.

'I wonder what happened to the actor?' Reuben said.

'Missed the train or something,' Frank said. 'Well, I reckon that's it then,' he added, trying not to sound too relieved.

'You or Ed could always go to the solicitor's. Say you're him, the actor, and ask for the letter.'

Frank laughed briefly. 'C'mon, Books, it's a bleeding law office. And anyway, they'd need identification. Plus the fact they were supposed to open here last night, so he's probably come and got the letter himself, and gone again.'

'And they might know where to.'

'Books, they're lawyers. In a small town. They won't have to be told what we are if one of us turns up there. And then if you did find this Jack Savage and sort it, they'll have a face to remember. C'mon, guv'nor, you know that's right…'

Reuben stared at the door, at the padlocked chains, and the notices, at the message to Jack Savage, a message that seemed in that moment to also be addressed to him.

And because he knew it couldn't be, and didn't understand how he could think that it could, bewilderment and something like fear added fuel to frustration.

His meaty hands shot out and the doors shook as he yanked and pulled at the chains as if to try to break them, as if they were meant for him, meant to shut him out from the answer inside.

'Guv'nor,' Frank said warningly, the two men looking nervously around.

And then the sudden rage that had gripped him like a spasm passed, leaving him spent and defeated looking.

Back in the Ford, Reuben slumped on the back seat as the car turned for home.

He was silent for most of the journey, busy with his thoughts. Thoughts that had one foot in reality, knowing that so far in pursuit of the actor he had simply been unlucky, the other in instinct telling him something else. Something said as it were from the shadows, a whisper in a life lived by them, slipped to him in clubs and bars, and passed on in the street, the instinct that had taken him to the house on the hill.

The instinct that was telling him something he couldn't have put into words, couldn't have talked about, even if he had someone to talk about it to. And it was that instinct that he was listening to now, as if something passed on to him, brooding on it all the way back to South London.

Chapter 20

Chinatown, in dockside Limehouse, where the air smelt of the Thames and its mud, and the steam whistles of tugs on their approach to the wharves sounded in a river mist.

The sooty London brick of its narrow streets, the shops and pubs, the seamen's hostels and missions, the gaming and opium dens, the dancehalls and brothels that waited their custom. And the houses in between with respectability in their shining windows and starched muslin curtains, where dogs barked behind doors and Pekin ducks and chickens scratched in the backyards.

And in one of those streets, in his shop, the Yellow Emperor, Henry Long was learning that his Monday had turned unexpectedly poorer.

He was working in the spicy dimness, among the ancient texts, wall cabinets of apothecary drawers, and porcelain storage jars painted with clouds and dragons, listening to the news Johnny Lee had arrived with.

Henry was grinding chaga mushrooms in a stone pestle, his movements carrying the force of anger, the chaga turning to dust under his hand.

Johnny Lee had come back empty-handed from the West End, where he'd gone to pick up the monthly protection money paid by various premises there, including the Burbage Bar. And found that

Books Kramer had taken over the lot, the money picked up by two of his men, who had left a couple of places smashed up, and a club doorman carted off to the Middlesex Hospital, to make sure that next time they paid up without argument.

Johnny Lee waited, respectfully patient, while Henry was still, his eyes closed on his inner turbulence, seeking the calm of samatha, his breathing slowing in his mind to soft breezes in a green place, and the singing of birds.

Then he looked at Johnny Lee. 'I want,' he said, 'discourse with the Bookmaker.'

Johnny Lee hadn't known what the word meant when Henry had first said it a few years back. But had soon learned, when Henry, on his first venture into crime, selling cocaine, had been threatened by a rival dealer. A threat that was instantly taken back when Henry returned to have discourse with him carrying a meat cleaver under his jacket. Johnny Lee both respected Henry's white coat, the ancient healing art it stood for, and his persuasive way with a cleaver.

Henry Long was in his early thirties, personable, good looking even, and, when needed, charming. His accent was the product of the public school his father, a respectable businessman, insisted he attend. The diploma on his shop wall qualifying him as a practitioner of traditional Chinese medicine was also gained in deference to his father's wishes.

A Confucian, Henry had been a conscientious observer of the doctrine of filial piety, which meant his father. He barely remembered his mother, who died when he was very young, a loss that had been felt in the family home like the warmth of a fire that had gone out.

His father had then died. And Henry, a young man, free of filial obligation, discovered Limehouse, finding freedom in it, more space to be Henry. And when the rest of his family in leafy Bexleyheath had finally shut their doors to him, he had then moved there permanently, buying the shop and the flat above it with money his father had left him.

Showing, as he saw it, deference to his shade while wearing his white coat, and letting the Henry he had found in Limehouse off the lead when not.

That evening he sent Yan, of the two Chen brothers, to the Hen and Chickens public house in Lewisham, a pub known locally as the Bucket of Blood, from the days of bare-knuckle prize fights of long and bloody duration in the back yard.

Yan was to establish if the Bookmaker, who regularly played cards there, was doing so tonight, and to phone him if he was. Yan reported back that he wasn't, and hadn't been in for some time.

He hadn't been seen anywhere else either, when Henry sent both brothers and Johnny Lee touring the pubs and his drinking clubs with a cover story of a big drugs deal in the offing. Everything was big with the Bookmaker. He ran in South London an empire of crime. He was what his father used admiringly to call certain businessman and politicians: a big cheese. Henry, on the other hand, to use his own words, was small time.

And the Bookmaker wanted that as well. His next move would be into the East End, into Limehouse, to take what little was left. Except that he wouldn't. Henry intended making sure of that. For a greedy man, he reminded himself, even his tomb is too small. But to avenge the insult, the loss of face, he had first to find him.

It came as no surprise to learn when looking through the telephone book that he wasn't listed. But a search of the electoral roll in the Lewisham public library gave him his address, and closing his shop for the morning, Henry drove over to Blackheath with his meat cleaver.

Chapter 21

He found the road and the Ridings, the name of the house he wanted, and parked a few doors down from it, trying at the last minute, with his late father in mind, to salvage something after arriving there without thinking.

'Why didn't you think first, Henry?' his father seemed constantly to be asking, giving him that quizzical look, the sort that also had patience and love in it.

Henry didn't know then, and he didn't know now. He had simply driven straight there without a second thought. He knew nothing about the Bookmaker, only that which was common knowledge. He didn't know if he was married, if he had children, didn't know if there were children there, playing happily, unaware that a stranger, a demon, was on his way to murder their father. The only advantage he had, if it was an advantage, was that Reuben didn't know him, didn't know what he looked like.

He considered walking past the house, and then returning to his car. Considered it still as he found himself walking up the drive, the house, like its neighbours, a large, imposing early Victorian residence, its upper storey half-timbered Elizabethan style.

The double doors of the garage were closed. So he didn't even know whether or not the Bookmaker was at home. Not that it mattered, not now. He had surrendered what happened next to fate.

The door was opened by a woman in her late thirties, early forties, fair hair carefully dressed, and in pearls and an expensive-looking green silk dress.

He lifted his Anthony Eden hat. 'Good morning, I—'

'I'm sorry. I don't buy at the door,' she said, glancing at his brown leather briefcase, in it the meat cleaver wrapped in a copy of *The Times*.

He laughed as if he found her mistake charming. 'Madam, you misunderstand. I may be driven to it one day, but at present business is in perfectly good shape. And it is business that brings me here,' he said, improvising. 'Is Mr Kramer at home, may one ask?'

'No. No, I'm afraid he's not.'

He wasn't sure if it was disappointment he felt, or relief.

'Ah,' he said, 'what a shame. It's – er – it's just that I had a rather important meeting arranged with Mr Kramer, which I have unfortunately to now call off. My secretary, who is otherwise perfectly competent, had a moment of incompetency, and lost his telephone number. Hence my turning up uninvited on your doorstep.'

She took all this in, said with his accent, and returned the smile that lit his dark eyes.

'Well, I can sympathise with that,' she said, 'having been a secretary once. And I'm sorry to have – er—'

'Not at all, not at all.'

'I mean, you certainly don't look like a pedlar,' she said, approving the rest of him, the black jacket and pin-striped trousers in the manner of a Harley Street consultant.

'Well, I'm not sure what they do look like, but thank you. And may one ask if you are Mrs Kramer?'

'Yes. Yes, I am. Look, do please come in.'

'Well…' He hesitated, while knowing he was going to.

'Leaving you standing on the doorstep, like a...'

'A pedlar?' he suggested, chuckling with her as he followed into the house, standing with his hat off in the hall while she closed the door.

'It's the maid's day off, so I've had to remember how to answer the door,' she said with a smile. 'To be frank with you, Mr...'

'Tan, Mrs Kramer. John Tan.'

'To be frank with you, Mr Tan, I've no idea where he is, or when he'll be home. But I'll write the telephone number here down for you, and anything else I can think of that might help,' she said, leading him into the sitting room off the hall.

'Thank you. It's very good of you. Ah, what a charming room,' he said.

'Oh,' she said, sounding surprised. 'Oh, I'm so glad you like it. I won't be a moment. Please, do sit down.'

She invited him to do so expansively, with an almost theatrical flourish of a hand, and on a sudden bright note, and he wondered if she'd been drinking.

She returned with the telephone number jotted down on a sheet of notepaper.

'I looked on his desk in his study to see if there was anything that might help. I don't know what it's about. He's certainly never shown an interest in the theatre before,' she said, handing him the programme for *Love and Miss Harris*.

Henry, who had no interest in the theatre either, muttered vaguely and glanced at it. He saw the name of one of the cast members, Jack Savage, ringed with a pen, and remembered a bit of gossip that one of the Yan brothers had brought back after checking out the drinking clubs. It concerned a young actor who had attacked the Bookmaker somewhere in the West End. It was the Burbage Bar, he also remembered then, making another vague connection. And under the actor's name was written: *The Palace Theatre, Collington, Kent.*

He handed it back. 'No. No, I don't think it's anything to do with the business we had in mind. But thank you for the phone number.'

'I'm just sorry I can't be of more help. My husband doesn't confide in me, not when it comes to business,' she said with a little wifely laugh.

'Well, I mustn't take up any more of your time,' he said, standing. 'I'll be in touch.'

'Oh, but I don't mind. Quite honestly, Mr Tan, it gets quite lonely here sometimes,' she said, and smiled, as if apologising for it in that large house, in a roomful of the best of Liberty's soft furnishing and home accessories.

'What, no coffee mornings with the neighbours?' he said, thinking of the social rituals of his two married sisters.

'No. No, they're not like that here. At least not with us. I'm afraid we're not really accepted, not yet anyway. They're, well, they're quite snobbish. And—'

'But you are not.'

'No, I don't think so. No, I'm not!' she said more definitely.

'Then they are not your equal, Mrs Kramer. The great Chinese philosopher Confucius advises you should have no friends who are not equal to yourself. One day, you might allow them into your beautiful home. When, that is, they have proved themselves worthy of it, proved themselves to be your equal in friendship and enlightenment.'

'What a lovely way of looking at it. I must remember that. Thank you.'

'But forgive me, you have no children?'

'No,' she said, and shook her head, an abrupt, dismissive gesture that spoke for the future as well.

'I see. Well, what about friends, family? If I'm not being too personal, that is!' he said, looking suddenly alarmed at the thought. A man used to keeping people at a cool distance, he had surprised himself.

'No, no. No, it's rather too far for my friends to visit regularly. I was living in Romford when I met Mr Kramer. And my family, well, I'm afraid they don't approve of the marriage. So...' She shrugged.

'I see,' he said again.

'But I shouldn't be talking to you like this, embarrassing you. I—'

'But you're not. You're not. My family disowned me,' he said, surprising himself again. It was the first time he'd told anyone.

'Oh!' she said. About to say more about her family, she immediately switched her attention. 'Why?'

She tossed the programme she'd been holding onto a coffee table with a sort of impatience, and, as if it were of far more importance, indicated that he should sit with her on the sofa.

'Complicated Chinese stuff, Mrs Kramer. And we can get very complicated.'

'How very sad. And what about your immediate family, Mr Tan? Do you have children? Oh, now it's me being personal.'

'I'm not married.'

'But you've got friends,' she said, as if offering consolation.

He had to think about that. 'Do you know, I don't think I have. Not really. Not what one would call friends.'

'Oh, dear,' she said on a laugh. 'What a couple we are.'

Henry, sitting with his Anthony Eden hat on his knees, his briefcase with the meat cleaver in it at his feet, laughed with her, losing himself in it, not keeping his usual distance, and not caring.

The two of them laughing together, looking at each other and shaking their heads and laughing.

And then, as if it were nothing to laugh about, as if mildly reproving him for it, she said, 'It's very sad. Never mind,' she added, brisk as a nurse, 'I know exactly what we need.'

A short while after that, Henry, sitting with his third sidecar cocktail, was half-wondering what the Bookmaker would do were he to walk in now, and half-listening to some problem she'd had with Liberty's and a wardrobe, when, as if losing interest in it, she stood suddenly.

'Do you like my dress, Henry?'

She twirled in front of him, showing off the stiffened flared silk skirt. 'It's Christian Dior, his New Look, called Springtime. I've got a pillbox hat, with an eye veil and net and ribbon on top to go with it. But I'll spare you having to say something about that as well.'

'It's lovely, Connie,' he said, was startled into saying, and found that he meant it.

He was never usually short of words to flatter, a repertoire of glibness it amused him to use, and see believed. But this was different. His words this time were not only meant, they were all he could find to say, while meaning so much more.

She was older than he was by some years, and to call her beautiful would be to be kind, or to flatter. Nor was he looking at her the way he looked at Effie, the barmaid in Charlie Brown's, or Daiyu, the beguiling restaurant waitress, who could make a reading of that day's dim sum menu sound more like captions in the *Kama Sutra*.

But he didn't feel for them anywhere near what he felt now, felt for the first time. Felt suddenly, unexpectedly, when about out of habit to say more, without having to think about the words. It was like opening the wrong door, and walking into a bright place he could only wonder at, with nothing more to say about such a thing than that her dress looked lovely.

She bobbed a brief curtsy. 'Thank you, sir,' she said, and then clapped her hands together and leaned down to him. 'Do you dance?'

'Dance?'

'Hold on,' she said, and, skirt of her emerald dress swinging, darted across to the polished dark walnut of a radiogram.

'Victor Silvester,' she said, returning on a swell of music, the brassy warmth of an alto saxophone reaching above it.

She held out a hand in invitation.

'I'm not very good at it,' he said happily, getting up.

'Well, no one's looking. You're doing fine,' she said then, as they shuffled around on the fitted cream carpet. 'You haven't trod on my feet yet.'

'You make it very easy,' he said.

She sang as they danced, sang 'Hear My Song, Violetta', sang it soft and low, as if to herself.

But he knew it was to them both. And he knew then what happiness was, what others had meant by it. Or had remembered what he thought he had long forgotten.

And he was about to tell her that, and much else, when he was saved, as he thought of it afterwards, by remembering why he was there. And remembering also his guiding light Confucius, and the *li*, the master's Fifth Virtue, that of correct behaviour.

And knew that if he was to avenge the Bookmaker's insult, as he must, as *mianzi*, the saving of face, and the honour of his ancestors, demanded he should, then he must never see her again. That to lie with a woman he had made a widow would be to show disrespect to his ancestors, and to invite ill luck to follow him all his days.

Chapter 22

Mr Hobson, the tobacconist in Collington, had sat behind his counter since the early 1920s, when he'd inherited the shop.

He'd smoked clay pipes as a schoolboy, followed by the more grown-up briar, which he'd smoked when in uniform, bound for France. And then, in his first week in the shop, he had discovered the carved beauty of a meerschaum, and Gawith, Hoggarth & Co Special Virginia Flake. Its cool, flavoursome smoke over the years painting the ceiling above the counter, up to where his thoughts drifted, aloof from whatever was happening in that other world outside.

He had smoked his way through the General Strike, the Great Depression, and another war, when Collington, five miles from Dover, was caught in the shelling from the heavy guns in Calais. He was puffing away when history was being made in the skies above him, in the Battle of Britain, and again when Luftwaffe bombers had demolished a good bit of the high street.

And with the rest of Europe under the Nazi jackboot, when there seemed little question that Britain would be next, that any day now Germany would goose-step its victory through the town, Mr Hobson, on his stool behind his counter, puffed on, as if none of it was any of his business.

The two imposters who turned up in the same week, first a London spiv professing to be a theatre lover, and then a Chinese male with the sort of hat favoured by Mr Smedley pulled down low, and trying to disguise his voice with a sort of pigeon English, barely gave him pause.

He simply told them what he knew, and returned to his pipe.

* * *

And so, first Reuben after Jack, and then Henry after Reuben, followed the trail to Surrey from Kent, to the Little Theatre in Godshall-on-the-Water, and then to Bishop's Alton and the Alhambra Theatre.

And at the end of it both pursuers returned empty-handed to London.

Chapter 23

Meanwhile the Red Lion Theatre Company had returned to Kent, which is where Jack caught up with them.

As it would be far more convenient, and save on petrol travelling to London and back again to the Home Counties, George, knowing how welcome they'd be, had suggested that they pool the housekeeping money and move into Ravenscourt Manor for the week, leaving from there for their next venue in West Sussex on Monday. They had done Surrey, the remaining theatres there already booked, when Titus was trying to get dates before the tour.

And on Saturday of that week, they, or most of them, were sitting in the kitchen of the Manor, drinking tea at the big pine table and listening to Wells talking about American vaudeville.

'It was part circus, part theatre, and part freak show. Then add out-of-tune singing waiters, animal acts, drunken prize fighters, and any other leavings they could fill a Saturday bill up with. We had a vent act, the old man and me. I was his feed. We were doing well, even in Peoria, a town in Illinois. They used to say that if it worked in Peoria, it would work anywhere. And I kept reminding him of that, of what we had, when things started to come off the road. But by then he had stopped listening.'

Wells trailed off into silence, after giving a glimpse of a past he usually kept to himself, and keeping the rest of it to himself now, his lips moving as if sucking on something.

'Do you ever hear from any of your family over there, Wells?' George asked, breaking gently into his thoughts,

'No,' Wells said with an abrupt shake of his head, as if denying her something. And then, 'Well, I've got a cousin over there I write to. He's OK. He's doing all right. He's a booker, acts and shows for the circuits. Got an office in New York.'

Simon, fascinated with a theatrical world before he was born, and knowing Wells had played the music halls as well as vaudeville, asked what the other differences were between the two.

'You know, apart from drunken prize fighters and singing waiters, and—'

'We had a singing waiter,' Dolly cut in. 'Well, singing cocktail barman, actually. Sam Parr. Used to tap his way off holding a full tray of drinks.'

'Sing outta tune?' Wells demanded, defending vaudeville in an accent that owed more to that time than the years since.

'No. No, not Sam. Sam had a sweet voice. A tenor. Could quieten a house with it. Had quite a following among the ladies. He had this beautiful barnet, dark and wavy, and—'

'These guys were so bad,' Wells said to Simon, getting his audience back, 'that people would stop their ears. They only put them on for the house to chuck things at. But to try to answer your question, the one thing that stuck out for me was that the headliners – and I'm talking about in the big cities here – the headliners were just part of the crowd once out of the stage door. While here, on the halls, the public not only knew their names, they took their acts out into the streets. People echoing the catchphrases, shop boys on bicycles whistling the songs sung in the pubs. The music hall belonged to everyone.'

'As if they owned it sometimes,' Dolly added.

'And the other thing is, Simon,' Wells said, 'that while vaudeville may have had its faults, it wasn't coarse in the common way the music halls were. And they had the good sense to stop selling booze. Which quietened things down out front. Shut the drunks, the critics, up.'

'It was banning drink out front, and then the house bar, that helped kill the halls,' Dolly told him.

Hector looked up from a copy of the *Kent Crier*, and a fascinating double-page spread on a sale of farm equipment. 'It was a liberty. A diabolical blooming liberty!' he said, an indignation remembered from his youth.

'And they weren't coarse, Wells,' Dolly said. 'They were vulgar. It's not the same.'

'Good old British vulgarity!' George said robustly, on Dolly's side, even though she'd never actually been to a music hall.

'Something that Shakespeare, if allowed off his pedestal, knew all about,' Titus put in. 'A man may break a word with you, sir, and words are but wind. Ay, and break it in your face so he break it not behind.'

Robin, Earl of Maidstone, cheerful in a house that felt lived in again, laughed. 'Splendid! Our common humanity, or at least our plumbing, meeting across the centuries.'

'Plenty of common humanity in Shakespeare, Robin,' Titus said. 'Whether or not a poperin pear actually was a fruit, it wasn't what he meant by it. And if you knew what the word "nothing" was Elizabethan slang for, Much Ado About it takes on a new meaning. The reason the good Dr Johnson, among his other criticisms, called him gross and licentious. But then the good doctor never had to play to the penny tickets. Because in the theatre of that time, like the music halls, you had to get the rowdies on your side.'

'Yes, that's right,' Dolly said. 'It's what got them coming back, and you booked again. It's what paid the rent. When you weren't doing a moonlight, that is.'

'And waiting for the pawn shops to open,' Wells added.

'Conditions were bad,' Dolly said. 'Something dear old Marie Lloyd, God bless her, stood up for during the strike.'

'You went on strike?' Simon said on a laugh.

'Nineteen seven,' Wells said. 'I was on the picket line. We were all out. Back of house as well.'

'Started at the Holborn Empire,' Dolly said, 'and spread right across London. Our union, the Federation, made sure of it.'

'People had had enough!' Wells added. 'They were squeezing more and more work out of us, and then piling on matinees. All for a couple a quid a week. The dirty crooks!'

'Marie came out not for herself and other stars, but for people like us further down the bill. She was a good soul. A good Hoxton girl.'

Wells shook his head. 'That wink of hers. Should have required a licence for it,' he said, managing to sound both prim and amused.

'It's not the songs, she used to say, it's the filthy minds of the audience,' Dolly said.

'*She'd never had her ticket punched before!*' Wells sang out raucously. 'She told the local watch committee that it was simply about a young lady who had never travelled on a trolley bus before. And she got away with it, too. She could do the big innocent eyes as well as the fruity wink.'

Dolly laughed. 'The first line of one of her songs went, "she sits among the cabbages and pees". And when they objected to it, she changed it to "she sits among the cabbages and leeks". Brought the house down.'

'What happened with the strike?' Simon asked, fascinated by the idea of it.

'They gave in after two weeks. We were hurting their wallets,' Wells said. 'We got better pay and conditions. Behind the curtain as well as in front.'

'And then a few of the managers tried to claw some back another way,' Dolly added, 'by fining acts that ran over ten minutes, because they weren't licensed for it. Anything over that came under legitimate theatre.'

'On the vaudeville circuits you could get away with a one-act play,' Wells said. 'But on the boards here, well, as Dolly says...'

'They used to deliberately let you run over so they could fine you. One of the worst for it was the Old Mo Drury Lane, when Pearson was there. Come across him?' she asked Wells.

'Yes. Yes, I have. An old Victorian macaroni. Wore more slap than the artistes.'

'A sly, greedy man. Honestly,' Dolly said, sharing her indignation with the others, 'they were worse blinking robbers than Smedley, some of them. At least he was a straightforward thief.'

'Ah, our Mr Smedley,' George said. 'I'd have dearly liked to have seen his well-deserved comeuppance. That's the business I told you about, Robin.'

'Yes,' Robin said, 'I'd have rather liked to have been there for that as well.'

'You should have sold tickets for it, darling,' Dolly said to Titus.

'Jack had a front-row seat,' Simon said.

'Where is Jack?' Daphne asked then, looking round the table, and as if surprised to find him not there, as if just back from some distance of her own, a journey that had tired her.

She'd been sober now for over a month. But at times the steps she was taking to get there led her briefly to some other place, and left her there, exposed and defenceless. She had more or less adopted Shoveler and Gus, and was standing at the range heating up dried biscuits with juices from last night's stew, the dogs sitting and watching her steadily.

'With Lizzie, Daph,' Simon said.

'Oi-oi!' Wells said suggestively, glancing up towards the ceiling and the bedrooms, and with a wide wink as if to the cheaper seats.

'Not in my company they're not!' Titus said. 'He's been warned about—'

'They're working, ducks,' Dolly told him. 'Keep your wig on. Went for a walk with the new opening scene. Innocent as lambs in the spring, la, la. They left after you'd toddled off to shake your arborvitae,' she added, Wells's laughter at it pure music hall.

* * *

The new first scene was added to the scripts, typed up by George on the machine in the estate office, a relic from a time when the estate needed an office.

Jack and Lizzie were walking with their copies in the fringe of ancient woodland on the edge of the estate, pieces of its iron boundary fencing tangled up in the undergrowth here and there, broken and falling to rust. Stray birdsong drifted across the wood in the silence, deepening it, and above their heads a wood pigeon, startled, volleyed out of a sycamore.

They hadn't started rehearsing the scene yet. Jack was still telling Lizzie, at her invitation, asking in a half-jokey manner, about Sunday. It was the first time in their week there that she had shown any real signs of thawing.

A week that had given him time to work on the story of the party he'd told Titus, telling her that there he had drunk home-made poteen, with a fellow Sligo man, out of sheer foolishness and nostalgia for the old country, for home and hearth, trying for a bit of Irishness to win a smile, Lizzie expressionless as he went on, 'A drink with the force of a shillelagh, that had me wrapped in its arms and delivered like a sleeping babe by British Rail to the city of Glasgow, and left like a foundling on its doorstep.'

He stopped and smiled ruefully at her. 'It is no coincidence, acushla, that the Irish for hangover is "poit". So that now my folly is laid bare, stripped of everything but the sad, lamentable facts. A lesson to all who like a drink. Especially if it's the colour of peeled potatoes and comes in milk bottles. And now to work,' he added on a sharper note, suddenly irritated by her expression, or lack of it, just standing there looking at him, her eyes weighing up the evidence.

'Tom Yardley,' he read, walking on and reading the stage direction from his copy of the play, 'is on a stepladder in the hall of the family home working on a ceiling light, when Miss Harris enters from the street. Well, go on,' he added. 'It's your line.'

'Oh, hello,' Lizzie, as Miss Harris, said.

He stopped. 'Oh, hello?' he repeated in the same flat voice.

'That's the line,' she said.

'The direction, Lizzie, reads – "Her commonplace greeting cannot entirely hide her immediate interest in him". You just sounded depressed. You sounded as if after a hard day you come home and find me there. This is the start of a fire which would consume us.' He leaned towards her. 'So you'd better start poking a bit more heat out of it than that, hadn't you. It's a love song, and your supper, girl. So start bloody well singing for it.'

She glared at him, her blue eyes sparking with it, the glint of sun on ice.

'You're not the director!' she hissed.

And when he said nothing, just stared at her, she said on a sudden, more professional note, 'OK, OK. Give me a moment.'

She stared off into the middle distance, her expression changing there, softening to a smitten Miss Harris.

'Oh, hello,' she said, walking on, script in hand.

'Hello. A problem with the light fitting. A loose wire, I think. It shouldn't take long, but I'm afraid the electricity's off for now.'

Jack waited for Lizzie's next line.

'What's her name?' Lizzie said.

'What?'

She stopped. 'What's her name?'

'Who?' Jack said.

'You know who I mean. All that blarney you gave me. Who is she? Was it the ASM Alma?'

'It was, Lizzie, as I told you it was. And I'm not going through it again. So let us get on, shall we.'

She stared at him, and then dropping her script stepped up and took his face in both hands.

Jack thought she was about to rake him with her nails, the way she was looking at him, and was about to pull away when she kissed him, full on the lips, as Alma Cooper had.

And then slapped his face. 'You bastard!'

Jack looked shocked at the word. 'Miss Harris!' he said.

He said it again some moments later, both their scripts on the new grass with them. Murmuring it then in the shelter of a beech tree, under small green fists of leaves opening to spring.

Chapter 24

When Reuben had arrived back to the house in Blackheath from his stay in the West End, Cornelia, or Connie, as her family and friends called her, was as usual there to greet him, the discreet wife who never asked the questions she had already more or less guessed the answers to.

She had offered her cheek to be kissed when he came in, the extent of any normal intimacy between them. When he wanted sex, driven by urges not altogether sexual, he simply went from his bedroom to hers and had it, took it. Getting into her bed without a word, as if there was no need, as if he'd made it clear by doing so what he wanted. And then talking about something else while fumbling at her, usually something domestic, as if hiding what he was doing from her, or from himself, his need a furtive, near violent thing, under the covers and in the dark.

And if there was a difference in her when he arrived then he didn't notice it. She looked as she always looked, and was where he expected her to be, like the three-piece suite, the American television set, and the cocktail cabinet.

But it wasn't the same Connie. This Connie had opened the door to more than Henry that day, and now carried its song with her, singing it to herself, and Henry, singing it, soft and low.

The day after that Nancy Dunn was back in Reuben's study with the phone, ready with her Inland Revenue rebate story again. This time, she was ringing the Red Lion Theatre, the phone number and address on the programme for *Love and Miss Harris*.

She would do this for the following three afternoons and into the early evenings, bringing a book with her to read in the intervals between calls. Happily earning the fee for each session they'd agreed on, while Reuben grew more morose as the phone on the other end continued to go unanswered.

Until he was finally forced to conclude that the company was still on tour somewhere. And that, having already covered three counties at the start of it, that somewhere could be almost anywhere. Even abroad, remembering the copy of the *Stage* newspaper he'd bought, hoping for a lead, an article in it about British theatre touring companies doing well in America.

That evening, he and Connie ate as usual in a dining room with oleographs and gilt on the walls, the light of a pair of Georgian candelabra, lit as if for romance, adding polish to the reproduction antique table. They sat, as usual, either end of it, making the occasional small talk. Connie doing most of it, saved up from a day short of any sort of talk, Reuben coming back from wherever his thoughts were and making the odd contribution.

And looking at him, gazing into some distance of his own, and looking lost there, she surprised herself by feeling sorry for him for the first time in their lives together, if not in the least sure why.

She had told herself once that she loved him, that he was a happy ending after a previous violent marriage and several failed relationships. That for her had been the real gift.

Reuben had what he had come out of the slums to take, a house on the hill. And she had shared that with him in the beginning, when more of her friends had visited, delighting in showing off the house and garden. But it had for her stayed just that, a house, not the home she'd wanted to make for them there, with the children it was not too late to have, but which he didn't want, not even the marriage she thought she had. Just a house.

Its rooms, empty of the future, the lives, she had once imagined there, scented still with the best of soft furnishing Liberty's had to offer, as if only recently delivered, only recently unwrapped, waiting still to be used.

A showpiece, with not even these days, apart from the odd visit from a friend, anyone to show it to. The gossip about Reuben, and his presence, even when he tried for charm, never entirely free of menace, keeping others away. Not that she blamed them. She intended leaving herself, when she had enough money saved from the housekeeping to keep on running, knowing that she couldn't involve her family.

Reuben startled her then, by abruptly pushing his unfinished meal away, and telling her that he had to go out.

'What!' she said, annoyed. 'In the middle of dinner?'

Whatever else she was about to say went unsaid. He had never hit her, never even raised his voice, but there were times when her husband frightened her in a way she had never known and couldn't explain. His look then, as now, was unnerving enough, but it was something far more than that. A suggestion that something caged behind it was far worse.

He went upstairs, to his bedroom, for the Cobra Colt he'd put back under a floorboard after returning from the West End. He had to go out. He couldn't, he'd told himself, do nothing with that out there.

'That' being a conspiracy against him, undefined in his mind, but which had taken on substance. He knew it was nonsense, but at times like this carried on believing it anyway. As if he knew better, one jump ahead as usual of who or whatever. One jump ahead at times like this even of himself.

He was going to the East End, to get the answers he wanted from either the theatre or the Bargee pub. That was the way he had always done it, always worked, taking it to the enemy.

But this time he was not without fear. Not only of the sort that had humiliated him in the Burbage Bar that night, and that he had picked away at since. But also of something in himself, some place he hadn't gone before, not even in the worst of his violent career. That thing his wife saw sometimes of something caged in him, something he felt that once let out would take him with it, consume him as well as the actor.

He got the Bentley out of the garage and opened the street gates, the lights of South London below the hill like scattered sparks in the darkness, like the last of a fire that had raged there.

Chapter 25

Henry had found the words to a song he hadn't known he'd been carrying in his heart, until that morning in Blackheath. A song of something in waltz time to the music of Victor Silvester. Something bright and enchanting heard, it seemed now, as if from a room in someone else's life, as if through a door opening briefly on it, and then closing.

Because he must now live without it, turn his back on it, if he was to appease *mianzi*, and honour his ancestors.

He had just got back into his car outside the Red Lion Theatre in Dean Lane, was about to leave, to return to his flat over the shop, to search the *Analects of Confucius* for words to ease something he had no medicine for downstairs, when another car, coming in his direction, pulled up in front of the theatre.

He paused with a hand on the ignition, thinking it might be the theatre owner. A dark red Bentley, the colour of a blood blister in the gaslight from a lamp post a couple of yards behind it.

He recognised the driver then, when he got out, appearing as if his thoughts had conjured him up.

He could hardly believe it. But it was the Bookmaker all right, his unforgiving face as clear as a mug shot in a wash of gaslight as he crossed to the theatre entrance.

Reuben had gone to the Bargee pub first, but if the landlady or any of the regulars he'd bought drinks for knew where the tour had gone after Collington, which he suspected they did, then they weren't telling him. So now he was here, trying the locked entrance doors of a darkened theatre as if it were him they'd been locked against, and then walking down to the side door, on the edge of the circle of light from the lamp post, as Henry had. Both men, for different reasons, seeking an answer to the same question.

For Henry, failure to find Reuben and do what he must do, was not only to dishonour his ancestors, but to carry the stigma of it throughout his life, to come among them even more unworthy, when it was time for him to take his place in the nether world.

And now the Bookmaker was there, suddenly, a few yards up from where he was sitting in his car.

He gave awed thanks to his ancestors, swore solemnly and hurriedly on all their lives that he would not fail them, and fumbled for the meat cleaver under his seat.

He left the car quietly, using the passenger door, away from the pavement, and crept across to it on elaborate tiptoe like a cartoon cat, before rushing him, the raised cleaver carrying brief light on its blade.

That part of Reuben that lately was never entirely still, never entirely relaxed, caught the movement out of the corner of an eye.

He shot back a couple of steps and the cleaver thudded into the door frame. He backed away, shocked, and fumbling for the Colt, dropped it, picking it up as Henry was tugging at the blade.

He glanced swiftly around, checking for witnesses, an instinct with him, and Henry, seeing the gun, forgot about the cleaver and fled, darting round the back of his car, as Reuben fired, like a banger going off and leaving its burnt smell on the river air.

Henry took to the pavement, to the shadows of the buildings, sending up a wordless prayer like a sky lantern. Ducking then, when it would have been too late, at the crack of another near miss, and then, quickly, another and another, like someone trying furiously to stamp on something.

And he ran as if for help into his past, into a memory of a Chinese New Year's Eve, and a winter garden in Bexleyheath, when he was very young and the night held terrors. His father lighting another firecracker to ward off the monster Nian, and other evil spirits, he told him, kneeling at his side, the remembered brandy and cigar smell, his eyes behind his round glasses kind with understanding.

'You're a good boy,' he used to say, as if assuring his son of it, leaving guilt behind the many times that his son wasn't.

But his father, with his mother, was now with their ancestors, and the monster Nian was not only still there in the night, he was chasing him.

Henry glanced back, hope flaring for a moment when he couldn't see the Bookmaker, losing him to the long shadow of the shoe factory, and then seeing him, running, arm raised.

The shot didn't find him, but he knew it was simply part of the countdown to how it was meant to end, to *ming yun*, to his fate, for his failure to do what he had just sworn solemnly to do, and for his past waywardness, under the frowning ancestral heavens.

He was making for Limehouse a few streets away, a place that didn't judge, where doors had been open when those of his family had closed on him, making for shelter.

He turned off into a narrow unlit alley running between courts, where the air smelt of bad drains and crowded lives. In some of the windows tallow light gleamed behind the grime, others with panes missing; some hung forlornly with muslin curtains that had once been white, bright clean flags of pride and hope in the future, now limp with dirt and defeat. In the common yards, where there was always life, always people there, as if the houses were breathing out, figures watched with interest from the shadows as Henry ran past.

A door of a corner pub opened, light falling across the cobbles and the sound of voices, the door shut hastily then, at a gunshot in the night.

And Reuben, pulling the trigger again in the alley, heard the hammer strike on an empty chamber, and watched his target as he disappeared.

He had fired his last bullet, as he had the others, without taking aim properly. Doing it in anger, as he would with his fists, or a blunt instrument. When he had used the Colt before it had been close up, so that they knew who it was, knew who had had the last word.

It was anger that had carried him there, in an alley smelling of his past, of the slum he had climbed the hill from. The dim lights of candles dotted along it speaking directly to him of the lives lived there, and a stillness in the tainted air as if people were listening.

It was anger stoked by being right. Its heat burning out any doubt now, allowing no other explanation.

Henry was young and dark-haired, and in shadow Reuben had taken him for Jack Savage. That was what the conspiracy he had tried to tell himself wasn't a conspiracy added up to: the actor knowing where he would be at a certain time and waiting for him with a hatchet.

From now on, he thought, as if vindicated, and, for him at that moment, making perfect sense, he would listen only to himself.

He walked back to his car, calming himself with the promise, made to himself and the actor, that next time it would be personal. That next time he would again have the last word.

Chapter 26

On the Monday morning, following their week at Ravenscourt Manor, the yellow and black Rolls and the tour bus were waved off by Lord Maidstone and Shoveler, on the road again with the story of Miss Harris and love.

A story that belonged to the past of both George and Robin. A story of their shared youth, born again and dressed in cream pasteboard and blue silk ribbon, the name of it a christening, written with ceremony in copperplate that day in the East End. A story with an ending she had longed for all those years ago, and which she had given in the play to the young Miss Harris.

And now that ending was at last hers, sprung on her yesterday evening by Robin. He had taken her aside and had just come out with it, suddenly, a man who had at last got something off his chest he'd been carrying for longer, far longer, than her recent re-emergence in his life. Looking at her as if asking her to tell him it was not too late, or challenging her to say that it was.

And George had simply thanked him, and said yes.

'Well, you got him in the end, George,' Dolly said cheerfully, sitting with her in the back of the Rolls, while Titus, knowing that Dolly also had him in mind, buried himself in the copy of the play he was holding.

'Diamonds?' Dolly said, looking at George's left hand, no longer ring-less, as it had been that day in their kitchen.

'Yes. Diamonds. And rose gold. It had belonged to his mother.'

Dolly hesitated, and then said, 'George – George, not that it matters, darling, of course. Of course it doesn't, but don't you, you know, wonder how—'

George laughed. 'Dearest Dolly. You mean how many other hands it has been on?'

'Well, yes. But as I say, not that—'

'He said that I was the first, after his mother. He said that if he couldn't put it on my hand then it wasn't going on anyone else's. Do I believe him?' George smiled. 'I don't know. Does it matter?' She shook her head decisively. 'No. No, it doesn't. It's come home now,' she said, smiling again, smiling and gazing at it, while Dolly looked weepy and hugged her.

Leaving the drive of the Manor, followed by the bus, Jack turned the nose of the Phantom south, towards the coast, Gus sitting upright next to him, watching with that perplexed air the mystery of the world coming and going.

Jack was taking the route he'd followed on Saturday, when he'd papered the shops in Camberford Bay, their next date, with a batch of newly printed playbills, with review quotes from the newspapers of two towns. Travelling again under the wide skies of Kent, but this time heading for the Weald and the Sussex border.

'Oast houses, George. Where they dry the hops,' Dolly told her then, on their way through hop country, past the conical roofs of the kilns, the hop gardens looking devastated, spiked with tall, bare hop poles waiting for harvest, the fields of late summer and Dolly's childhood.

'Oh, the times we had,' she said. 'All mucking in together, singing away. Kids everywhere, babies in hammocks strung between hop poles. It was hard work, sweating away with plant lice crawling all over you, and your hands cut with the vine stems. But it was our holiday. Time off from smoky old London drizzling soot on us. All that green and everything so bright and clean. And we could see the stars. We thought they only had them in the country. We used to cook outside under them, and have sing-alongs round the fire. There were other things going on under them as well, George,' she added, giving her a nudge. 'And sometimes, nine months later, out popped little hop babies.'

Dolly clasped her hands with an expression of maidenly modesty. 'They say hopping's naughty, but that's just not true. We only go a-hopping to earn a bob or two,' she quoted, her look saying something else, and as if letting the gods in on it.

They were singing in the bus again, a while later, singing their way through a downpour, a mist billowing up in it to the rolling hills of the Kent High Weald, travelling down high-banked lanes, the new green of the hedgerows glittering in the rain.

An exuberant rendition of 'Jeepers Creepers', giving the bus a holiday charabanc air, Hector in his cab below moving in his seat to it, and tapping it out on the steering wheel, with the odd double toot on the horn.

It had stopped raining by the time they'd crossed the Weald into Sussex, the air gathering to it the Atlantic light as they neared the coast, where the Seven Sisters chalk cliffs, gleaming like salt in the new bright day, met the Channel.

As the Rolls and the bus followed the coast road, the last of the rain clouds sat out at sea where there was sunlight, the horizon lifting them slowly on its wide, shining shoulders, like a curtain going up, like a new day beginning.

'A good omen,' Dolly decided.

'Look – they've got a pier. And a bandstand. A proper seaside!' George said a while later, as the coast road met the promenade of Camberford Bay, her voice sounding much younger than her years.

They sang about that then, on the upper deck of the bus following on behind, led by Wells, sang about how they did like to be beside the seaside, a song from his first job on these shores, on the beach at Brighton.

'What sort of chap did the manager sound like?' George wanted to know.

'All right,' Titus said. 'As much as one can tell on the phone. It's not a chap, by the way. She sounded rather like one, but it was a woman. A Violet du Pree.'

'A Violet du – oh, my Gawd,' Dolly said. 'So she went into management.'

'You know her,' Titus said.

'Yes, I know her, all right,' Dolly said. 'If it's the same one. And if it is her, I'm surprised we can't hear her from here. She used to do a drag act as a sergeant major. You didn't need to buy a ticket for it. You could listen to it in the street. Not,' she added, 'that it was ever worth listening to.'

Chapter 27

The Empire Theatre was on the promenade, but Jack, after turning right, went past it and then took a first left, for the rear of the building and the stage door, sitting between a labour exchange and a barber's shop.

A neat line of candy-striped deckchairs had reserved a parking space for them, facing the passing traffic as if offering views of it.

The Rolls and bus pulled up behind them. Jack went into the theatre and came out with the ASM, a small middle-aged man, shirtsleeves rolled up, thinning grey hair plastered in strands across his scalp like pale flattened winter grass, with NHS wire spectacles and a club foot in a black heavy surgical boot.

'You've started already, I see!' he said, when he saw Titus in his Edwardian smoking suit and flowing silk scarf, his black wide-brimmed hat worn with a musketeer tilt.

Jack laughed. 'That's the boss.'

He introduced him to Titus and Hector, who were clearing the deckchairs away.

Hector nodded at the labour exchange. 'Be handy if nobody turns up,' he said, with a sort of glum conviction that that might well be the case.

'Well, if they don't you can always drown your sorrows in the Queensbury,' Davy said, pointing out a pub sign a few doors down from it. 'But don't worry, mate. We've taken a few advance bookings already. You'll get your dinner money anyway.'

'Don't spoil his day,' Titus said. 'When it comes to pessimism, Hector is King Lear.'

As in Kent, people stopped to look at them quite openly. They were like a carnival, or a circus come to town, exotics visiting from another world. The red and white London bus emblazoned with its legends of love, the scenery flats when unloaded from it, painted rooms of make-believe appearing in that grey reality of a Monday morning high street.

'The curtain goes up at eight,' Titus told them, working the gathering audience. 'Advance bookings are coming in all the time, so don't miss out. When it premieres after this tour in the West End, all London will be talking about it, but you can say you saw it here, saw it first.' He indicated the bus with his cane, where the rest of the cast waited to be taken on to their digs. 'Daphne Langan, international star of the silver screen, has chosen this particular play for her long-awaited return to the stage. Bring an extra hankie, ladies – the word "love" in the title is not an idle one.'

They took the deckchairs in after the flats and stored them in the props store, where Davy kept them. When the summer season started he was a deckchair attendant by day on the beach, and an ASM there in the evenings. The ladies, as he called them, the two women who ran the theatre, had the beach concession for the chairs, as well as the ice-cream pitch on the prom, his wife serving from a van in a two-tone pink uniform and a sailor-like hat.

When Titus carried on with Dolly to the manager's office to pick up the keys to their accommodation, which, they had learned, was a small row of corrugated-iron huts on the beach, Davy and Jack took a cigarette break in the props store, sitting on a couple of the deckchairs.

'I'm ASM here, under Vi, who's manager, right? Now,' Davy went on, settling down to his grievance, leg out resting the burden of his boot. 'Now, I do props, furniture, set building and dressings, OK? I do the calls, the lights, sound, and supervise the flies, especially for panto. I do offstage cues, blocking notes, and supervise the casuals for the scene changes. Yes? So what does Vi do? Eh? Tell me that. I mean, she's stage manager, right? So, apart from walking about poking her nose in where it don't belong, what does she do? Wardrobe. Wigs and costumes, that's what,' Davy told him with a sort of triumph, when it was obvious Jack didn't know. 'Wigs and costumes. I mean, we're mostly variety, so panto aside, how many times do we need wigs and costumes? Eh? Yeah, that's right, you've got it, mate,' he added, when Jack obligingly nodded understanding.

While in the auditorium Titus had stopped on their way to the office to try the acoustics, standing stage centre and sending words from a favourite part of his, Sir Lucius O'Trigger in Sheridan's *The Rivals*, across the empty seats to Dolly, the ears of an audience, at the back of the stalls, and then had to be reminded by her that the rest of the cast were waiting on the bus.

And when they did reach the office, she put out a hand, holding him back, and poked her head round the door.

'Elsa Johns,' she said, grinning round it at the woman sitting behind the desk.

The woman stared at her. 'It's Dolly! It's Dolly Burke,' she said, getting up, head shaking and making little twittering sounds of pleasure. A tiny woman, coming not much higher than Dolly's breast, she darted across to her as if to jump up, and flung her arms around her waist.

'You haven't changed a bit, Elsa,' Dolly said, getting a good look at her.

'Nor you, dear. I recognised you immediately, I did. It must be...'

'Oh, let's not go into that, darling. It's lovely to see you again, Elsa. Honestly it is. I wondered if you'd be here, you know, with Vi, when I heard.'

'Yes. Yes, we're still together.'

'How is she?'

'Oh, she's fine. Quietened down a bit these days. Getting on I suppose, like the rest of us.'

'Is she here?'

'Not at the moment, no. She's at a WI coffee morning. But wait till she hears—'

'At a WI coffee morning?'

'Well, as I say, she's quietened down. And the president's the wife of the councillor for sports, recreation and entertainment. Which has its uses, I can tell you. But are you legitimate now then, Dolly?'

'No, only the odd standing in. Otherwise, strictly back of house these days, love.'

'Like Vi. Doesn't even do her turn now. I do the front, and she does wardrobe and back – or gets under Davy's feet there, according to Davy. Anyway, it suits us.'

When Dolly introduced Titus he swept off his hat, bowed and said in his Captain de Granville tones, 'Delighted, ma'am.'

Elsa twittered at it, and added to the performance by saying his name in full, and then twittering again.

'What a mouthful, eh, Elsa?' Dolly said. 'I'll try to get him to trim it when we get hitched.'

'Ohh!' Elsa said, twittering again. 'How lovely! Have you got a date?'

'Not yet,' Dolly said, and winked at her.

'Excellent acoustics you have, Elsa,' Titus said, as if he hadn't heard. 'And a very pretty house. I particularly liked the ceiling. Blue skies and clouds, shot with the golden light of a better world to come. And plenty to look at elsewhere if the play bores. The baroque influence playfully at work, suggesting, I suspect, variety.'

'Yes, that's right, dear. We're on the circuit. It was redecorated from a hall in Victorian times. We're still mostly turns, especially in the season. We couldn't have booked you if it had been some gloomy modern piece. But you've got "love" in the title.' She lifted her shoulders in sudden delight. 'And Daphne Langan's in it. I'm looking forward to meeting her. The locals are reviewing it, and if Daphne's all right to do interviews—'

'Yes, she's fine. And well done,' Titus said. 'I wish all management was as organised and as helpful.'

'That's Elsa for you,' Dolly said. 'I know for a fact she kept a couple of halls back then from going under by organising—'

'Oh, no, Dolly. I just—'

'Yes, you did, Elsa Johns,' Dolly insisted. 'And kept a few more out of the sticky as well. At one time and another she did the books for every gaff in London. Everyone wanted her.' She grinned at the other woman with sudden affection. 'And she once threw a glass ashtray at Pearson at the Old Mom, bless her.'

'Fancy you remembering that.'

'Made my week, that did. He was a dirty old thing.'

'We'll have a good old chinwag later, Dolly, when you've settled in. Has Davy told you about the accommodation?'

'Only that it's on the beach.'

'Well, not actually on the beach,' Davy, who'd just arrived, said. 'They're up in the sand dunes, on a sort of shelf of concrete slabs. They're warm and dry. Well out of the reach of any tide. But handy for a paddle. They were put up for Land Army girls at the start of the war. The farmer used to pick them up and bring them back on the trailer of his tractor, singing their little hearts out.'

'They were lovely girls,' Elsa said. 'We gave them special rates, lumped in with our service people. Now, about the cooking and heating. There's gas fires, to warm you up when you've finished of an evening. We use Calor gas, and there's enough in the cylinders to last you – no charge for that – and a Baby Belling and a range to cook on. And there's Barker's Restaurant round the back here.'

'Cheap and cheerful,' Davy said. 'Do a good meat pie and chips.'

'Water's laid on, and there's also a hip bath in each hut,' Elsa went on. 'We rent them off the council at a pound a week per hut, and we charge our acts thirty bob a week. The extra ten bob covers our laundry and cleaning.'

'Sounds fair enough,' Titus said.

'There's five huts,' Elsa said. 'All with two beds in them, sharing. I'll get you the keys, one for each hut, and Davy will take you over there and show you what's what.'

'Then the Roller can park at the back here,' Davy added. 'And the bus in front.'

'Normally, there's no parking on the prom,' Elsa said. 'And they're strict about it. But we've got permission for the bus to stay there for the week. Something else to thank the WI for.'

'Along with the deckchairs and ice cream,' Davy said, winking at them.

* * *

Dolly and George, who were sharing a hut, brought their suitcases in from the bus, and stood looking at the sitting room. A bright clean room with pale wood tongue-and-groove panelling on the walls, a sofa for two with matching armchairs of blue cloth, two slatted wooden chairs, and daffodil-yellow curtains at the windows.

'How charming,' George said. 'Like a dolls' house for grown-ups.'

'I'm not sure theatricals can be called grown-ups, George,' Dolly said.

'I'm not sure that any of us can, Dolly. I remember a family friend, a priest, who worked well into old age, and when retired said that a life spent listening weekly to the sins of others had left him with the conviction that there was no such thing as a grown-up.'

'I'd have liked to have been a fly on the wall for all that naughtiness,' Dolly said.

After unpacking in the shared bedroom, they were drinking tea and discussing Elsa and Violet du Pree. The phlegmatic Gus, after a quick sniff round at the new quarters, had managed to fit himself onto the sofa, his large head on an arm, and was snoring gently.

'I wonder,' George said, 'I wonder if they – er – you know...'

'What?'

'You know...' George said, and indicated with her head the direction of their bedroom.

'George!' Dolly said, 'What's a lady like you doing knowing about such things?'

'Because a lady like me, when young, read about Sappho.'

'Who?'

'An ancient Greek poetess.'

'Oh, the Greeks! Well, no wonder.'

'And it's love that's important, isn't it. Not who does the loving.'

'That's true, George, yes. And where would any of us be without it? We'd all be lost, that's where. Out in the blooming cold, like children without a home.'

'Well?' George prompted. 'Do you think they – er...?'

'Who, Elsa and Vi? No. No, I don't think so, darling. Comfort cuddles, maybe, but that's all.'

'Ahh,' George said.

'That's all I suspect it ever really was.' Dolly thought about it. 'Perhaps the odd awkward kiss when younger, because it's what lovers do, but which embarrassed them both. You see, they're both a bit... well, a bit odd, you might say. And when they met they were no longer so odd, no longer so alone. And together, the two made more of a one, if you see what I mean. Whatever they had, or have, wouldn't frighten the horses. But it's enough I think for them. And in the end, as you say, darling, that's all that matters.'

'Good. I'm glad. I like Elsa,' George said. 'Little Elsa.'

'Yes, little Elsa. And I think that's part of it for Vi. Gave her someone to mother. Poor old love. She's a big, awkward thing, she is, but her heart's sound under it. She grew up shouting at the world, and the world, I suspect, gave her a lot to shout at.'

George, sitting on another of the wooden chairs, got up, went across to her friend, and kissed her on the head.

'What's that in aid of?'

'It's in aid of you being a good soul, Dolly Burke, and a wise old duck.'

''Ere – not so much of the "old". Come on, gal, grab your coat and we'll get some lunch. See who wants to try the restaurant Davy recommended.'

* * *

They had a full rehearsal in the afternoon to get the feel for a new place and borrowed furniture.

Davy had rigged up a ceiling light for Jack to work on in the added scene, and had also supplied a front door flat. Which, when Lizzie, as Miss Harris, tried to open it, stuck, and she had to push it, shaking the rest of the flat.

He was working on it with a plane when Violet du Pree arrived.

She came down through the auditorium to the stage, creaking with corsetry, her handbag carried like a weapon. She wore a hat dressed with silk flowers and nets of pressed chiffon, the coat of her royal blue suit buttoned to the neck like an awkward embrace, the frilly collar of a blouse escaping from it there as if for air.

'Welcome to the Empire. I'm Violet du Pree,' she called, her voice sweeping with it the three cast members waiting for their cues in the front row.

Titus introduced himself from the stage, and Vi went up the steps one side of it and, indicating Lizzie and Jack, said, 'Are these two young things the love interest?'

161

She sounded indulgent, almost sentimental, startling Dolly in the prompt corner. Said by Vi in the old days it would have sounded more like a threat. *Elsa was right*, she thought, *she has quieted down, stopped shouting at life.*

'You look well, Vi,' she said, coming out on stage, meaning more than that, and pleased about it for Elsa, for them both.

When they'd greeted each other, Vi said how much she and Elsa were looking forward to seeing the play, and that when she'd left her in the office she was taking another booking over the telephone.

'Excellent,' Titus said.

'And Elsa tells us she's got your two local papers to cover us,' Dolly said. 'And a nice interview with one of them for Daphne Langan.'

'Yes, the bigger of the two, the *Mercury*. Nice to have a name on the bill. I met her once, at a charity do. There was drink available...' she said, letting the rest hang in the air.

Titus's head went back, as if to get a better look at her. 'If by that you mean, madam, as I suspect you do, will she be falling over the furniture when the curtain goes up, then—'

'No, no, I simply—'

'Then allow me to assure you that the answer is of course no. Daphne is a professional, as am I. She would no more dream of going on drunk than I would of letting her. Your question, I have to say, Miss du Pree, unspoken as it was, insults us both.' Titus, who had once gone on drunk, when appearing at a theatre with a pub next door, bristled indignantly.

Vi bristled back. 'And let me assure you, Mr Llewellyn-Gwynne, that I most certainly did not mean—'

'No, no, of course she didn't!' Dolly said, heading her off.

'But I am management,' Vi went on. 'And have a responsibility to the house.'

'A responsibility we don't have,' Dolly added, before she could get going again. 'And one that will still be here when we've moved on.'

'Yes,' Vi said, somewhat mollified. 'Yes, thank you, Dolly.'

'And people have gone on drunk before,' Dolly added, looking a warning at Titus, a woman armed not only with the details but one prepared to share them.

Titus appeared to reconsider. 'Yes, well, I have to say that put like that you both of course have a point. One tends sometimes to think, I'm afraid, no further than that home in the house, the stage.'

Vi, about to reply, was distracted by Davy trying the scenery door, opening and closing it.

'A small problem,' Titus said, 'being ably addressed by Mr Hado.'

'Or perhaps the flat itself is the problem. Have you checked the bracing, Davy?' she asked.

'Yes, Vi, I've checked the bracing,' Davy said heavily.

'We had trouble with the bracing at Christmas, on Cinders,' Vi told them.

'Always gets people in, that show,' Titus said. 'You shall go to the ball. We all want to be told that.'

'The wall of the kitchen set almost collapsed,' Vi said, watching Davy. 'While Cinderella was on her knees under it, scrubbing.'

The ASM indignantly stopped work. 'Excuse me, Miss du Pree, it did not almost do anything of the sort. It shook a bit, that's all. And Cinders had stopped scrubbing and was leaning against it doing her exhausted bit – and going over the top about it, if you ask me. And the wing nuts had come a bit loose, the work of one of the casuals. Because I can't be everywhere. Can't do everything.'

'Nobody's blaming you, Davy,' Vi said.

'Yeah, well,' Davy said, trying the door again.

'The poor old ASM has a lot to bear,' Titus said.

'He has a lot to blinking do, as well,' Davy muttered. 'See,' he said then. 'It was nothing to do with the bracing. Just needed a bit off the stile that side,' he added, referring to one of the two vertical framing timbers.

'Thank you, Davy,' Titus said. 'Can't have love shut out on the night.'

'Nah. Sweet as a nut now, look,' Davy said, watching Lizzie trying it, going out and entering again. 'You'll have no more trouble with that, guv'nor.'

Chapter 28

Davy was right, almost. They had no trouble that evening, the door opening as it should. Lucinda Harris entering, putting her latch key in her handbag in the hall of the family home, as if she'd done it countless times before, and then looking up and seeing Jack on the stepladder.

And Titus, waiting in the wings at the start of the second act to go on as Edmund Brownlow, to offer more avuncular advice to Miss Harris, seemingly torn between her head and her heart, heard out front what for him was another kind of silence.

The welcoming one of an audience returning from the bar or foyer sweet kiosk, not dawdling and chattering, and laughing among themselves, as they would with a slow play, as if what they had to say to each other was more entertaining than what they had paid to see. A silence broken only by the odd whispered exchange and the stealthy unwrapping of sweets, an audience settled and waiting for what comes next.

An audience that in the first act had warned Lucinda not to drink the soup her wicked uncle had made her, advised by a woman in the front row, shouting it with sudden alarm, as if in her sleep. That had alerted her to Jasper's midnight stalking with a pillow ready to suffocate. And, not knowing until the last scene that Lucinda is an heiress, was untidily and vocally divided among its female members on whether she should follow her heart with Tom Yardley, or, pragmatically, in these hard times, her head with the ambitious and socially superior Rupert Kenton-Browne. An audience for whom the story was now almost as much theirs as it was the actors'.

* * *

The next day, after a promotional walk around the town with the company, Jack and Lizzie had lunch at Barker's Restaurant, Jack trying Davy's pie and chips, Lizzie a cheese and potato flan with greens. And then went for another stroll round the town, where Lizzie had gone into Timothy White's the chemist, telling Jack, as his mother might have done, to wait outside, leaving him, as she disappeared into the shop, with something else to add to the mystery of the female.

And shortly after that, for the first time in their careers, they were asked for their autographs.

An elderly couple stopped them in the street. The man looking embarrassed by it, the woman smiling indulgently at them, a triumph of love, and digging into her handbag, bringing out a programme of the show. They signed next to their cast photographs with a flourish, as if perfectly used to it.

'Hey! We're famous,' Jack said, when they were walking on. 'We should ask Titus for more of the gate.'

'And get a pair of dark glasses like Daphne's,' Lizzie said, almost prepared to forgive her for them in that happy moment, when life seemed somehow suddenly bigger and brighter, as if of a radiant dawn, the first light of a shining future.

After they'd seen the rest of the town, Lizzie dragging him into a clothes shop, trying things on and parading them for him like a wife, and diving into a Dolcis shoe shop as if in relief at finding one there, they turned for the sea and the promenade.

They had two cornets of ice cream on the house from Rita, Davy's wife, and walked on to the pier eating them, where they had photographs taken by a beach photographer, posing with a stuffed camel at the entrance, and bought coloured picture postcards of Camberford Bay from a kiosk.

Jack could only think of one person to send it to, a woman behind the bar of the Act Two Club in Soho.

Thank you, was all he wrote on that one, knowing she'd know what he meant, her sheltering arms when war had found him again in his sleep.

They changed silver for copper for the machines in the penny arcade, where 'Happy Days and Lonely Nights' over a tannoy competed with the laughing policeman machine. And bought candyfloss on a stick from a large, jolly-looking woman singing along with the tannoy, jiggling her ample weight from foot to foot as she spun it, smiling over at them as she did so, her audience of two, taking their money and giving change without saying a word or missing a beat.

Some of the rides on the pier were under covers still, but they clutched each other and screamed in mock terror, getting their money's worth on the ghost train, played crazy golf, got told off by the operator for head-on bumping on the dodgems, and Jack, holding a gun again, won a teddy bear for Lizzie on the rifle range.

They were walking back towards the entrance, as three young men, loud with horseplay, were coming up from it. Jack saw them notice Lizzie, saw the elbow-nudging, and watched as they veered towards them.

'Hello, darling,' the hardest-looking of them said, his grin including Jack, insolently, in it, before dismissing him. ''ere,' he said then. 'You're from that play at the Empire, ain't yer?'

'Yes, that's right. We both are. Have you been to see it then, or are you going to?' Lizzie asked.

Jack could only wonder at her naivety in thinking they'd be interested in a play, particularly one with 'love' in the title. They were local petty crooks, thugs, in trilby hats with the peak pulled down, and wide-lapel tailoring, their ties splashes of garish colour, and wearing two-tone correspondent shoes. And carrying, maybe, to go with the style, a sheathed cut-throat razor in the silk of an inside pocket.

'Nah. Someone had left programmes about it in a pub. You're Lizzie something, ain't yer. Well, I'm Alfie, see. So now we've been properly introduced, like, you can come and have a drink, can't yer. You and the bear,' he said, sharing his wit with the other two, who laughed on cue with him.

'Come on, chaps,' Jack said, smiling it, as if he understood, as if he'd done that sort of thing himself, but asking them in turn to understand his position.

'Yes! I'm with my friend here,' Lizzie said indignantly. 'Now if you don't mind…!'

'Yeah,' Jack said. 'Nice try, lads, but—'

'Button it,' Alfie snapped, barely looking at him.

Jack took Lizzie by the arm. 'Come on, Lizzie.'

'No you don't,' Alfie said, blocking their way. 'She stays with us. You can go, though. Go on, orf you trot, chum.'

'We're both going,' Jack said, and Alfie made a move towards him.

Jack held out his hands, as if showing them empty, or in appeal. 'Look,' he said, and the hands lifted Alfie with sudden force under his armpits, Jack's thumbs stabbing up into them, deadening his arms, and he found himself perched, swaying, on the sea rail, his trilby hat flying, sailing towards the water.

He tried to lift his hands, lift arms turned into enfeebled flippers, and looked down in panic at where his trilby had gone and he might any second follow.

There had never been as much to Alfie as he believed, and as others had led him to believe. And what little there was of him now

168

was caught between a high tide one side, slapping and sucking at the pier's pilings below him, and Jack's expression, looking quickly away from it, his eyes stretched with fear.

'Keep your feet still. Can you swim?' Jack asked then, as if he'd been considering the options, and the sea was one of them.

Alfie's head wobbled in his eagerness to tell him that he couldn't. 'No, no, I can't!'

'Jack,' Lizzie said, her voice low and urgent with alarm, lightly touching Jack's arm, adding to Alfie's terror, as if they were the words of some sort of keeper.

Jack glanced at the other two men, who looked as if they had decided to make a move. 'Don't,' he advised them. 'Or he goes over. And you'll follow him.'

'No, don't, lads!' Alfie added, with what sounded like a brief laugh at the thought.

'If I let you go, let you down, I want you to behave yourself,' Jack warned him. 'If—'

'I will, I will,' Alfie got out, nodding furiously at it.

'If not, if you bugger me about, boy, then this time you go straight over without the option. Got it? Understood!'

'Yes. Yes,' Alfie said, the words a plea.

Jack lifted him off the rail like a toddler.

'Now piss off,' he said.

He watched them go, watched as Alfie, with a safe distance between then, turned and looked back. 'It's not over yet, mate!' he shouted.

'What do you think he meant by that?' Lizzie said.

'Nothing, probably. An attempt at face-saving.'

'I just hope it doesn't mean they'll disrupt the play in any way.'

'Is that a criticism? Of the way I handled it?'

'What? No. No, of course it isn't. I was just wondering what he meant by it.'

'As I said, nothing, probably. And if they do something like turn up and heckle, I will come down among them from the stage and turn the night into *Titus Andronicus*.' He smiled at her expression. 'But it won't come to that, or anything else. They're just words. Which is all he had left,' he said, sounding suddenly tired, as if wearied by his knowledge of such things.

'What did you do in the army, Jack?' Lizzie asked then, breaking a silence between them on the way back to the entrance. 'What were you in? You know, what—?'

'The catering corps,' he said.

Chapter 29

The next evening, some twenty minutes before the curtain was due to go up, Jack was called to Elsa's office. Vi du Pree was there, with Titus and Dolly, and a tall, middle-aged man in a suit, but who somehow gave the impression of wearing a uniform.

He was introduced to Jack as Detective Sergeant Deeprose from Camberford CID. A charge, Jack learned, had been laid against him of attempted murder.

The room waited for his reply.

'What?' he said on a laugh. 'Ah. Wait a minute.' It dawned then. 'Don't tell me. Alfie, right?'

'If you're referring to a Mr Alfred Lee, sir, then yes. He alleges you tried to tip him off the pier after he accidentally bumped into you when walking along with two of his friends, and even though he told you he couldn't swim,' the sergeant said, in an accent with the sea or the Sussex High Weald in it.

'I have difficulty believing that of Jack, Sergeant,' Titus said, looking at Jack.

'He didn't accidentally do anything of the sort,' Jack said. 'He was about to hit me. I got in first. It was self-defence. If I had wanted to tip him off the pier he would have gone off it. He lied to you, Sergeant.'

'Well, sir, I have to say that Mr Lee is not unknown to us, so I think I can tell you that the charge will probably be reduced to assault, of the attempted grievous sort. An important difference when it comes to the length of a sentence,' he added, sharing it with the others.

'Oh, dear!' Elsa said, looking almost tearfully at Jack.

'I speak theoretically, of course, madam,' the sergeant assured her. 'It may not come to that.'

'But this is nonsense,' Vi said briskly. 'This Alfred Lee, you tell us, is known to you. Which means anything he says, surely, must be in doubt. If not a downright lie, as Mr Savage said.'

'Yes, madam,' the sergeant said, speaking patiently for the law, 'but he made a complaint, and as a citizen it must be investigated.'

'And quite right, too,' Titus said. 'We are all equal under the law. A democratic principle that stands shoulder to shoulder with a free press, fundamental human rights, and universal suffrage – the voice of the people aired in that raucous heart of British democracy, the members of which themselves are not above the law, and are equal before it – that stands as a bulwark against tyranny. And I would deny no man, no matter how undeserving he might be, its shelter. No man,' he insisted, striking the floor with his cane.

'I'm glad you understand, sir. So if you'd get your coat, Mr Savage.'

'What – now?' Titus said.

'Yes. Shouldn't take long.'

Titus snatched a look at his watch. 'But, Sergeant, in almost fifteen minutes from now the curtain goes up here. And he's in the opening scene. There are people out there already taking their seats.'

'Well, I'm sorry. But there's nothing I can do about it. My instructions are to invite Mr Savage to attend the police station. And that is what—'

'And suppose Mr Savage declines the invitation?' Titus said, clutching at a straw.

'Then I'd have to oblige him to do so by arresting him.'

'But why now, Sergeant? Why tonight? He can do it in the morning, surely.'

'I'm afraid not, sir.'

Vi looked at Titus. 'No understudy?' she said, more of a statement than question.

Titus shook his head, bowed his head to it, the fate that he had tempted by cutting corners.

'We'll have to cancel, Elsa,' Vi said briskly.

'Oh, dear,' Elsa said again, her head rearing, shaking with dismay.

'Sergeant, I say to you,' Titus said gravely, 'that your actions will not only turn this house dark tonight, they will in all likelihood derail the tour we are on. And I do not exaggerate the situation.'

'I'm sorry, Mr Llewellyn-Gwynne. But I'm afraid it changes nothing. Mr Savage must accompany me to the police station. Those are my orders.'

'And what then?' Titus asked.

'Well, he'll be formally charged, cautioned, and a statement taken. If it's the lesser charge he'll no doubt be granted police bail. Be back with you before you know it. Now, Mr Savage, if you'd—'

'And what if it isn't the lesser charge?' Titus said.

'Well, sir, in that case he'll be held until the Assize Court next sits in Lewes, our county town. On remand in their prison there.'

'And when does the Assize Court next sit?' Titus asked, expecting the worst now, knowing what war can do to people, knowing what Jack might have done, and feeling responsible for him.

'Yes, well,' the sergeant said, and made a brief sound like a laugh. 'Unfortunately we've just had an Assize. Had a black cap job then, incidentally,' he added, sharing a death sentence with them, seeing that they were theatricals. 'A dentist in Worthing, murdered his wife with an axe. You may have read about it. He chopped her up, packed her in a couple of suitcases, and deposited them in left luggage at West Worthing railway station. It was only—'

'Interesting bit of local colour, Sergeant,' Titus broke in. 'But perhaps you'd kindly tell us when it sits? If the worst happens. A week? Two weeks?'

'Oh, a little longer than that, I'm afraid, sir. The last sitting this year was the spring Assize. There used to be a summer sitting, but that was scrapped. Now there's just the two. So the next one is the autumn Assize. End of October.'

Jack broke the silence that followed.

'Look, I think I ought to say that—' he started, when the door was flung open and Lizzie Peters came in with Dolly, who'd slipped out to find her.

'They're taking him away, Lizzie,' Elsa wailed, hand to her chest. 'To Lewes Prison. Till October.'

'You are a police officer?' Lizzie demanded of Sergeant Deeprose.

'Yes. I—'

'Did he tell you all? He didn't tell you all, did he,' she said, directing it accusingly at Jack. 'He's got this silly army, or man thing, or something.'

'All I know is, Miss—' the sergeant started patiently.

'He is innocent. He did it defending me,' Lizzie said, as if offering herself in Jack's place.

Betty Hutton in *The Perils of Pauline*, Jack thought.

'This Alfie person is the one you should be arresting,' she went on. 'He wanted me to go for a drink with him and his pals. And when I of course said no, he became aggressive, and tried to strike Jack, strike Mr Savage, when he stood up for me.'

'Is this true?' the sergeant asked.

'Yes, yes, it is, as I was about to say. I was about to tell the officer that,' Jack said pointedly to Lizzie.

'And there was a witness to it,' Lizzie added. 'The man on the rifle range. He saw what was going on, and looked as if he was about to come over and help. Then he saw that Jack didn't need it, even though there were three of them. You can ask him. Ask the man on the rifle range.'

'Connor Ryan is the stallholder's name,' Sergeant Deeprose said. 'Yes, Mr Ryan is very public-spirited.'

He thought about it, and then asked to borrow the desk phone. He spoke to his inspector while the room waited, Titus looking again at his watch and tapping a foot.

'Well, we're holding off until we've talked to Mr Ryan,' the sergeant said then, putting down the phone. 'If you present yourself to the police station at, say, eleven tomorrow morning, Mr Savage, we should have a better idea of things.'

'Thank you, Sergeant,' Jack said.

'Yes, indeed,' Titus added.

He glanced again at his watch, and stabbed a finger at Jack and Lizzie. 'Right, you two – never mind make-up, into costume and on!'

* * *

The house sounded good to Titus, standing in the wings just before the curtain went up, but it was left to Davy, during a scene change, to tell him how good, that he had put the House Full board out.

When the theatre was dark again, the entire company, including Daphne, who was still sticking to soda water, decided to celebrate with a drink at the theatre pub, the Queensbury Arms a few doors down. Elsa and Vi were also invited but Vi said it wouldn't do for a WI member, and one about to be elected to a committee, to be seen in a pub, especially a singing pub, and Elsa loyally stayed with her.

They went into the lounge, the biggest of the four bars, busy with theatre goers. And Jack and Lizzie, for the second time in their career, found themselves, along with the rest of the cast, giving their autographs.

Wells, happy with his share of the evening's takings, and heady with signing programmes, and a couple of large brandy and sodas, sat at the piano on a small raised platform one end of the room.

After starting with a bit of grandiose, as he put it, a bit of Chopin, sitting down to play it as if at the Wigmore Hall, he waved Dolly up to sing.

'You must remember this,' she sang, like an end-piece to the play most of them had just seen.

She took the room with her in the chorus of a music hall Saturday night favourite, 'I'll Be Your Sweetheart'. '... *if you will be mine. All my life, I'll be your Valentine. Bluebells I've gathered, keep them and be true. When I'm a man my plan will be to marry you.*'

She turned 'Red Sails in the Sunset' into a drama that could be heard in the street, and her version of 'You Made Me Love You' had no wistful notes to it. He'd started it, and she was going to finish it.

'*Gimme, gimme, gimme, what I cry for,*' she growled, her eyes on the prowl among the men in the audience, '*You know you've got the brand of kisses that I'd die for. You know you made me love you!*'

And Titus, sitting with Jack Savage at one of the tables, fingered his black beard and eyed her as if sighting a tasty prize off the starboard bow. The grey in her dark hair was silver in his eyes, her lines, the years she wore on her face, an adornment.

She had on her large hooped earrings, and was wearing a red spotted neckerchief with a wide-sleeved emerald blouse, a flared skirt and her broad, ornate silver-buckled black leather belt, a gift, Titus knew, from a former lover of long ago, a Spaniard who'd had an abracadabra act.

He had given into jealousy once, and asked her what he was like. Whatever he'd meant by it she answered it with a slow smile and mischief in her eyes.

'Magic, darling,' she'd said. 'Sheer magic.'

When Wells was sitting at the piano, lost in a dream perhaps of concert hall glory, head moving merrily to one of Chopin's livelier pieces, Titus had brought up the incident on the pier. He had approached it tentatively and with humour, as if, just between the two of them, finding it amusing.

Jack had laughed. 'Titus,' he'd said, 'what you really want to know is, am I likely to end up murdering somebody.'

'No, no, no, not at all, dear boy. Not at all. Unless of course we get a bad notice from some local hack, then feel free.'

Jack smiled at it, and then said, 'I do understand, you know. I mean, I'd feel the same in your position. But I can assure you—'

'Dear lad, I—'

'Look, Titus, as I told the sergeant. The man tried to stop us walking on. He mistook politeness for weakness. The two with him were nothing, but he needed a scare thrown into him, or we'd still be there now. That's all.'

On the stage, Dolly, 'with apologies to our Vera', ended with 'We'll Meet Again', the words of the song coming back from those in the room like an echo. It was their song, their memories they were singing about, the weight of them for some too brittle still not to break, old tears shed again.

And tears from Jack Savage as well, wiping furtively at them, head back out of Titus's eyeline.

It wasn't the first time his war had caught up with him. And lately he had found himself crying a couple of times for no reason at all. He had no idea what that had been about, as he had no idea what had happened when briefly he'd held Alfie's fate, held both their fates, in his hands.

He had no memory of what he'd intended doing, before returning from wherever it was he'd been for those seconds. Blank seconds that could have ended with Alfie drowning, followed by him going up the steps to answer a charge of murder or at the least manslaughter.

He wasn't sober when he went to bed that night. He intended that he shouldn't be. But it wasn't long before the dreams found him again, a kaleidoscope of war, of the things done in it.

The things he had been trained to do, sometimes stealthily, in the dark, with a F-S fighting knife, embracing his enemy then like a lover, before silencing him. And holding his warm weight afterwards he turned for that moment inward, to a self before manhood and the things he now knew, for a sort of prayer. A few words, ill-formed and hardly there at all in the heat and clamour of his mind. A prayer said for both of them to a God he had left behind in Ireland.

And the dreams returned him again, as lately they almost always did, to Southern France and 1943 when summer was in the hills. And the enemy, frustrated in their search for them, had bombarded the area with heavy mortar, saturated it, and scored a direct hit on the squad's hide, a structure built only to keep out the weather. He had returned, half running, half tumbling, from a hilltop reconnaissance to find them among the rubble, the human leavings of war, the brilliance of their blood in his dreams like a heat on his face, driving him sweating from sleep, struggling to escape what always came next.

The eyes of the men still alive, men who had shared their lives with him in the waiting hours. Men he had talked and laughed with only hours before, pleading with him, a last conversation, while he stood over them trying to hold the revolver steady, administering death like a sacrament.

And when he woke, his face was wet with tears as well as sweat, and the guilt again of leaving them behind.

He dressed while Titus, in the next bed, rumbled and blew in his sleep as if coming up for air, and lit a cigarette outside the hut, and stood looking out to sea.

A new day was beginning, shining above the horizon, the starched whiteness of gulls, rising in flight with it, carrying its light higher and higher, their cries like those of lost children who no longer expected to be found.

Chapter 30

Nancy Dunn knew it was far too soon to start grafting again. She was already getting visits from the local CID, following the circulation of crime sheets with other people's crimes on them, and hoping like the last time that she'd oblige them with an easy arrest.

And Reuben had said there was a hundred notes in it, a hundred pounds, if she could come up with a solid lead, just a good lead. Offering it with a sudden distracted sort of smile that she'd found unnerving, after the last phone session had left them with no more ideas, nowhere else to go.

'Otherwise, that's it,' he'd gone on. 'Unless you can come up with something, I just have to wait till he gets back to the Smoke, and put myself about then. Which makes it a lot more risky. But he's coming for it, one way or the other. He has to. Nancy, he has to,' he said, as if talking more to himself.

Nancy got up from his desk and picked up her handbag, hoping he'd see it as a signal to pay her. 'Well, all tours end,' she said. 'And he's an actor, London is where it is. He'll be back.'

He looked at her as if he hadn't heard, as if he didn't see her even, the look of someone lost in some place they neither understood nor knew how they had got there.

'Don't worry, Uncle. You'll find him,' she'd said, on a softer note, feeling something like pity tugging at her, and using a term for her godfather she hadn't used for a long time. An endearment that had withered slowly in the face of what she had begun to see in him as she grew up.

'Well, I'll be off then,' she said briskly, and waited.

'Yeah,' he said, his shoulders slumping. 'Yeah, all right, Nancy, I'll get your wages.'

'Thanks, Uncle. And don't worry. If he's still in the country we'll find him,' she said, telling herself that, as well as him, with his offer in mind, breezy with a confidence she didn't remotely feel.

* * *

She was still thinking about the hundred pounds when her bus got to Catford, travelling through the streets she had always known. The corner pubs, and the bomb sites waiting still to rise again. The courts of back-to-back houses where she was brought up, until, like her father, she'd had enough of the 'uncles' her mother brought back from the pub, uncles she was often left to fight off alone. The milk bar and fish-and-chip shop, hangouts of her youth, and the small park where she had dallied with boys after school, its grass threadbare, its iron railings, taken for war, still to be replaced.

The local library, where the fiction shelves took her to other worlds, and that other refuge from who she was, the Ritz Cinema. Where for one and fourpence she could leave herself behind for an hour or so. Live a life in a world of sunshine and blue skies in glorious Technicolor, or love brooding in black and white, sharing, in the dreaming, red-plush dark, all their hopes and tears, and their happy endings.

Before the house lights went on again, and she was back into the real world as if evicted, through the gas-lit streets of Catford, and something on toast for her supper.

* * *

The next morning Nancy, reluctant to say goodbye to Reuben's bonus offer, left the bedsit she'd moved into after her last prison sentence, and made her way to her uncle Wally's scrapyard, her refuge often as a child from what was happening at home.

She didn't particularly need the money. She knew about need, and thanks to earning off Reuben and a recent generous birthday present of cash, a drink, as he put it, from Wally to his favourite niece, she wasn't currently in need.

But she also knew all about rainy days, which in her world were always just around the corner. And she had an idea. It wasn't much of one, and it wasn't new – she'd been there before, ringing Jack Savage's agent twice. The first as an Inland Revenue clerk, the second as the same clerk saying that the rebate cheque sent to Jack Savage had been returned as no longer at the address. She had then learned from Equity, she'd said, that he was on tour and did they know where he was currently?

A different female answered then, one far less friendly, who without answering the question said all they could do was to pass the information on when their client next phoned in.

This time she was returning as Jack's sister. A sister with news of their father, seriously ill, and not expected to live. Her brother had left his lodgings in Earl's Court and his landlord knew only that he was touring in a play. Jack had mentioned the name of his agent in one of his letters home, and she had nowhere else to turn.

If it was the same receptionist as last time, she was hoping to find her heart, to open it up a little. And she was phoning from Wally's yard, where she wouldn't have Reuben pacing up and down, or breathing intensely over her.

She was in the dilapidated caravan Wally had bought in the 1920s for scrap, and which had turned into his office, its rotting tyres giving a slight tilt to the floor, the inside walls that were once cream-coloured stained where the rain dribbled in.

She was sitting at the kitchen table that served as his desk, waiting for the phone to be answered. Through the open door she could hear her uncle in the yard telling whoever that if they didn't like the price he was offering for whatever they could always go elsewhere.

'That's the opening figure, my son, quoted by the Exchange when they opened this morning,' he said, 'plus my overheads. Plus we both know it's hooky, off somebody's roof. But please yourself.'

'Hello! Yes, I'm sorry to bother you, but I wonder can you help me,' Nancy said then, and went into her spiel,

The receptionist on the other end said she was sorry to hear about Jack's father, and Nancy was encouraged, recognising the voice of the woman who had obligingly given her his address when first she'd called there.

With an accent picked up from Mairead, a barmaid in the Harp of Erin pub, Nancy painted a picture of a man dying and wanting only to see his son's face, or hear his voice again, almost moved to tears herself, as if in the one and fourpences in the Ritz.

There was a silence on the other end, then the woman told her to hold on.

Returning after a few moments she said in a voice meant for Nancy's ears only, 'I don't think I'm supposed to do this, so you didn't get it from me.'

And like a fruit machine paying out with a last pull of the handle, and with little expectation of a win, down the phone came the name and address of the theatre the tour was currently playing.

She thanked the woman, almost losing her Irish accent in gratitude, and putting down the phone looked at what she'd been given, scribbled on the back of a British Scrap Federation form, a jackpot of one hundred pounds.

She picked up the receiver again, and had started to dial Reuben's number, when she came to a halt, as if struck by a sudden thought.

She put it down, slowly, on what she was doing, on what she had almost done.

It was only then, when about to give Jack Savage to Reuben, that it had caught up with her, cornered her. Forcing her to fully face for the first time that which she had known all along, but had looked away from. That it wouldn't involve just a couple of probably well-deserved slaps for a lippy actor, as she had told herself it would, rewriting it for her conscience.

She knew what it would mean for him. She had seen that look on Reuben's face once before.

She picked up the receiver again with a sense of urgency, almost snatching at it, as if someone else might get to him first, as if Reuben, by the sheer blind force of his obsession, might somehow get to him first.

And when the exchange answered, she asked for the number of the Empire Theatre in Camberford Bay.

Chapter 31

The woman she spoke to at the theatre didn't know where Jack Savage was, and there wasn't a phone where he was lodging. All she could tell Nancy was that he had to be in the theatre in time for the eight o'clock curtain.

Nancy declined the offer to leave a message, and sat thinking about Camberford Bay, the name taking her away from Wally's scrapyard and the waiting streets of Catford.

She saw in it that other world that she'd discovered when a child, gaping in grubby wonder at the elegant figures lounging in cool, flawless whites on seaside posters, the glowing blue skies and sapphire seas, and the golden beach-ball sands busy with summer and fun. And later watched on the newsreels after the barbed wire and mines were cleared from the beaches, and life took a holiday again in a kiss-me-quick hat along the prom, and danced in the evenings under a glitter ball.

A seaside she had never been to, had never seen the sea. She had never been on holiday, never packed things in a suitcase and gone on holiday like other people, like normal people.

And it didn't take her long to decide that she would have a few days' break from sooty old London and take a look at the seaside.

And then come back refreshed and sort her life out, turn it in some direction that didn't risk it ending again in prison. Use the money in the post office to take a secretarial course maybe, then as a properly brought up young lady enlist with the exclusive Brook Street Bureau in Mayfair, armed with a glowing reference from Wally, as a managing director with a double-barrelled name of something called The London Metallurgy Company, Ltd. And end up marrying the boss of some large firm and living in a nice house in Esher or Virginia Water.

Life, her new life, was beginning to look promising already. She rang the exchange again with a feeling that her holiday had already started, asked for train enquiries.

* * *

She pulled her suitcase off the luggage rack as the train made its steamy entry into Camberford Bay station with a sort of triumph. It had taken her all those years to get here, but here she was, on holiday, at the seaside.

She left the station's booking hall and walked into air salted with what she knew was the sea, knew it as if she had known it before, as if remembering it from those long-ago posters. And a light that filled her with a sudden uplifting feeling of freedom, of horizons far beyond those she had left behind.

She took a taxi off the rank, sitting in the back, a holidaymaker on her way to the bed and breakfast the driver had recommended.

The driver was a woman, middle-aged, in a short grey nylon coat, a collection of enamelled badges on its lapels, and an official-looking peaked hat. Nancy had never met a female taxi driver before and told her so.

'This is nothing. I drove double-decker buses during the war. In Lewes.' The driver tapped the civic crest on the front of her hat. 'Lewes Borough Council. They fired me when the men came home. Got my notice on Friday in me pay packet.'

'What, just like that?'

'Just like that. Without even trying to find me anything else, and knowing my old man was ill. I was of no more use, see. So when I left there the hat and coat went with me.'

'Quite right, too. They didn't deserve anything else,' Nancy said. 'I hope your husband got better.'

'He died,' the driver said, waving a car on out of a side road.

'Did Lewes get bombed much?' Nancy asked, changing the subject.

'Yes, they were always chucking stuff at it. Trying to get the railway line, see. I ran the bus nose down into a bomb crater once during a blackout. Flattened me against the windscreen, but the passengers were all right, apart from the odd bruise. The front wheels were locked in the clay and the rest of the sign I'd smashed into. They'd gone off to fetch lamps for it. The bit I could see, just a few inches from me nose, said "bomb", in red letters on white. And they don't warn you of a bomb unless it hadn't gone off yet.'

'Blimey!' Nancy said.

'That's what I said – well, that and a bit more. But as luck would have it, I had a group of squaddies upstairs and they got the other passengers off. I couldn't reach the connecting window at the back of the cab, so I had to wait for firemen and a ladder. Then, because of the way I was jammed up against the steering wheel, it was decided it was best if I shifted me bum round and left backwards. We do see life, one of the firemen said. Fortunately, that's all they did see, because on that shift I was wearing slacks.'

The woman laughed, as she would have laughed, Nancy knew, at the first telling of it, or even when climbing backwards up the ladder. She had heard laughter like that before, on mornings after a bad raid, from women gathered together in the street. Laughter blooming in the ruins, the lives and homes destroyed, laughter and tea brewing somewhere.

It was what they did, who they were, and it could never be silenced for long.

She thought of telling her she was brave, but knew she'd only argue about it, so asked instead where in town the Empire Theatre was.

'It's on the prom. I'll show you how to get there after I've dropped you off. It's not far.' And then, glancing at her in the rear-view mirror, the driver added, ''ere, you're not an actress are you, love?'

Nancy, flattered, was about to say that, actually, yes, she was, but found herself reluctant to lie to her. She said she was just visiting, taking a short break. She'd seen the play advertised in the station and liked the sound of it. She was, she added, between jobs at the moment.

Which was true. She'd worked away from London before, and would be doing so exclusively now for a while, taking a day trip by train to do it, a member of the county set in whatever country she was in, in tweeds and with a reassuring accent and Coutts cheque book.

'The reason I asked,' the driver said, 'is old Mr Critchley. He won't have actors staying there.'

'What, in this bed and breakfast?'

'Yes. His daughter wouldn't mind but he won't have them. He's got a notice one side of the front door. No circulars, hawkers, no actors, or artistes. Oh, and no dogs.'

'Well, I'm all right then,' Nancy said.

'Doris, his daughter, she actually runs the place, cooks and all that. But he owns it and likes to stick his oar in. Miserable old bugger he is. But you won't see much of him. He mainly stays in his room with the wireless. And Doris is lovely. She was engaged to the love of her life, till he got demobbed and met a Wren.' The driver shook her head. 'She still hasn't got over it.'

'That uniform, and that hat,' Nancy said, criticising an unfair advantage.

She had yearned to wear one herself, but they wanted workers at the sugar refinery in Woolwich. She was still there when peace was declared, and expected to go on working there. She considered that that, or something like it, was her station in life, that for her, and others like her, the train didn't go any further.

And then Alice Monroe, a kite flyer, a passer of forged cheques, suggested another way of making a living, and Nancy had jumped at the chance.

It beat working ten hours a day, six days a week, making jute sacks for sugar in the bagging department. Beat feeling, even in her free time, that she was only on loan to herself, that her life belonged more to Tate & Lyle than it did to her, at one pound eight shillings a week.

* * *

Mr Critchley was in his room on the ground floor with the radio turned up when she arrived at Ivy Lodge, the three-storey bed and breakfast.

Doris, his daughter, let her in, and took her up to her room on the second floor. She'd been on her way out, she said, and Nancy thought, *I bet you were, and not to the shops either, my girl, in your red swing dress, hair and make-up ready to meet the world, or whatever his name is.* Despite what the taxi driver had said, this was no Miss Havisham, her love gathering cobwebs. Whatever was going on in her life now it no longer had room in it for an errant fiancé and a Wren, in or out of uniform, with or without the hat.

After Doris had gone, Nancy looked around her, and found something extra in that perfectly ordinary-looking room. Something charged with a feeling of excited anticipation, a feeling that belonged more to a child than an adult, a child on the first day of a holiday at the seaside. The child she had left behind, had to leave behind to survive in her world, and who at times had yet to entirely catch up.

The furniture looked Victorian, polished heavy mahogany; the dressing table in front of a bay window with floral curtains had a lace doily on it, a glass ashtray and a guidebook listing local shops and the attractions of Camberford Bay. The bed was a double, with bunches of grapes carved into it either side of its headboard, and with a very clean rose pink shiny coverlet on it. There was a gas fire in a green-tiled fireplace, with a small print of a sail boat on its mantelshelf with the caption: *If I settle on the far side of the sea, even there your hand will guide me...*

Above the pay meter a typed notice said that it took shilling coins only, and warned that any use of unauthorised substitutes was illegal.

Nancy put an authorised shilling in, just to have a homely glow in the room while she unpacked.

She checked she had the two keys Doris had given her, and wearing her cream topcoat with the black velvet collar, an ill-gotten gain from Bond Street, and much admired by Doris, and with her wine-red felt fedora worn at a roguish tilt, left to take a look at the sea.

The sky as she stood on the prom wasn't burning with summer as the skies were on the posters; it was grey, and the sea with the tide out looked the same colour. And the sand, with few people on it, was just sand, left behind by the tide as if it had been rained on.

But you can't have everything, she told herself. And sometimes you got nothing. Life had taught her that as well, long ago, before she'd first sat down for other lessons at a desk in junior school. And so she gazed with appreciation, with happiness even, at what it had given her, and a pier still to explore.

When she left the pier she walked on along the prom, past the Empire Theatre, looking for a café, having not had time for lunch. She found one with leaping dolphins on its tiled blue and white walls, and sat down to a meal of fish and chips, with a side plate of bread and butter, followed by a pot of tea.

And then walked back to the theatre, wondering again now she was nearly there if she should forget about it, simply take her few days' holiday and leave it at that. She didn't care to think for long what Reuben would do if she did do it and he found out, the thought of it doing something briefly to her breathing.

She was still wondering if she should forget about it when she reached the theatre. The bus with the name of the play she'd seen on the programme was parked outside, and one of the double doors was open.

Elsa was in the box office feeding the ticket machine a new roll.

'Excuse me. I'm sorry to bother you. I'm looking for Jack Savage who's in the play here,' she said, as if saying it before she could change her mind.

'I don't think he's in, dear, but I can check for you if you wish,' Elsa said, her sharp, bird-like eyes taking her in, taking in her dimples when her smile came and went, and her urchin eyes, and finding something endearing in her, some quality of mischief and something like innocence.

'Thank you,' Nancy said, and found her mouth was dry.

Elsa phoned the stage door, where Mrs Westcott, who'd started there as a programme seller, and then usherette when young, now sat in her small room with her kettle, and seed catalogues and gardening magazines.

Elsa put the phone down and shook her head. 'He's not in, I'm afraid.'

'I think you're the lady I spoke to earlier today when I phoned,' Nancy said. 'You said he has to be in for eight o'clock. For when the play starts.'

She was starting to feel vaguely anxious, as if somehow running out of time, as if Reuben wasn't far behind, even glancing round at the entrance doors.

'That's right, dear,' Elsa said.

'Well, I'll – er – I'll come back then, shall I? At seven thirty, say?'

'Yes. Yes, do that. And you could always leave a message of course,' Elsa said, hoping to learn more.

'No,' Nancy said. 'No, thank you. It's – it's rather, well, complicated.'

'I see, dear,' Elsa said, and wondered if that meant pregnant, one of the girls in her London clothes handsome Jack had left behind.

Seeing Nancy's disappointment, Elsa hesitated. She liked Jack, but this wasn't one of the silly local girls who had turned themselves into a sort of Jack Savage fan club, and started waiting at the stage door each evening like bobby soxers. And if he had left something behind in London, then she wasn't going to help him escape it.

'Well, we don't normally do this,' Elsa said then, confidingly, 'but I can give the address of his digs. I can't guarantee of course that he'll be there, but—'

'No, of course you can't,' Nancy said. 'And thank you very much.'

Elsa smiled at her. 'And if he's not you can come back this evening,' she said, and gave her his hut number and how to get there.

Nancy was still telling herself that it wasn't too late to turn back, while on the path through the dunes, the huts sitting among them painted for war the colour of sand.

She found the number she wanted and knocked on the door.

Jack had his feet up on the sofa reading.

'Come in,' he called.

Nancy opened the door and walked in.

'Mr Savage?'

Jack, expecting another member of the company, looked startled. 'Yes,' he said, standing.

She glanced at his feet.

He smiled. 'I was cutting my toenails.'

'Mr Savage, my name is Miss Clifford, Genevieve Clifford,' she said, a name to go with the cover story she'd come up with, ignoring that part of her nervously telling herself to forget it, to just enjoy the break. And a life afterwards not having to look over your shoulder.

But it was as if some practical part of her was simply getting on with what she knew had to be done, leaving that other part to dither about it, fearfully.

Chapter 32

'What can I do for you?' Jack said.

'Well, it's rather a long story.'

'Then you'd better sit down. Can I get you a cup of something? We've got—'

'No. No, thank you,' she said, taking one of the blue cloth armchairs, handbag on lap. 'Mr Savage, you know I believe a Reuben Kramer. You had an argument with him in the Burbage Cocktail Bar in Shaftesbury Avenue. Before leaving on your tour,' she prompted, when he looked blank.

'Oh, yes. Yes, I know the fella.'

'Well, he intends to murder you.'

Jack stared at her. 'What?'

'Perhaps I'd better explain.'

'Yes, please,' he said on a laugh.

'I work in a West End firm of solicitors. As legal secretary to the senior partner, Mr Warrington-Ore,' she said, using the name of a Master of Foxhounds she'd seen in *Country Life*. 'And our Mr Warrington-Ore is Mr Kramer's solicitor.'

'I see,' Jack said, not altogether sounding as if he did.

'And after phoning to make an appointment one day, Mr Kramer asked would I like to make some extra cash in my free time making a few phone calls for him. I had, he said, what he called the right sort of voice.'

Jack nodded. 'Secretary, business-like. Yes, I can see that.'

'So I did.'

'Made the phone calls for him?'

'Yes. Yes, well, the money—'

'Yes, yes, of course. What were the calls about?'

'You. There were made to try to find you. So that he could finish it his way, as he put it. I didn't at the time understand quite what he meant by it.'

'But... but surely he's not serious? I mean, we all say—'

'Mr Savage, if I didn't think he was serious, I would not have taken all this trouble to warn you, would I.'

'No. No, I suppose not.'

'For your own sake you should also take it seriously.'

'You mean he's prepared to risk a murder charge, risk getting hanged, because I hit him? Hit him, let me add, because he was about to hit me. Is he mad?'

'Yes, I believe he is. Or heading that way. He told me about it in order, I think, to gain my sympathy, to make him more of a victim, tying it in with the money he said you defrauded him of. But I believe—'

'I defrauded him of money?' Jack said.

'Yes. A substantial amount. Five grand – as he put it,' Nancy added quickly, remembering who she was supposed to be. 'Five thousand pounds. An awful lot of money, however you say it. Did you defraud him of it? You can speak freely. I'm not here in any professional capacity.'

'No! No, I did not defraud him of it. That or any other amount. I didn't even get a drink off him.'

'I thought that that might be the case. And even if you had it would not of course be a defence or mitigation for a charge of murder,' she said, remembering something like that from a visit earlier to Catford public library. 'But I believe the real reason lies in you hitting him. There are rumours in the office about Mr Kramer, and by the sound of it he's not the sort of man prepared to forget something like that.'

Jack shook his head. 'I don't understand this. If he murdered me, your evidence, all you've just told me here, would put him straight in the dock, surely?'

'As I have said, Mr Savage, he's not entirely sane. He's obsessional. He sees nothing but revenge. And office rumours have it that he's done it before, several times – and got away with it. He shoots people, Mr Savage.'

'This is... this is ridiculous!' Jack said then, unable to think what else to call it.

'I know,' Nancy agreed, standing. 'But I thought I ought to warn you.'

Jack stood with her. 'Yes. Yes, of course. And it was good of you. Coming all this way. I really do appreciate it,' he said, showing her out.

'I would not wish your death on my conscience, Mr Savage,' Nancy said, with the quiet intensity of Ingrid Bergman in *Joan of Arc* when it was on at the Ritz.

And then, remembering her visit to the library's reference section, went on with her legal secretary's voice, 'Besides which, I would be criminally liable under the law to the same extent as the principal. The murderer,' she explained.

'Ah, I see. Anyway, some people wouldn't have bothered, traipsing all the—' Jack stopped, struck by a thought.

'But how did you know where to go, where to find me?' he said, suspicion sending his eyes to the door, thinking of some sort of conspiracy, of being set up for whoever to come through it, to finish it his way, and something in him jumped when it opened.

Titus, who was sharing with Jack, stood in the doorway.

'Hello,' Nancy said. 'I was just going.'

'Hello. Titus Llewellyn-Gwynne,' he said, smiling a welcome at her, in case she was local press, or on some official committee.

'Genevieve Clifford. How do you do.'

'How do you do,' Titus said, shaking her hand, and looked at Jack.

'Titus, I'm afraid I've brought trouble again,' he said. 'I'm jinxed in this place. First the pier and now this.'

When the pier stallholder had told him what he'd witnessed, Sergeant Deeprose's superior had reluctantly decided against charges of any sort being brought. He took the view that Jack, as an actor, must have done something – if not attempt to murder or grievously assault one of the town's citizens, then at least to offend in some way against its morals.

'Trouble you had to sell your shoes and socks to get out of?' Titus said.

'What? No, no. I was cutting my toenails. No, it's – but you want to get off, Miss Clifford. I've taken up enough of your time. Miss Clifford came all the way from London to—'

'From Surrey, actually,' Nancy said. 'From my home in Virginia Water. Not quite so far. And I think perhaps it's best if I explain it to Mr Llewellyn-Gwynne. As he was witness to and involved in the incident.'

'The Burbage Bar, Titus. This goes back to the Burbage,' Jack said. 'The Books Kramer business.'

'Are you a lawyer, may I ask?' Titus said.

'Legal secretary,' Jack told him.

'Ah,' Titus said.

'For a West End firm of solicitors. I'm—'

'Look,' Jack said, 'why don't we sit. Please, Miss Clifford.'

Nancy sat again, and when she had finished repeating her story for Titus, he said that none of it surprised him greatly.

'I said to you, Jack, just after you'd left the bar, that Mr Kramer is the sort of man who keeps his wounds green.'

'And, frankly, is quite mad,' Nancy said, a prim legal secretary, sitting again with her handbag on her lap.

'You know, it's just occurred to me,' Jack said, 'that that must have been what my ex-landlord was on about. He phoned the theatre and warned me that someone he called a razor boy had been asking for me. Well, everything was over the top with him, so I thought it was just one of the blokes I used to drink with. But maybe not now.'

There was a small silence, broken by Titus, who said, 'One of those phone calls you made, Miss Clifford, presumably bore fruit? Led you to us.'

'Yes, I was going to ask about that,' Jack said.

'And, thankfully, without the homicidal Mr Kramer in tow,' Titus added.

'Yes,' Nancy said. 'As I did with the other calls, I told him I'd had no luck. But I did have. The call was to your agent, Mr Savage.'

'And they told you?' Jack said.

'Lucky, and I imagine, Miss Clifford, persuasive,' Titus put in. 'I'm with the same agency, and they don't give that sort of information out to just anybody.'

'Yes, I was lucky. She was a very friendly, chatty sort of woman.'

'Jessica Fowler,' Titus said.

'Bubbles,' the two men said almost together.

'Known as Bubbles,' Titus said, 'throughout the acting fraternity. There are two receptionists. You'd have got only what she was paid to say from the other one. And that would have frost on it.'

'What did you tell her?' Jack asked.

'Ah, yes, well, I have to confess that I was the tiniest bit out of order there, I'm afraid. I told her that I was your sister, over from Ireland for a few days, and unable to contact you,' she said, giving an edited version.

'Miss Clifford!' Jack said.

'I know,' she said, and smiled ruefully at him, dimpling contrition, and was thrown by him winking at her.

She felt she'd been caught in the act, his wink like a camera shutter falling, exposing Genevieve Clifford from Virginia Water to be Nancy Dunn from Catford. The Nancy Dunn of Catford, her life there, she was never able to leave behind.

She glared at him, spurred by sudden anger. 'I had to think of something. I had to find you to warn you. And you do realise I hope the risk I am taking by doing so. Mr Kramer is not a man to get on the wrong side of.'

'I do indeed, I do indeed, Miss Clifford,' Jack said quickly, putting his hands up to it. 'And please believe that I meant no offence by it. And I have to say that, although Bubbles is English with an English ear, most people putting on an Irish accent give themselves away in no time, tripping over their begorrahs and top-of-the-mornings.'

'I hope I am more subtle than that, Mr Savage,' she said, ignoring his offering of a smile. 'A girl at the office is Irish. I listened and learned. It's been said that I am good at mimicry.'

Alice Monroe had said it, while sitting with her at the bar in one of Reuben's drinking clubs, after Nancy had imitated the accent of one of the northern businessmen who'd tried to pick them up.

'You're good at mimicry, gal,' she'd said. 'And that's what the trade's about, copying people. The rest is confidence, coming on with as much front as Harrods. You expect them to take your cheque, and be quick about it. Always of course done with courtesy and a smile. And the smile is important. Don't show all your dimples like you normally do. You want the smile of a titled lady dealing with the servants.'

'Miss Clifford,' Titus said. 'We are indebted to you. Forewarned is forearmed. It's now just a question of deciding what those arms will be. We can't go to the police,' he added to Jack, 'because it would of course involve our good friend here. We'll have to think of something else. But we will, my boy, we will. Meanwhile, Miss Clifford, as I say, we are indebted to you. Are you going back today?'

'No,' she said. 'No, I'm taking a few days' break now I'm here.'

'Well, if you'd like to take in our humble offering at the Empire Theatre, there will be a complimentary ticket waiting for you at the box office. We had our matinee yesterday, on Wednesday, but we're on tonight, Friday, and our last performance here is on Saturday.'

'That's very kind of you. Yes. Yes, I might well do that,' she said. Something else she had never done before, never been to the theatre, never seen a live play. 'Thank you.'

'Not at all, not at all. And tomorrow, Miss Clifford, if you wish, and have nothing better to do, Jack here will take you to what I'm told is a decent little restaurant, and give you lunch on the company. Won't you, dear boy?'

'There's really no need—'

'It will be the company's pleasure. Where are you staying, Miss Clifford?'

Nancy, not knowing the name of a good hotel in the town, said, 'A rather sweet little bed and breakfast called Ivy Lodge, in Northumberland Road. I prefer a good bed and breakfast to a hotel. I like the homely touch.'

'Oh, you can't beat it,' Titus agreed. 'Well, I'll book a table for, say, one o'clock, and have Jack on your doorstep at twelve thirty, nails clean, boots polished, and on his best behaviour.'

Chapter 33

Later that day, among the evening drinkers in the public bar of the Bargee pub in Dean Lane, a lighterman, that lorry driver of the Thames, and a black cab driver were discussing with traditional scorn their respective thoroughfares.

'The Tideway talks, cock,' the lighterman said, 'and you've got to understand what it's saying. Got to understand when the waterline on one part of it downriver tells you what arch of a road bridge upriver to take your load through. That's why – that's why, chum,' he said, tapping the bar counter sharply, 'it takes five years to get a Lighterman's Certificate.'

'The London Knowledge—' the cabbie started.

'And to be able to navigate through a fog by the smell of the different wharfs. And—'

'The London Knowledge – the London Knowledge,' the cabbie said again, upping the volume, 'requires you to learn three hundred routes in this city through—'

'On roads that never change. Not like the river, when—'

'Through twenty-five thousand streets – three hundred routes through twenty-five thousand bleeding streets, mate!'

'Keep it down in there!' the landlady snapped, poking her head round from the snug where she was talking to a customer. 'Not everybody wants to hear your nonsense.'

'Sorry, Ma,' the cabbie mumbled.

'Nor your language,' she added, before going back to her customer in the snug, who told her then that she'd had a postcard from Dolly.

'Oh, yes,' the landlady said. 'How is she? Where are they now?'

'She's fine. She's in Sussex. At a theatre run by a couple of old pals of hers from the halls.'

'Oh, that's nice for her.'

'Said she'll have a paddle for me. They're at the seaside there. Place called Camberford Bay. Looks nice. Got a pier and all that.'

Sitting with her Guinness at the public bar counter a few feet from the snug, with a view across into it, a shabbily dressed old lady made a conscientious note of the address, because she was sure people had once asked that about her, where is she now?

She lived on overheard scraps from other people's lives, words hoarded as she hoarded other things. Words she took away with her to fill the silences of a life with little in it, apart from two tides a day, and a past she still hoped one day to remember.

She had caught the word 'theatre' said by the woman in the snug, and remembered the man in the pub one evening mentioning it. She had thought at the time that he'd looked troubled, and she understood now why. Because it was what had happened to her once. He'd been troubled because this Dolly was missing, as she herself had once been. Missing and never found.

The old lady wore a grubby raincoat a couple of sizes too big, and the hat of a senior officer in the Russian Merchant Marine, something else the river had given her. Its broad top helped to keep out the weather, the salt stains dried into like added decorations, the insignia of the sea.

Her name was Gabby, short for Gabrielle, she'd say, whether asked or not, said with imperious clarity, a small triumph of memory, and as if imitating in old age the upper-class accents of her youth.

She was a mudlark, a scavenger on the foreshore of the Thames, her day, her life, following the rhythm of the river's tides. The debris when they ebbed like gifts left behind for her to find.

It was mostly junk, fragments of the past, pushing it to her room in a couple of wooden fruit-boxes on pram wheels. Lengths of rope, rusty metal, broken pottery, bits of Roman floor tiles and Tudor bricks, old coins, and broken clay pipes and other leavings, the long history of London written in the mud of its river.

Things she put a value of her own on, and sometimes things of actual value, dug from the preserving silt, silver plate, candlesticks, snuff boxes, and once a silver Georgian wine cooler.

It never occurred to her to sell them. They were far too valuable, far too precious for that. She decorated her room with them, cleaning them and polishing them industriously, as if trying to make out a hallmark, a clue to another age, another life. They touched something in her that made her cry sometimes, while not altogether knowing why, a memory of something that was like a jigsaw with most of its pieces missing, a past also in fragments.

She had the card still in one of her raincoat pockets, hoarded with pieces of strings, marbles, pins, and other bits from the river beaches. It was one of the cards the man in the pub that evening had handed out, and which she'd taken simply because it was free.

Reminding herself what she had to say, repeating it to herself as she went, she left the pub, and parking her cart outside the telephone box by the Biograph Cinema, rang the number on the card and asked to speak to a Mr Baxter.

Chapter 34

The daughter of the house, Doris, opened the door to Ivy Lodge, when Jack presented himself at twelve thirty the next day, wearing his demob suit, a clean white shirt and a tie, both pressed obligingly by Davy.

Her eyes, as she let him in, approved him, as his approved her. Doris was on her way out again, and dressed for it.

'Genny'll be down in a minute,' she said, with a faint smile, a suggestion of female intimacy between them before he'd arrived.

'Genny?' Jack said, standing back for a family packed for the beach, the children hugging shop-new buckets and spades, the front door opening again on sunshine. In one of the rooms on that floor somebody was arguing with the radio.

'She asked me to call her that. Short for Genevieve.' She made a face. 'My parents just called me Doris. Have fun,' she added cheerfully, waving goodbye with a brief dance of scarlet nails.

'You're on time,' Nancy approved then, coming down the stairs, as if he were there for an appointment with Mr Warrington-Ore.

What, he wondered, had happened to Genny?

'You're looking,' he said, 'if I may say so, very fetching,'

She was in a blue and white polka-dot dress, and a beret that suggested the French Navy, with a red pompom.

'You may. Thank you. You look very smart yourself. And you're wearing shoes and socks.'

'In your honour,' he said, opening the front door.

'You know you really shouldn't have been allowed in,' she said, when he'd closed it after them, pointing to the notice one side of it.

'Quite right, too,' he said, 'the way some actors behave. But what's a dog ever done? Although on second thoughts perhaps it's best not to ask.'

On their way to the restaurant she turned to him, and on a note of sudden enthusiasm said, 'I loved the play, by the way. Really loved it,' she added, as if she'd surprised herself.

'Good. Tell your friends.'

'I've told Doris, at the bed and breakfast. She's going on Saturday with her friend. You were good,' she said, giving him a friendly nudge with her elbow.

'Thank you,' he said.

'Yes, I really enjoyed it,' she went on, and was about to add that it was her first time in a theatre, before deciding that for Genevieve Clifford that would be most unlikely.

'Thank you,' she said, after pausing at the restaurant door, expecting it to be opened for her, a woman used to the courtesy.

The restaurant Titus recommended was called The Captain's Table, with a large ship's wheel on one wall, and the other walls and ceiling decorated with lobster pots, pennants, ship's lamps, fishing nets and floats.

Under its influence Nancy ordered baked stuffed haddock with jacket potato. Jack got no further down the menu than steak and ale pie with chips.

He answered her questions about his short acting career, and what the pier business he'd mentioned yesterday was about, and she told him about her work as legal secretary to Mr Warrington-Ore. A fearful bully with a red beard, a thunderous presence in the practice, the scourge of incompetents, slackers and larking juniors. Only she, as his secretary, saw another side to him, the services he gave freely to widows and orphans and the deserving poor of the city.

'Tastes nice,' she said, taking another sip of the house red, and wondered if that was the sort of remark Genevieve would have made.

'Indeed it does,' Jack agreed. 'Good luck,' he said, lifting his glass.

After they had eaten, Jack, feeling in something of a holiday mood, asked her would she like a spin.

'A spin?'

'A drive out. Take a look at the countryside.'

'Yes – yes, why not!'

'Come on then.'

'And it's a nice day for it,' she said.

'Sussex, I am told,' Jack said, 'is the sunniest place in Britain. Mind you, it was a Sussex man who told me, so I can't guarantee its truth.'

When they reached the Empire's stage door, and Jack stopped by the car, Nancy said, 'It's a Rolls-Royce...'

He looked at her. 'Yes, of course it is. Is there any other sort of car?'

'Well, I mean – it's not yours, is it?'

Jack lowered her voice. 'No, but I know how to start it. Quick – get in!'

'What?' she said, alarmed, and looked quickly around, as if for witnesses, a reflex born in South London.

Jack laughed. 'Don't worry, I've got enough problems. And no, it's not mine. I'm just the driver. It belongs to George, who wrote the play you saw, and whose proper title – one she'd not in the least insist on – is Lady Devonaire. And don't worry about me cunningly running out of petrol in some secluded spot. I filled her up yesterday. In you go, Lady Genevieve,' he said, opening the rear door for her.

'What – in the back?'

'Well, certainly not up front with the chauffeur. This may be the new era, but this lady,' he said, patting the Rolls, 'belongs to a more proper age. And that's a speaking tube if you want to issue instructions. Just blow down it first, to get my attention. In you go, me lady.'

'OK,' Nancy laughed, leaning back on the cushions as Jack closed the heavy door with the discreetest of clicks, and touched an imaginary chauffeur's cap with a finger.

Here I am, Nancy thought, as they drove along the promenade, *Nancy Dunn from Catford, not only at the seaside but looking at it from the back of a Rolls-Royce driven by an actor. We do see life, as the Lewes wartime fireman would have said.*

Jack followed the road out of town the way the company had arrived, along the coast, and up over the chalk cliffs above the Channel.

He pulled the Rolls up to take in the view. The afternoon sun burnt a path of glittering white fire to the horizon, and met it in an explosion of light, the blue of the sky above it flushed white with it, white and shining like marble.

They watched a small boat steadily heading out under power disappear into it, swallowed by its light as if a sea legend, as if never to be seen again.

Nancy blew into the speaking tube. 'It's lovely, isn't it. Lovely,' she said, was all she could find to say, even to herself, while meaning much more.

They drove down narrow winding lanes of cow parsley and flowering blackthorn, past meadows and fields where cattle and sheep grazed, and small farms among apple orchards pink with blossom.

Jack reversing to let a tractor pass on the edge of a village, the driver as he went by peering down curiously at the passenger in a

Rolls-Royce, Nancy returning a small regal wave when he touched his cap. And stopping again then, a herd of cows being moved from one field to another, Nancy delightedly finding the dark, dewy, long-lashed eyes of one of them gazing frankly in at her through the open window.

They found a teashop in the village, that was also the post office, and sat at a table in the front garden eating Sussex gingerbread biscuits with a pot of tea, and exchanging pleasantries about the weather with customers on their way in.

They strolled through the village afterwards, the spire of its church standing over it. A high street of mellow brick houses patched with flint, Tudor gables and Elizabethan half timbers, and black and white cottages with summer growing in front gardens. The villagers friendly, and openly curious, word of the Rolls-Royce parked outside the post office travelling before them.

The ancient church of St Margaret's stood at the end of the high street within singing distance of the village pub, in a churchyard that looked scythed, the parish dead of the centuries gathered to it in etched stone and marble.

Jack pushed the great oak door open, its hinges squeaking in a silence that smelt of damp hymn books and mice.

Nancy followed him in cautiously. Something else she hadn't done before, seen the inside of a church. She was relieved to see no one else there, that she didn't have to find something to say to such a remote a figure as a vicar.

On one of the lime-washed walls, Jack saw the Royal Sussex Regiment star and plume badge on a white memorial stone commemorating the men of this parish killed in two world wars.

He remembered them, saw them again, what was left of them, on the road to Cherbourg, bedraggled, half-asleep and half-starved, with their wounded and their battle honours, rallying to the voice of their colour sergeant on the approach – 'Bags of swank! Bags of swank!' Straightening and singing their way into the town, the marching song they'd made their own, 'Sussex by the Sea', singing their way to the port and home.

'Were you in the army?' Nancy asked.

He nodded. 'Yes.'

And on the same wall a dozen plain wooden crosses, their sharp ends stained still with what had once been mud. Crosses from the makeshift graves of local men who fell in the Great War, and who lie in France still, facing the sea and home.

'Are you all right, Jack?' Nancy said.

Jack had turned his head away and wiped at his eyes.

'Yeah, just a touch of hay fever. Get it every year around now.'

After wandering around the rest of the church, they sat on one of the long bench pews with winged animals carved into its ends.

A jewelled light from the stained-glass windows above the altar was like twilight in the gloom. The Crucifixion and Christ in Glory, and the Life of Paul, in emerald and yellow, crimson and cobalt blue, and St George in shining white and gold, with pale flames in his gilded hair.

'Do you believe in God, Jack?' Nancy asked him then, breaking a silence, her voice a near whisper.

'Yes. Fervently, in moments of extreme danger.'

'Did you have many of those?'

'Only as much as any bloke did who carried a rifle.'

'It's very quiet, isn't it,' she said then, as outside a car or van went past.

'It's a church, Genevieve. Do you?'

'What?'

'Believe in God.'

'I don't know,' she said, sounding as though she didn't believe, but didn't like to say so there.

They sat in silence, Nancy, sneaking glances at Jack, who seemed to be lost in thought.

'Jack,' she said then, decided to say. 'Jack, my name isn't Genevieve Clifford. I said that to protect myself. In case, you know, anything got to court, and in the papers. Well, you can see that, can't you?' she demanded, when he didn't answer.

'Yes, yes, of course I can.'

'Well then. I just thought I should tell you. My real name, if you must know, is Nancy, Nancy Dunn. And I don't live in Virginia Water, I live in Catford, actually. In South London. It's how I know about Books Kramer. In fact, to tell you the truth, he's my godfather. That's why he asked me to make the phone calls for him.'

'So the legal secretary—?'

'I made that up.'

'I see,' he said.

'You don't seem very surprised.'

'No... No, I don't think I am entirely, for some reason.'

She shifted in her seat as if to get a better look at him. 'What's that supposed to mean?'

'I'm not sure. I—'

'Are you saying I don't look like a legal secretary?'

'I—'

'What, so you're some sort of an authority on what a legal secretary looks like, are you?'

'N-o,' he said patiently.

'Well, if it wasn't that, then what was it, may one ask? What was it this great authority on legal secretaries found wanting in me? Was it the voice, the accent? Do tell me,' she said sweetly.

'Look, I don't know why it's important to you whether or not you come across as a legal secretary. I mean, I... unless, of course,' it occurred to him, 'you want to be a legal secretary. Is that it? Is that what this is about? What do you do now?' he asked on a kindly note, expecting to learn she was a shop or factory worker with aspirations.

And then, with hardly any hesitation, and for reasons she wasn't at all sure of, she told him what she did do for a living. *That's what you get for going into churches*, she thought on the train home – *you cough the lot*. She left nothing out, even throwing in her two prison stretches, sitting, head bent, like a penitent with her sins and her confessor in silence and a stained-glass twilight.

Then she sat back and waited.

'I see,' he said.

She looked sharply at him.

'Is that all you've got to say? A person lays her life bare for you, all the errors of her ways, and all you can say is, "I see".'

'Well, what do you want me to say? That you're a bad woman? That it's wrong to steal. Either with a gun or a Montblanc fountain pen. You know all that.'

'Well, you're quick enough to tell me I didn't look or sound like a legal secretary.'

'I didn't say that.'

'No, you didn't say it, but that's what you meant. You just didn't come straight out with it. You hadn't the—'

'I didn't say it because I didn't mean it. So what would you like me to come straight out with now? What, Miss Cliff— Miss Dunn, would you like me to say?'

'Well, use your imagination. You're the actor.'

'What's that got to do with it?'

She had no idea, but that didn't stop her. 'Or do you need someone to write the lines for you? Yes, I thought as much.'

'What the hell's wrong with you?'

'Language,' she said. 'Remember where we are. Well, I'm off,' she said, picking up her handbag. 'I've got things to do if you haven't. Perhaps brush up on my legal secretary, as you immediately saw through it. Goodbye,' she added cheerily. 'Thanks for the lunch.'

'Hold on,' he said, getting up.

'Oh, don't bother yourself. I'll get a cab back. Bye-bye.'

'Don't be daft, woman. This isn't South London. You'll never get a cab here. And if you try to walk back you'll get lost. End up sleeping under a hedge.'

'That's my problem.'

'No, it's not. It's mine. I brought you here and I'll take you back,' he said, following her out of the church.

'Will you indeed? I've got news for you, chum.'

'Look, Gen— Nancy. Look, the truth is,' he said, walking with her back up the high street, and as if for her ears only, 'the truth is, that if I don't take you to your door, and it gets about that I didn't, as these things have a way of doing, I'll get into trouble. OK?'

She stopped. 'What sort of trouble?' she said, an authority on all sorts of trouble.

'Probably one that means one of his fines. And I can't afford another one.'

'Whose fines?'

'Mr Llewellyn-Gwynne's. He's got a series of them, one for every misdemeanour. Forget that avuncular front. That's his character in the play. In real life he's a dictator. A ruthless dictator.'

'But why? Why does he insist that you take me to my doorstep? What's the reason for that?'

Jack laughed briefly, a laugh that spoke of what he knew of the man, and what she didn't.

'Reason doesn't come into it. It's simply because of what he is. And whatever that is, I'm sure psychiatry has a word for it. I expect them to come for him one of these days. But meanwhile he's Napoleon, and there's nothing we can do about it.'

'But why are you here then? With the company? Why—'

'Because I couldn't find other work, doing anything. They cut my dole off because they said I wasn't looking, and I couldn't pay my rent. It was either this tour or a shop doorway. Get the picture?' he said, the bitterness of that picture there briefly on his face.

She smiled at him, the smile of a woman giving a coin to a street beggar.

'All right,' she said. 'Come on.'

* * *

On Monday, before the company moved on to their next venue, Jack was again at Ivy Lodge, picking up Nancy to take her to catch her train home, as, he had told her, Mr Llewellyn-Gwynne had ordered him to.

When her train pulled in, and Jack had deposited her suitcase on the carriage luggage rack, he came to a decision.

'Before you go, Nancy,' he said, standing on the platform after she'd dropped the carriage window down, 'I also have a confession to make.' He smiled a little sheepishly. 'When I—'

'Is this,' she broke in, 'about Mr Llewellyn-Gwynne's fines? Oh, I wasn't entirely convinced about that for some reason.'

Jack laughed. 'Touché.'

'Goodbye, Jack,' she said.

'Goodbye, Nancy. And good luck.'

And then, as the train started pulling away, he said, 'Hey! Why did you accept a lift then?'

'Because I had no money on me,' she said, and winked.

Chapter 35

The Red Lion Theatre Company, on that same day, left for the small market town of Church Mere in the same county of Sussex.

They travelled away from the coast, up onto the Downs, under a sun behind rain clouds, and down again into fleeting, wheeling sunlight, and something to look at on a dull Monday for people in the villages, a carnival of two passing through.

When they arrived in Church Mere, Jack led the way to the Gate Theatre. Some of the shops he'd visited on Saturday had playbills in their windows advertising their opening there that evening.

But there was different news waiting for them at the theatre.

The manager of the Gate, who was also the owner of the building, and several other properties, as he'd lost no time in telling him on the phone, when he made the booking, wasn't there when Titus went in to introduce himself.

But his secretary was. Her name, she told him, was Miss Henshaw. Hilda, she offered, as if hoping it was all right to do so. He guessed she was probably in her early twenties, in an office uniform of neat white short-sleeved blouse and dark skirt, and with a diffidence behind the secretarial manner. He found her immediately appealing.

'Alan – Mr Morrison,' she corrected herself, but not before he had heard a story there, there and in her bare ring finger. It was unrequited love, he decided, rather than an affair. That's what he saw in her eyes, a yearning to give going to waste behind the secretarial glasses, and in a smile she seemed to find awkward, as if she wasn't sure if she'd meant it for Alan, or, politely, for the visitor.

'Mr Morrison is away on business at the moment,' she went on. 'But I'm afraid there's a problem,' she added, as there was a knock on the office door and Jack came in, followed by a sandy-haired middle-aged man.

'Hello,' Jack said, and winked at Hilda. 'Titus, we can't play here. The electrics are shot.'

'I was about to tell you, Mr Llewellyn—'

'Titus, please, Hilda.'

'It's not just the wiring,' the other man put in. 'Parts of the backstage are now unsafe.'

'Neil's stage manager here,' Jack said.

The introductions were made, and then Hilda said, 'You see, we had a fire here on Sunday. Fortunately it didn't take complete hold.'

'Aye, a bit odd that, I thought, looking at it,' Neil said. 'And where's our blessed manager when he's needed? Where's—'

'I've told you, Neil. He's in London. On business.'

'Is he? Well, I just hope he's coming back, lass.'

'Of course he's coming back!' Hilda said sharply. 'Don't be so *silly*!'

She was staring heatedly at the stage manager, and looked to Titus alarmingly near to tears.

'Well, these things happen,' he said, the avuncular Edmund Brownlow offering it to Miss Harris. 'And as for us, we'll simply move on,' he added with a flourish, if not sure to where. The next venue was not ready for them until the coming Monday.

'Mr— Titus,' Hilda said, 'there's a small theatre in the town hall here, used by our local amateur dramatics group. If you agree, you could use that. I mean, I know it's not what you expected. I'll quite understand if—'

'No, no, no,' Titus said, with some relief. 'If it has seats and a stage it is a home.'

'Good. Good. And it's all arranged. I spoke to Mr Gibbings, the town clerk, earlier. In case, you know, you did agree.'

Titus beamed at her. 'Hilda, even on our very brief acquaintance such efficiency does not in the least surprise me.'

'Och, Hilda runs the place, mon,' Neil said. 'She has to, with his nibs playing at it.'

'Neil,' Hilda said.

'All right, lass, all right. Look, they have an old London bus out back, with their luggage and scenery in it. Give me the addresses, and I'll go with them to their digs. Then carry on to the town hall with the flats and settle them in there.'

'Oh, that would be a great help, Neil. Thank you,' she said, and smiled at him, as if once again finding his softer side.

While Titus went with the bus, Neil, cut from the good, honest, no-nonsense cloth of Lowland Scotland, found himself a passenger in the back of a Rolls-Royce, that vehicle of the English upper class and colonial splendour, issuing directions to the digs down the speaking tube to the chauffeur.

They moved on to the town hall after that. They off-loaded the flats, but found that the bus couldn't park there for the week; it was against the regulations. The uniformed porter informed Titus of it, asserting himself among the sudden and highly irregular upheaval.

The bus would have to be left at the stage door of the Gate, which deprived them of immediate advertising outside their new venue. And Jack and Simon had then to get busy in the high street, advising the shopkeepers advertising the play about the change of venue, and writing it on all the playbills.

While inside the small theatre, Titus, remarking it really was small, found that it had a seating capacity of just on sixty-four.

'And I don't think it's ever been full,' Neil said. 'Mostly family and friends. Now, there's a lavatory backstage, but nay dressing rooms. There's clothes hangers for costume changes in the wings. There's no fly system, so the curtains are opened on lines – but take note, mon, that they stick.'

'Better than nothing,' Titus said. 'We have a stage, and all the world on it.'

'Aye,' Neil said.

When Titus asked him then what had caused the fire in the theatre, Neil said his lips were sealed.

'But I'll tell you this for nothing,' he added, 'there's more to it than meets the eye. And I'll tell you something else, mon,' he decided. 'Don't trust Mr Alan Morrison. And I'll say no more about that. Except to add that he wanted to pay me and my ASM monthly. I insisted that it must be weekly. Which it now is. But that will give you some idea, d'you ken?'

Titus was relieved to find that there was enough furniture stowed backstage to dress the sets, and set up the opening scene with the help of Neil. Then before the afternoon run-through in a new venue, visited the offices of the *Town Crier*, the local newspaper, seeking coverage about the change and the reason for it, and throwing in the visit of a film star, Daphne Langan, to their town.

The assistant editor he saw was friendly enough but regretful. 'I'm afraid, Mr Llewellyn-Gwynne, that this newspaper will not have any more dealings, financial or otherwise, with Mr Alan Morrison until he pays his considerable advertising bill. Sorry, old man, but there it is. Have to draw the line somewhere.'

Leaving the offices Titus realised that he hadn't really expected anything else. He'd already suspected that the town was against them. Not the people – the town, its buildings. He had experienced it before in his long years of touring, and thought he recognised it again now. He thought that here it might be the puritan spirit of

England sulking in the seventeenth-century brickwork, affronted at the brazen parading of a play.

But a visit to Boots Lending Library in the high street after the newspaper offices told him that the town had been a strong supporter of Charles I.

Whatever it was, they were stuck with it until the end of the week, which dragged miserably on.

As the play was contemporary, the cast simply changed into costume in the evening in their digs, and walked to the town hall. There was no box office, just Hector with a ticket roll from the Gate, programmes, and a biscuit tin on a folding table for the money.

Not that there was much of it, on the first night and throughout the week. Despite the board outside the town hall advertising the play, and seats at gallery prices.

Despite plastering the bus with hand-written notices giving the new venue, hand-written because the town printer said he couldn't handle a rush job. And despite the cast courting the citizenry in the high street with handbills.

None of which, of course, came as a surprise to Titus. He was a Celt, and he knew what he knew.

There was no nightly share-out. What money they did make Titus took in to Hilda the next day, and after she had punctiliously entered the ticket and programme sales into a ledger, she gave him the company's share.

And on the following Monday, shortly before leaving for the next venue, when he called in with the takings from Saturday night, she told him that the police had just left.

'Alan, Mr Morrison, has been arrested in London.'

'Arrested?' he said, as if wanting to get it straight. Going by her expression and tone of voice she might have been quoting the day's weather forecast.

'Multiple mortgage and insurance fraud, arson elsewhere, and he'll face attempted arson here. Our theatre. The police believe he got someone in the town to do it, someone fortunately who wasn't very good at it. Probably didn't pay whoever enough. That would be Alan all over.'

She looked with a quizzically amused expression at the bunch of mixed flowers he was holding.

'For you,' he said. 'A small farewell thank you.'

'Oh, how *lovely*. How nice of you, Titus. Thank you.'

She put her face to the blooms and drew in their scent.

'I knew all along what he was, of course. But chose to ignore it,' she said, as if gently chiding someone else, someone less wise in the way of men. 'Just wouldn't listen. As I wouldn't listen to Neil.'

'Yes, well,' Titus said vaguely.

'And now,' she said brightly, 'I must put your lovely gift in water.'

After they had said goodbye, she kissed his cheek, and smiled at him. A kind smile, as if she were the older of the two, and he was too young to understand.

Chapter 36

Titus and his company left for Burton and Boxgrove and its Phoenix Theatre, where, after their week in Church Mere, things promised to be different.

And they were. But in a way that threatened not only to end that tour, but to prevent the company touring in the future.

Courtesy of Hilda, Daphne had given a telephone interview on Wednesday of that week to the *West Sussex Times*, and photographs, including Daphne on stage as Agnes, Lucinda Harris's mother, were dispatched ready for their Monday morning edition. A nice warm-up for the company's week there, backing up the playbills Jack had visited the town with on Saturday.

The Phoenix had a seating capacity of over five hundred. And on their opening night there, when Wells, as Lucinda's wicked uncle Jasper, came on to make his first attempt on her life, creeping with murderous stealth across a bedroom landing set, large kitchen knife in hand, he would never be more Wells Cheslyn than then, when playing to a full house, or something very much like it. He had judged the size of the audience almost immediately he'd entered earlier for his first scene, the darkened auditorium had told him it in a language that over half a century of performing had taught him.

Lucinda Harris has retired, and Jasper is about to open her bedroom door, knife raised, ready to strike, when Lucinda's mother enters as if from a staircase.

'I thought I heard someone up here. I – what on earth, Jasper, are you doing with that knife?'

'What...? Oh, this!' Jasper titters nervously. 'Yes, I was – er – I was making sure the door knob was secure.'

'Making sure the door knob—?'

'Now, you know perfectly well, Agnes that I've been complaining for the past week about the lack of security in the house, how anyone could break in and murder us in our beds. So I've been going round tightening things.'

'With a knife?'

'I couldn't find a screwdriver. And anyway, I thought you were going to the cinema with Mrs—'

'It turned out she'd seen it, so we had coffee and a chat instead. And as—'

The door of one of the bedrooms opens and Lucinda wanders out in a nightdress, hair in curlers.

'I heard voices. Is everything all right? What's Uncle Jasper doing with the knife?'

'He couldn't find a screwdriver,' her mother tells her, as if it should be obvious, and after pausing for the laugh it almost always gets there, adds to Jasper, 'And as regards security, I phoned Tom Yardley, the young man who—'

'Tom Yardley!' Lucinda's hand flies to her curlers. 'He's not coming tonight, is he!'

Her mother eyes her suspiciously. 'Is there something I should know, Lucinda?'

And Lizzie, as Lucinda, and usually line-perfect, is about to deliver a vehement denial when, for the third time that evening, she dries, and has to be rescued by Dolly in the prompt corner.

Something that was understood by those with her on stage, if not altogether forgiven. She had learned earlier that day that she had got the film part she'd auditioned for last week, travelling from Sussex to a rehearsal room in London. It wasn't a big part, but it was her first film, and when the rest of the company congratulated her on it, most of them even meant it.

But it left Titus with a problem he'd spent most of the day with, sitting with his contact book and the telephone in the manager's office.

The film company wanted Lizzie in London for a read-through on Monday of next week. Titus had insisted that she must go, indulging her performance of being willing to stay, a performance so half-hearted it amounted to a plea to let her go. And if he didn't get a replacement for her within the next couple of days, it wouldn't leave him enough time to get whoever ready to go on at the next venue.

Otherwise that venue, and the rest of the tour, would have to be cancelled. Which would also mean that he could forget about any future dates at those theatres, or anywhere else in the country. It would be reported in the *Stage*, and gossiped about wherever theatre people met, a reputation for unreliability passed on like a contagion from management to management.

The next morning, Jack, on his way to buy a newspaper and cigarettes from his digs round the corner from the theatre, saw Titus disappearing into it.

Returning from the newsagent's, he found him sitting at the desk in the manager's office.

Titus indicated his contact book open in front of him.

'We are finished, Jack. The last person who might have stepped into the breach is working. So you may have your desk back, Alex,' he added to the young manager, standing watching Titus with his hands clasped, an audience to Titus's drama. 'And thank you for being so obliging. Do let me have the bill for the calls.'

Alex waved it away. 'No, no, no. Not at all. Art, Titus, as you have said, must be served,' he said recklessly.

Alex, an accountant, recently appointed by the council, the owners of the building, had started the job with an anticipated sense of glamour, of art and the theatre. Something which, after a few months managing a venue on the variety circuit, he had soon lost.

Then Titus had swept in, as if off a stage, and he'd found it again. Titus was precisely what he had meant.

'And art and I both thank you, Alex. But alas, it was to no avail. And it's all my fault. *Mea culpa, mea maxima culpa.* Because I should have not set out, not *thought* even of doing so, without safety nets, without understudies for both principals. A couple of small parts easily added, or even off-stage cover. But I wanted to keep the numbers down, you see, Alex, for a bigger share-out, a more tangible reward for those who serve that art, who give without stint and for small reward.'

'Yes, of course, of course,' Alex said, wringing his hands.

'Sheer folly. And now, with only rubble to go back to, and doors these days closed to an old player of parts, his hour fret upon the stage, I am finished. To come no more, no more,' he said on a dying fall.

'Oh, dear,' Alex said, looking anguished and sharing it with Jack, who was leaning against a filing cabinet with his newspaper, smoking and looking at the headlines.

'Titus,' Jack said then, putting the newspaper aside. 'I've been thinking. And I might – might just know someone.'

Titus lifted Welsh-dark eyes, liquid with misery.

'Someone prepared to work without the guarantee of an Equity wage?' he said, and smiled a little, sadly, as if at Jack's naivety, and at a world that places such things above art.

'Yes. Yes, she might well.'

Titus shrugged. 'Then phone her, dear boy. Phone her,' he said, getting up from the desk and indicating the phone. 'I'm sure Alex—'

'No, of course not!' Alex said, hands out, offering his desk again.

'I don't have a phone number for her. But I think I know where I can find her. But to do that, I have to go to London.'

'Then go. Jack. Go. Take the Rolls. See Dolly, she should be up by now, for petrol money, and go. After all, we've nothing to lose now. Nothing at all,' he added, waving a hand as if careless of the loss.

But Jack caught the look in his eyes before leaving the office, saw what cancelling would mean to him, and saw hope there.

Hope he took with him on a journey he already regretted saying he'd make, with so little chance of success. Saw another's hope and felt its burden like guilt.

* * *

Following directions he'd stopped to ask for, he found the Harp of Erin pub shortly after arriving in Catford.

It had just opened, the public bar, with a few early customers in it, smelling of disinfectant and last night's beer. Jack caught the sound of home, or at least Dublin, two of the customers vigorously debating over the back pages of a newspaper the merits of runners in the first race at Brighton.

Jack didn't need to be told that the man stacking a shelf behind the bar was the landlord. He was built for Saturday night and a rough house, and wearing an immaculately clean and pressed white shirt with metal sleeve garters, a jewelled stick pin in his tie, his hair centre parted and slick with Brylcreem.

He greeted Jack with a smile enlivened with two gold front teeth.

'What can I get you, squire?' he said, resting meaty hands on the counter, chunky gold rings on both of them like knuckle dusters.

Jack was about to said he was hoping to speak to Mairead the barmaid, when a middle-aged woman, carefully made up and coiffed, trailing scent and two white miniature poodles with diamanté collars, swept into the bar from a side door.

She took in Jack with a glance like a pawnbroker's.

'Is that your Rolls-Royce out there?' she asked, her tone making it clear that if it was, then she didn't believe he'd come by it legally. 'May one ask,' she added just in case she was wrong, and smiled as if careful of her make-up.

'Well, it's not mine, I'm just the chauffeur. But yes, it is. I was—'

'Because we can't be held responsible for it. You understand that, I hope.'

'They're like that round here, chum,' the man said cheerfully. 'Have it jacked up and the wheels off in no time. Or just half-inch the lot.'

'You don't look like a chauffeur. They usually have a uniform, don't they?' The woman smiled again, as if to offset her rudeness.

'It's my day off. I get the use of the car then.'

'That's my missus,' the landlord told him, by way of explanation. 'Perhaps I can finish serving the gentleman now, Betty. Unless you want him to make a statement first. Or take his fingerprints.'

His wife glared at him and swept off through another door with the dogs.

When Jack was assured that the cellar man responsible for keeping the draught Guinness was Irish, he ordered a pint of it, and bought the landlord a pale ale, which was put out of sight on a shelf just below the countertop.

The landlord told him that Mairead had phoned in sick earlier. But if it was actually Nancy Dunn, her friend, Jack wanted, then he didn't have a telephone number for her, but did have her address, because it was where Mairead used to lodge.

The house was a short distance from the pub, at the end of a street half of which was given over to a used clothes market.

When Jack spotted the house number he wanted he parked halfway up on the pavement with a couple of stallholders for an audience.

'Come the revolution!' one of them shouted.

Jack waved airily at them, one of the filthy rich rubbing it in.

Nancy's surname was under a small piece of plastic above a bell push one side of the front door. He rang it a few times, and when there was still no answer went and sat in the back of the Rolls with the morning paper, apart from the headlines still unread.

Shortly after that someone knocked on the side window of the car. Jack looked up, expecting to see the helmet of a bobby, the way he was parked, and found Nancy Dunn peering in at him.

She opened the door. 'What on earth are you doing here?'

'Waiting for you. I've got a proposition you might be interested in.'

'What sort of a proposition?' she asked suspiciously.

'Get in and I'll tell you. Cigarette?' he said, when she was seated.

She took one and said, 'Well, what is it?'

He blew out smoke, and, sitting back with the cigarette like an impresario with a cigar, said, 'How'd you like to be an actress, Nancy?'

She pulled away to get a better look at him, and laughed, 'Wha-at?'

'How would you like to be an actress?'

'What are you talking about?'

'It's quite simple. Lizzie Peters, who plays Miss Harris in the play you saw, is leaving at the end of the week. She was offered a film role, out of the blue. That's what can happen, let me tell you, Nancy, when you're an actress. And we have to get a replacement for next week, for the new venue.'

Nancy stared at him. One of the stallholders across the way was shouting his goods to anyone who would listen.

'Are you serious?' Nancy said.

'As ever was.'

She laughed again. 'Don't be daft! I'm not an actress.'

'What – never impersonated anybody, pretended to be somebody you're not?'

'That's different.'

'Yes, it is. Actors don't get sent down for it – I'm not saying some shouldn't, given their performances. But mostly people are just terribly nice and clap.'

'There is—'

'And you get paid for it. Not a lot, mind you. Just a share of the door. That's why we've having difficulty getting someone. But we've been doing good business lately, and—'

'Jack – Jack, there is a difference, and it's a big one. I have never been on a stage in my life.'

'Ah, away with that. We can teach you that stuff in a couple of hours. Nothing to it.'

Nancy stared at him.

'No,' she said. 'No. I'm just not cut out for that sort of thing.'

'Not cut out for it? What are you? A gingerbread man or a living person with the mind God gave you? You decide what size, how big or small, or what shape, you want to be. You decide who you are, you and no one else. Not cut out for it! People carry that about as if they were born with it stamped on their bum.'

'Look,' she almost pleaded. 'Look, I—'

'It's about possibility, Nancy. The road to what is possible. You could of course do nothing, simply stay here, waiting for life to do it for you. And in five or more years end up like those old demob suits out there,' he said, pointing to a rack of them across the street, 'still waiting for a decent offer.'

'Thanks a lot,' she said, but without heat.

Jack wound down the window his side and dropped the end of his cigarette out.

'Nancy, Shakespeare wrote that there is a tide in the affairs of men, which taken at the flood leads on to fortune. But omitted, not taken, not *taken*, Nancy, all the voyage of their life is bound in shallows and in miseries. Don't waste your life paddling in the shallows.'

'Or piddling in them. As we used to in the swimming baths when I was a kid,' she said, and laughed, a woman who had made up her mind before Jack brought Shakespeare into it. 'All right. I'll have a pop at it. Why not? Why not!'

'Good girl!'

'When do you want me there?'

'Well, now, today. Lizzie's leaving on Monday.'

'Today?' she said doubtfully.

'Now, now, none of that. Is your rent up to date?'

'Well, yes. Till the end of the week.'

'There you are, you see. Fate is already giving you a hand. God knows where you'll end up at this rate. Kissing Clark Gable by Christmas, I wouldn't be at all surprised.'

'I don't like men with moustaches. Can you make it Cary Grant?'

'I'll give him a ring. Meanwhile, have you much gear, furniture and things?'

'No, no, just a few clothes, and odds and ends.'

'You're a woman. What does a few clothes mean?'

'I came here with two suitcases and a grip. And that's it. You don't need many quality clothes, and I dress from Bond Street,' she said, and when he looked at her she winked.

'I see,' he said. 'And what about – what's this you call them? Kite books?'

'No, they're stashed with a friend. And they can stay there for now. Because you never know.'

'True. That is true. I mean, look at yourself this very morning.'

'Yes. Yes,' she said. 'I was going to sign on today for a secretarial course in Streatham. And now here I am, Nancy Dunn, actress.' She laughed. 'I must be mad.'

'I was going to say about that, the name. I don't think you ought to use your own. You know, just in case.'

She looked at him. 'You mean Reuben…'

'Well, yes—'

'Crikey! I hadn't thought about that.'

'As I say, just in case. That's all.'

'I hadn't thought about that…' she said again, doing so now, what it might mean in her eyes.

'Because of the publicity, the printed stuff. I don't think you ought to have your real name on it. You know…?' he added, his voice trailing off.

And then he said, 'Nancy, I owe you an apology. There is a risk to you, of course there is. And it's a big one. And one I hadn't given anywhere near enough thought to. And it was stupid of me. Stupid! Take the secretarial course, it's far safer. I'm sorry. I'm sorry, Nancy. I've messed you about.'

She stared at him, her face fierce with thought, and then burst out, 'No! No, bloody well sod him! He's not running my life. I'll do it!'

'Nancy—' he began.

'Don't start that again! Do you want me to do it, or not? Make your mind up.'

'Well, yes, of course but—'

'Then you can give me a hand packing. Come on.'

A short while after that, Nancy sitting this time in the front passenger seat, because, as he said, she was now staff, Jack closed the boot on her luggage.

And turning to the small audience of stallholders she had exchanged waves with, he said, 'She's only after me for my money.'

'Have you got much then, Jack,' she said, when he got in.

'No. Hardly any at all.'

'Trust you,' she said, and then, 'Trust me. Where are we going then?' she asked cheerfully. 'Camberford Bay?'

'No, we've done another week elsewhere since then. All the same county. We've opened now in a town called Burton and Boxgrove.'

'Burton and Boxgrove. Two towns in one?'

'Yes, for whatever reason. An English compromise maybe after a long stalemate in the mayor's parlour when it came to the naming of it, with the Burton councillors voting for Burton, and the Boxgrove lot for Boxgrove, and the pubs near closing.'

'Well, whatever it's called, it beats getting the bus for Streatham.'

He laughed, and sounded the car's horn, two imperious blasts like brass clearing non-existent vehicles out of the damn way, on the road to Burton and Boxgrove, and to whatever came after that.

'And it's just the start, Nancy. A stop on the way to more possibilities. A place that our tribe are always, in one form or another, on their way to, always travelling its bright road. Welcome to your future, Nancy Dunn.'

'Genevieve Clifford,' she said. 'That's the name I've decided I'll use. Genevieve Clifford.'

* * *

The day before that, at precisely nine o'clock in the morning, a single bell tolled from the parish church of All Saints in South London, a ritual that gathered in the streets silent witnesses to a convicted murderer's last moments in Wandsworth Prison a mile away.

And so Joey Baxter, on remand in that prison for a bungled smash and grab on a Knightsbridge jeweller's shop, had something other than the bad food and his cellmate's feet to talk about when he next saw Doreen, his wife.

They were sitting across the scarred wooden table from each other in the visiting room, its stone walls a two-tone cream and green, the colours of his cell. Children ran about, playing, bringing in the sound of home, and there was laughter at other tables, and sometimes tears, shared despair, and promises at others made again, and this time meant.

When Doreen had finished talking about the job she'd had getting there, waiting about for the two buses she had to take, he told her about the hanging.

'The geezer who did the old man in Lambeth, Dor. All for a few quid and a Mickey Mouse watch. The topping shed's on E Wing, but you could hear the thud of the trapdoor when he went all over the nick. They locked us behind our doors just before, and there was a lot of shouting from the chaps, and banging of things, and that. But it all went quiet then, I can tell you. Never known a nick that quiet before, at any time.'

'And having to stand about in the rain,' Doreen went on, headscarf off and fluffing out her hair with a hand. 'And I only had it done yesterday. Specially for today. Not that you'd noticed, of course.'

'Course I noticed. I was about to—'

'And another thing. Who's Dolly?'

'Dolly…? I don't know no Dolly. What are you talking about?'

'Last week, some woman rang. Posh sounding. Asked for Mr Baxter and when I said you weren't there, she wanted to leave a message. She said it was very important and insisted that I write it down.'

Doreen rooted about in her handbag, and when a patrolling prison officer saw her, held up the piece of paper she'd found.

'It's just a phone message somebody left for him. Not a bleeding cake with a file in it,' she muttered to his back.

Joey, frowning into the middle distance, shook his head. 'I don't know no Dolly,' he told himself.

'Joey, listen to me. I'll read it to you,' she said, knowing he'd struggle with the words. 'It says – *Dolly is in a theatre in a place called Camberford Bay in Sussex*. Ring any bells?' she asked.

Joey shook his head again. 'No.'

'Perhaps she got the wrong number.'

'Must have. I don't know no Dolly. Anyway – 'ere, hang about. Did you say something about a theatre?'

231

'Yes. She said Dolly's in a theatre. In this Camberford Bay.'

'That's for Books. I know what that is, it's a message for Books Kramer. He gave me a drink to pass on any messages about a theatre, while he's waiting for his own phone to be mended. Said there'll be a few more quid in it if I do get something for him.'

'Why? What's that about?'

'I dunno. And I don't ask questions, do I. Look, my address book's in one of the kitchen cabinet drawers. Look up a geezer called Frank Collins, give him a bell, and tell him about the message. He'll pass it on to Books. He's Books's lieutenant,' he said, putting a swagger into the word, liking the gangster sound of it. 'Apart from the extra few quid, it pays to keep in with Books, Dor. You never know where it might lead.'

Chapter 37

In her room in Burton and Boxgrove, Nancy Dunn danced as Genevieve Clifford in her sleep to words that turned, in the way of dreams, into something like music. Words she had fallen asleep over in bed, her well-thumbed copy of *Love and Miss Harris* on her chest. Words, music, that in sleep had released Genevieve Clifford from the wings of the Phoenix Theatre, from the shadows Nancy Dunn had long looked on and envied from, to dance in a brilliance of lights, and the embrace of an audience like love in the velvet dark.

She woke to the real world, to cramming Miss Harris into another day and watching her at night on stage, following her lines as if lip reading. There were only two days between now and Monday, Monday and an eight o'clock curtain. And although it wasn't as bad as when she'd first moved into that room, it was something she still didn't care to dwell on.

Alex, the theatre manager, had come up with her lodgings on Tuesday, a single, in a large house a few streets away from the theatre and the digs of the rest of the company. She had no idea how many others were under its roof. She had heard people coming and going, and passed them in the hall, but had only spoken to one of the other lodgers, a middle-aged traveller in perfume, with a bow tie and a practised gentlemanly charm. He had tried on her second day there to tempt her into his room with talk of a free sample.

But although he didn't know it, it was the sophisticated actress Genevieve Clifford he was trying it on with. And Nancy Dunn had always been worth more than a free sample of anything.

After taking her turn in the shared bathroom on her floor, she dressed, in slacks instead of a skirt, ready for another day preparing for her debut as Lucinda Harris. Something which, for the first couple of days, had prompted panic and thoughts of writing a letter of apology to Titus and Jack, and taking the next train back to London.

But she was more at home now in the spaces of the stage, more sure of her moves after several blocking rehearsals. And, although often shakily so, starting to be more sure of her new job description of actress. Learning about timing, and cues, and how to stand, and things such as not sitting or moving on a line, or when somebody's talking, about stillness and projection, mentally aiming her voice at the back row of the stalls.

'You're not expected of course to remember it all on the night, or indeed for some time after that,' Titus had said. 'But it will come. I can promise you that. I see the child in you, Genevieve Clifford, that all good actors have in them. We were all born with a talent for acting, the reason children are so often good at it. But for most of us it gets lost in what is called the real world. As of course it must, because then we are called grown-ups. But you, dear girl, have kept more of that talent you were born with, more of that child, than most people. As you will see.'

And there were times when she believed him, the times when something she found within herself drove the doubt and uncertainty into the shadows, where, at those times, she knew they belonged.

And she was remembering more and more of her lines. With fewer desperate whispers of 'line!' to Dolly in the prompt corner. The other cast, knowing it was for the good of the tour, showed patience, keeping whatever complaint they might have had about full afternoon rehearsals, of a play they'd have to do again in the evenings, to themselves.

Lizzie Peters, of course, didn't have to be at these rehearsals, but at other times had made no secret of what she thought of a little amateur from South London, as she had put it, loud enough for Nancy to hear, being passed off as an actress, and a principal one at that. It was pointed out to her that she could afford to say that, now that she no longer needed the play.

But it was the little amateur, Nancy Dunn from Catford, not Genevieve Clifford the actress, who had the last word. She was alone in the female dressing room, experimenting with the stage make-up Daphne had given her, when Lizzie entered, and stood for a few moments watching her at one of the mirrors, seeming to find it amusing.

But she lost her smile then, when Nancy stood, walked up to her and, putting a bit of South London into it, told her quietly, just between the two of them, that if her manners didn't improve she'd be turning up for her film job on Monday with half her blonde hair missing.

'It's how we settle things, love, where I come from,' she explained to a girl from the soft heart of the Home Counties. 'And I'm good at it.'

Only Jack, Titus and Dolly knew where she had come from, knew about her past. But Lizzie got the picture, if not the details, immediately. There were no more remarks, or eye rolling, or that thing she did with her mouth, after that.

Nancy's digs didn't provide food, just a bedroom, and she had breakfast, a fry-up, at a workman's café she'd found, tucking into it with a mug of tea and Patti Page on the jukebox, before leaving for work.

The stage door of the Phoenix Theatre was presided over by a keeper known to everyone as Mr Nowak. Mr Nowak was an elderly Pole who wore whatever past he had brought with him from Warsaw on his face. He had never been known to smile. And he ignored those who smiled at him, doing so in a manner which suggested he considered that they knew no better. For Mr Nowak, if no one else, life remained a grim business.

With Nancy, when she came past his window each time, it was different.

Maybe there had once been a Nancy in his life who had smiled at him like that, a grin like mischief in her eyes, her cheeks holed with dimples. Maybe that's what he was responding to when he smiled back, a smile like a crack in something, like the very first movement of a thaw after a long hard winter. And what sounded like a chuckle then, when Nancy, before disappearing into the theatre, winked at him.

Chapter 38

Monday came round, as Nancy knew it would, like a dentist's appointment, or a court appearance. She even missed Lizzie Peters, because now it left only Genevieve Clifford, who that morning felt far more like Nancy Dunn.

But it was Genevieve Clifford on the programmes that had been rushed through, as her photograph for it had been, the brim of her fedora, with Reuben in mind, pulled down. And Genevieve Clifford on the publicity playbills Jack had gone ahead with on Saturday, the name on it seeming to her like an alias on a wanted poster.

And she was driven again to thoughts of writing that letter of apology to Titus and Jack, and leaving it with Mr Nowak on her way to the station in a taxi.

Thought about it while knowing she wasn't going to do it, knowing she didn't mean it.

It had woken something in her, set off something that she'd never felt before. Not even when walking away from Garrard & Co with a Princess Catherine ring.

* * *

She had got up earlier than usual, unable to sleep any longer, and making two trips loaded her luggage onto the tour bus.

She had her usual fry-up café breakfast, and then said goodbye to Mr Nowak, who patted her hand and told her to be a good girl. And chuckled again then, when she said she would, and winked.

On the bus, Nancy sat next to Daphne Langan, who was talking about the scene they shared as mother and daughter towards the end of the play.

'… do of course at all times remember the back of the stalls voice tip, Genny. But the truth of a scene won't be added to by shouting it at the audience. The odd missed word or two doesn't matter. If they believe in it, they'll follow it. They're not supposed to be there anyway. They're not supposed to be there, and we're not supposed to know they're there.'

Seeing Nancy's unconvinced expression, Daphne smiled. 'You'll be fine, you know, darling, you'll see. You'll see.'

As the bus was leaving the town, Daphne said, 'Goodbye, Burton and Boxgrove. You were good to us.'

'Burton and Boxgrove,' Nancy said. 'I've never heard of a town before with two names. I wonder why it is?'

Daphne said she didn't know. But Simon, sitting a couple of seats behind them, did. Simon collected town and county guides in pamphlet form from each date they played, and liked to air the contents.

'Hold on, and I'll tell you,' he said, rummaging in his haversack next to him on the seat.

'It was the result,' he said then, reading from the guide, 'of what in medieval times was called an incorporation, which merged the two neighbouring towns when they both expanded into a single legal body and affirmed the rights of its burgesses and courts.'

'Thank you, Simon,' Daphne said, without much interest.

'What are burgesses?' Nancy asked him.

Simon, sounding regretful, said he didn't know. He would have liked to have to known, seeing that it was Nancy asking.

The bus left West Sussex, and travelled for a while along the Surrey and Hampshire border up into Berkshire, heading for the town of St Anne's on the Hill, and the King's Hall Theatre.

Under the big skies of the Downs and a wheat-coloured sun, across the chalk grassland of Berkshire, its flat distances turning grazing Friesian cattle and fleece-fat sheep to stillness, to small, painted enamel animals on green cloth from a toy cupboard.

Simon, sitting across the aisle from Wells, who appeared to be asleep, had found the Berkshire county guide Jack had given him on Saturday.

'Berkshire,' he read to no one in particular, 'has been the scene of some notable battles throughout its history. Alfred the Great's campaign against the Danes included the battles of Englefield, Ashdown and Reading. Two English Civil War battles were fought—'

'There'll be another bloody battle in a moment if you don't button it!' Wells snarled. 'I'm trying to get some sleep.'

Daphne looked back at him. 'Another bad night, Wells?' she asked, indulging him, suspecting it was more drama than insomnia.

'Pretty bloody awful, quite frankly! Thank you for asking, Daphne,' he added with martyred politeness, before closing his eyes again.

A few minutes later, Simon, checking that Wells was asleep, pretended to read from the guide.

'The county is also known,' he said in a quieter voice, 'as seeing the first ever public appearance of Genevieve Clifford. She—'

If Wells had been asleep he was now suddenly awake. 'Simon!' he snapped, sitting up rigidly and glaring at him. 'That was not only unprofessional, it was also rather bloody unpleasant,' he said, surprising Nancy, who had got the impression that he disapproved of her.

Simon looked appalled. 'Oh, I didn't mean – I meant it as a compliment!'

He got up quickly and sat on the seat behind the two women.

'I meant it as a compliment, Genny. Honestly.'

'That's all right, Simon,' Nancy said.

'You ought to have more sense, Simon,' Daphne said.

'And better professional manners,' Wells added.

Simon was staring hopelessly at the back of Nancy's head.

'I meant it as... I think you're marvellous, quite honestly, Gen,' he said, stroking her hair. 'I think—'

Nancy pulled her head away. 'Don't do that! I've told you before about that. Don't do it. Unless you want your fingers bent again.'

'For God's sake, Simon,' Wells said. 'Go and read your damn guide things. Quietly, to yourself.'

Simon sat down again and stared, misunderstood, out of the window.

Across from him, Wells put his head back to sleep again, and then sat up and sighed heavily. Daphne looked back at him with a grimace of sympathy.

Wells lit a Woodbine in his amber cigarette holder, and sat gazing out without interest at the passing world.

They left behind a stretch of moorland, patched with purple heather and butter-yellow gorse, its wild ponies looking up from their grazing as the bus went by, and took the road signposted to St Anne's on the Hill.

Hector changed into first gear to follow Jack up the steep cobbled high street, past shops, and shoppers stopping to look, first at a Rolls-Royce regally passing, and then a bus plastered with exotic words like 'love' and 'theatre'.

Jack turned off down a side road and took them past the star-shaped ruins of a castle.

'The past through which the wind now blows,' Wells quoted.

'It's lovely,' Nancy said. 'Like something on the pictures.'

'The castle of St Anne's on the Hill,' Simon supplied, county guide in hand, 'was founded...'

He trailed off when he saw Wells looking at him.

'Carry on, Simon. You might as well, dear boy. I shan't sleep now,' he added, with a small doleful smile.

'It was founded by the Saxons after a series of ferocious attacks by the Danes. And—'

'How very unladylike,' Wells drawled.

'Danes, Wells,' Daphne said, laughing. 'Not dames.'

'And built on in the eleventh century by the Normans,' Simon went on, 'against attacks by rebellious English—'

'Cheek!' Daphne said.

'Certainly looks like somebody's given it a good bashing,' Nancy said. 'Poor thing.'

'Old misery guts,' Daphne said. 'Oliver Cromwell. He was always bashing things. When he wasn't banning them.'

Simon consulted his guide. 'No, it was before Cromwell's time, Daphne. It was—'

'*I'm one of the ruins that Cromwell knocked abaht a bit, One of the ruins that Cromwell knocked abaht a bit, 'baht a bit,*' Wells sang out, and was joined by Daphne, and Nancy, with a Saturday night Catford pub in mind, Wells conducting with his cigarette holder, while Simon, forgetting about history, sat grinning at the performance.

'*... In the gay old days there used to be some doings, no wonder that the poor old castle went to ruins!*' they sang, as the bus pulled up behind the Rolls at the theatre's stage door.

Chapter 39

Frank Collins could unfailingly read when a man was about to become violent almost without knowing he was doing so, the slight tightening of the face, something there suddenly in the eyes. And when that happened there weren't many who could beat him to the punch.

But he had little insight into people outside of that, and had no idea why what he saw lately in Reuben's eyes made him so uneasy. It was for that reason that, after Doreen Baxter, Joey Baxter's wife, had phoned with the message about Camberford Bay, he hesitated before passing it on, if not altogether sure why.

But not for long, considering who he'd be withholding it from.

He had other business to discuss with Reuben, concerning the West End protection they'd taken over. But had been unable to find him. Reuben's wife, Cornelia, when he phoned her again, said she still hadn't seen him, had no idea where he was, and didn't, he thought, sound much interested either way.

And then the landlord of the Hen and Chickens pub in Lewisham, the Bucket of Blood of Frank's trade, knowing he was looking for him, phoned and said Reuben had turned up there out of the blue and was playing cards.

When Frank drove over there, Books was sitting in his usual chair at the card table, back to the wall and with a view of whoever entered the small bar. Frank indicated that he wanted to see him in the back, in the landlord's private sitting room. He noticed that Reuben was badly in need of a shave.

The furniture in the sitting room was from a long firm fraud Reuben ran in the thirties, before the warehouse under the railway arches in Peckham had been raided. Above a tiled fireplace, a plastic Guinness wall clock had said it was twenty to seven for as long as either man could remember.

They sat in front of a lacquered black-and-red art deco coffee table, on a two-seater sofa in gold velour. And when they did so, Frank caught the smell of unwashed flesh and linen from the other man, a man normally fastidious about his grooming, the air around him scented with Pinaud Clubman shaving lotion.

They waited until the landlord had brought in the usual tray of glasses and water jug with the bottle of Bell's whisky, and had left, before Frank told him about Joey Baxter.

'Then we've got him,' Reuben said quietly, staring into some distance of his own. 'We've got him, Frank! We've got him!' he said again, and laughed, an odd, sudden, jarring sound that made Frank shift uneasily on the seat.

'Yeah, well, Books,' he said, 'we don't know when this was, we don't know when this woman phoned—'

'That's all right. That's all right, Frankie. No problem there, boy. We know it wasn't last year. So all we have to do is to follow the trail from this Camberford Bay place. Sweet as a nut, my son. Couldn't be easier.'

'Why don't we just ring the theatres, follow it that way.'

Reuben leaned towards him. 'We want to be on the doorstep, Frankie. Then when they open the door – pop!' he said, and unnerved the other man by widening his eyes at him, and then laughing as if at some joke of his own. 'Your time's up, actor,' he called into the air, and laughed again. Then he turned suddenly solemn. 'We go back a long way, you and me, Frank. Through thick and thin. Good times and bad. Times of plenty, as the Bible says, and times when we hadn't a pot to piss in. And you were always there, mate. Always! I never had to look. So here's to you, Frank. No, no, I mean it. Here's to you, son,' he said, lifting his glass.

'Yeah, well,' Frank said. 'Thanks, Books. Right, well, it looks like we've got a result then. I've give Ed a bell. Tell him—'

'No. No, I've been thinking about that, Frank, giving that a bit of thought. In fact giving it a lot of thought. He's a loose cannon, chum, that boy. And for a loose cannon he knows a lot. In fact, Frankie, you might even say that he knows *too* much,' he added, and waited.

Frank got it then and stared at him. 'You don't mean...?'

Reuben nodded, as if regretfully.

'What! Eddie?'

'Yeah, Eddie,' Reuben said, and shook his head as if at the death of one so young. 'It's something I'd rather not do, Frank, believe you me. There's his mum for one thing. He's all she's got. And then to stir up the Old Bill when they learn he worked for the firm. But what choice have we got, Frank? Answer me that. I mean, think about it – think about it, Frank. He's got the goods on us, boy. He could put his signature on papers that could get both of us up the Old Bailey steps. With me getting the black cap and you copping a good few handfuls. You'll be old when you come out.'

Frank was thinking about it. 'Yeah, well, put like that...'

'Nobody likes doing it, mate. But it's him or us. Him or us, Frank. Know what I mean?'

'Yeah. Yeah, I—'

'I'll do it. You don't have to be involved. I'll attend to it. I'll top him after the actor. I'll phone the shop and ask for an order of flowers to be delivered to that deserted Tipton's Yard on the river.

Then do it there, put it in his head there, when he's looking for the address. He won't know a thing.'

'Hey – hey, I've got an idea,' Frank said then, making a contribution to a future as a free man, as if surprising himself.

Reuben grinned encouragement at him. 'Go on then, Frankie, spit it out!'

'We could put him down to that Chinese geezer.'

'What Chinese geezer?'

'I couldn't tell you at the time because I couldn't find you. A Triad boss, by the look of him, from Limehouse, with a few of his heavies. They had the West End protection till we took it off 'em. I was in the Pelican when they were doing the clubs looking for you. They've been there before, I'm told. Anyway, I said that they could have the West End back. I—'

'You what…?' Reuben said quietly.

Frank put up a hand, as if to ward him off. 'Yeah, but hold on, boss, hold on. Two days before that I had a word from a mate of mine in Soho, who'd guessed we'd been at it up there. He said that West End Central had got involved, undercover plants, that sorta thing. So I told the Chinese that we couldn't afford a gang war, and so they can have the business back. I was expecting trouble. But the geezer just shook my hand. Funny lot.'

Reuben looked doubtful. 'Yeah, but people wouldn't have described Chinese blokes for the last lot, would they, Frank. So I don't see—'

'Ah, but hang about, guv'nor, that's where it gets really sweet. You see, it was Eddie who picked up the money, from the Burbage and the other West End gaffs, him and a geezer called Kirk Turner.'

'Kirk Turner?'

'A false moniker probably. They come and go these people. He stood in on a couple of the weekend doors for us. He was in the

Smoke for a few weeks, then moved back up North. Which leaves Eddie. Eddie nicking Triad money? Well, I mean, gotta end badly, that has, hasn't it.'

'Yeah. Gotta end up where Eddie ended up – Frankie, you're a bleedin' genius. And in that case, boy, I won't do the business with the Colt, but with a meat cleaver.'

'A meat cleaver?'

'Very Triad, that is. The actor tried to whack me with it, the one I've got, outside the Red Lion Theatre across the river one night. But I was too quick for him. I almost popped him then. But I won't miss next time.'

'I thought he was on tour...'

Reuben shrugged. 'Night off, or something. There to get something. The cleaver maybe. Maybe it's a stage prop. But it's real enough. You could shave with it. He left it stuck in the door post. Missed my nut by an inch.'

'Blimey,' Frank said.

'So, I'll do the Ed thing with it. Not so noisy either. Then we'll hand his topping by the Triads to the local Bill, give them a bell anonymously. And with Eddie tidied away, the lights are on green for the actor. This is fate, Frankie, this is bleedin' fate talking, my son!' Reuben said with sudden force, knuckles white on his whisky glass. 'Little Joey Baxter and his wife are no problem. And Nancy's practically family. So there it is, the actor, on a plate. We'll leave tomorrow morning. Pick me up here with the Ford at ten thirty. And bring enough gear to stay over for a couple of nights.'

'Right,' Frank said, and saw off the last of his whisky.

'No, hang about,' Reuben said then, standing with him. 'Better make it up the hill at my drum. Pick me up there. I could do with a shave and that,' he added, rubbing a hand over his face bristle, as if surprised to find it there.

'I've been sleeping in the car,' he added, staring at Frank, a sudden admission, and in his eyes at that moment, in that brief weakness, was a plea for help for something he hadn't words for.

Then he shot up a hand, as if angry with himself for it. 'Don't ask.'

Don't ask because he didn't know. He didn't know why, or what. He knew only the fear that drove him to hide from it, huddled out of sight on the backseat of the Bentley.

Afterwards, Frank, who rarely had insights into people, had one into Reuben, when driving back to Peckham. With Eddie tidied away, and Joey Baxter, his wife and Nancy considered no problem, who did that leave? Who, he asked himself, apart from them, could make a connection between Reuben and a murdered actor, not to mention two other capital jobs?

And the answer to that, when he remembered the look in Reuben's eye, almost made him drive through a red light.

* * *

After Henry Long, with Johnny Lee and the Chen brothers, had left the Pelican Club, Johnny Lee, buoyed up by Frank obviously thinking they were Triads, wanted to go back and demand the protection money they'd lost.

But Henry, carrying his briefcase with his newly bought meat cleaver in it, just smiled and shook his head at it, keeping his reasons to himself.

For one thing, what had happened meant he would no longer have to murder the Bookmaker. He had never murdered anyone before, and the thought of having to do so had stalked his days and turned into nightmares in his sleep. And for another, to take the money would be to throw what he had just been given into his late father's face.

For he believed, or perhaps chose to believe, that his father, whose wise, kindly eyes followed him approvingly back across the river to Limehouse, had arranged what had happened, had interceded on his behalf with his ancestors.

He had, at one Confucian stroke, made the South London firm give back the business they had taken from him, so satisfying the demands of *mianzi*, the saving of face, and handed him the means of his own redemption – to leave his criminal past behind him and to walk the path of correctness, under the blue skies of virtue and probity, under the smiling ancestry heavens.

Chapter 40

The King's Hall's ASM was called Roberta, Bobby. She looked about eighteen, with short dark hair, a man's shirt, slacks, and lots of lipstick.

She came briskly out of the stage door to help unload the flats, slowing only to take in Jack.

'Hello,' she said on her way past, her eyes saying the rest.

Their stage manager, she told Titus, had left to take a job with Birmingham Rep, and for now she was in charge backstage. And she left him in no doubt she knew what she was doing, when supervising the two casual hands when the set was going up, placing the furniture according to audience sightlines and blind spots. By the time Titus had returned from the manager's office the stage was rehearsal ready.

The manager's office smelt of furniture polish, the things on his desk arranged as if waiting inspection. The manager was impeccably groomed in a dinner jacket with wide satin lapels and a stripe down the trousers, a fussily precise man who seemed to wear a permanent frown, of disapproval, perhaps, of a world less precisely arranged.

Titus was reassured. It was his experience that men of this sort do not usually fiddle the figures. It was perhaps too disruptive to something in them to make, at the end of the evening, two and two anything other than four.

They had a rehearsal in the afternoon, during which Nancy needed even fewer nudges from Dolly. She left the stage buoyant with a new-found confidence, a feeling for the first time that she really could do this,

That lasted until the evening, sitting with Daphne in the dressing room they shared, where she felt it ebbing away.

Daphne was skilfully using a highlighter stick from a make-up box that had once held Fortnum & Mason chocolates, offering up the heaviness under her chin to it.

She was telling a story about one of her husbands, while Nancy sat smiling at it as if she'd forgotten the smile was there, and listened for the approach of Dolly.

She felt trapped there, a prisoner of her own folly, and of theirs. She had seduced herself with thoughts of being an actress, seduced herself and had been seduced.

She started, thinking she heard footsteps in the dressing rooms' corridor.

'Genny,' Daphne said gently. 'Those people out there haven't come to see you, Genevieve Clifford. They are there to see a play, one you just happen to be in. Along with five other cast members.'

Nancy nodded, clutching at a straw. 'Yes. Yes, that's a good way of looking at it, Daphne, isn't it. Thank you.'

'And there isn't an actor living, or dead, that hasn't suffered from stage fright. When I worked with Gideon Fyffe he used to regularly throw up in a fire bucket before going on.'

Nancy stared at her, as if trying to decide if that helped or not, then jumped, as Dolly in the corridor called for beginners.

'Genny and Simon to the stage, please.'

Dolly poked her head round the door and smiled at her. 'You all right, gal?'

Nancy nodded. 'Yes, thank you, Dolly.'

'That's the ticket, darling. They'll love you out there, you'll see.'

'Do your breathing exercises,' Daphne said, as Nancy made her way, as if sleepwalking, to the door.

'And hum to yourself,' Dolly added, 'when you're waiting for the curtain. Your voice is a bit up.'

'What's the house like, Dolly?' Daphne asked.

'Filling up nicely, dear, when I last looked,' Dolly said, standing to one side to let Nancy out.

Nancy walked with Simon as if to her doom along the corridor, forgetting about breathing exercises, and humming, forgetting about everything except what was waiting for her.

She left him in the wings and, crossing the bright emptiness of the stage as if on tiptoe, sat carefully in an armchair placed stage left, within whispering distance of the prompt corner.

She picked up the novel she was supposed to be reading when the front door bell went, her cue to say the first line of the play. She stared unseeing at the page, trying to stop her hands shaking, and listening to the audience on the other side of the curtain.

Then it went quiet, faded, she knew, with the house lights.

And when the curtain went up on the opening scene it was no longer Genevieve Clifford the actress sitting there, but Nancy Dunn the fraudster from Catford.

Nancy Dunn startled then, when Hector, in the wings and cued by Dolly, pressed the switch on the bell board for the front door.

She forgot her direction of checking, as a reader lost in her book, that there was no one else in the room, before calling, 'I'll get it!', the line coming out like a choked cry of alarm.

And when she left the stage, she left as if escaping from it. As she intended doing, from the stage and the theatre, had not Titus and Jack been waiting in the wings.

'That's it. I'm sorry, but I can't do it. It's not me. I'm not cut out for it. I'm a gingerbread man after all,' she added to Jack, with something that sounded like a laugh.

'No, you're not,' Jack said.

'Just watch me. I'll pick up my things and go. I'll sorry but there it is,' she said, while Simon, who, as Rupert Kenton-Browne, was supposed to be the one at the front door, gnawed on a fingernail and wondered what this threatened disaster would mean for his career.

'My dear girl,' Titus said, 'we understand. We've all gone through it. Gielgud walked out once as Richard the Second, abdicated between scene changes, and was found wringing his hands in full costume a couple of streets away. He then took that terror back with him and let it loose on the part. Agate, in his review of the play, said it was the finest Shakespearean acting he'd ever seen on the English stage.'

'So instead of running away from it,' Jack said, 'face it and use it, Genny. It's what we do.'

'Adrenaline,' Titus added. 'The actor's fuel. Johnny swears by it now.'

'Don't go back now, Genny, please,' Jack urged, waving a hand in a direction intended to be Catford. 'Not when you've come so far. You can do it, Genny. You can do it,' he said again, but with more desperation than anything else. This was the disaster he always knew was possible. His folly coming home.

Through the scenery door Nancy had left open he could hear the audience becoming increasingly restless.

She looked from one man to the other, then her shoulders slumped.

'All right. All right. I'll do it. I'll go on again. OK? I'll go back. But don't blame me, that's all I'm saying. Don't blame me.'

'Good girl,' Titus said, while wondering, as he had when she'd first read for the part, if he was doing the right thing.

'It'll be fine,' Jack added. 'It'll be fine, Genny. You'll see.'

She looked at him, her dark eyes darker, as if with a dreadful knowledge that was hers alone to bear.

'It won't, you know, Jack. But I'll go on…'

Margaret Lockwood in *Madness of the Heart*, Jack thought, and felt reassured.

She walked back on stage ahead of Simon as if at gunpoint, as if surrendering to it, their entrance quietening the audience.

Simon delivered his opening words as if continuing, as directed, what he'd been saying before entering. '... Yes, one of the barristers recommended it. Good nosh and a decent wine list. I thought we'd give it a whirl. What...?' he added then, the unscripted word jumping nervously out when he realised she'd dried.

Dolly supplied the line and Nancy echoed it in a mumble.

'Speak up!' someone shouted.

The audience, as Titus termed it, had turned insolent.

Under the greasepaint Nancy's cheeks burned with heat, while the rest of her felt chilled, as she stumbled on, remembering what she had been taught one minute, forgetting it the next. Dolly had never been so busy.

Then the curtain dropped for the scene change, in which Miss Harris and odd-job man Tom Yardley meet for the first time.

The sitting room set turned into the hallway of the house, Bobby, her two casuals and the actors pitching in, the furniture and dressings piled in one of the wings ready to go on.

In this scene, Lucinda Harris enters from the street, sees Tom working on the ceiling light fitting, and is instantly attracted.

Their script notes read that Lucinda looks at Jack, and Jack looks at Lucinda. Four beats of silence between them, as directed by Titus. Four beats of silence charged with things they haven't words for yet, a conversation that continues while saying the lines written for them, while speaking of something else.

But Nancy, as Lucinda, couldn't get in. The door flat which Davy at the Empire Theatre had made them a present of because he had them to spare, had stuck again. And what Nancy had to say then was direct and to the point, words said briefly and fiercely, before ramming the door with her shoulder, and then stumbling through it out onto the stage when it opened suddenly.

Laughter from the audience brought Titus out from the wings, and he and Jack went to her as if shielding her from it.

'Genny, the fault is mine,' Titus said. 'You weren't ready, and I should have seen that. Forgive me.'

'I suggested it in the first place,' Jack said.

'And I, as manager, agreed it.'

'Yeah, well, anyway, you did what you could, Genny,' Jack said. 'You can retire with—'

Nancy bristled. 'I'm not—'

'Hey! Have you forgotten us?' someone shouted from the audience.

'I'll go and speak to them,' Titus said, 'tell them we're cancelling.'

'You will not! I'm OK now. I'm going on,' she said, glaring in the direction of the auditorium, and more heckling.

'Genny, my dear girl,' Titus said, 'this sort of thing has forced actors, seasoned, top-billing players, permanently out of stage work. They do only films. I—'

'I want to carry on! I can do it. I can do it,' she said, out of a belligerent stubbornness, aimed at both men and the audience, rather than any conviction.

Titus looked at Jack.

Jack shrugged, meaning what had they to lose?

'Are you sure?' Titus said to Nancy.

'Yes, I'm sure,' Nancy said.

'All right. Good girl,' he said, touching her cheek, hearing more noise from out front, and as if wondering if he was about to do the wrong thing again. 'I'll have a word with them. Feed them something, the brutes.'

Titus came downstage and held up his hands for quiet.

'Ladies and gentlemen,' he said, as if about to announce a death, 'we owe you an apology and an explanation.' He paused, head bent over clasped hands, working on the explanation part of it.

'Ladies and gentlemen, as actor-manager of this company, the responsibility for what you have so far seen rests entirely with me. Miss Genevieve Clifford replaced at the last minute an actress who left to take up a film offer. Miss Genevieve came to us from the ranks of mute supernumeraries and bit parts, a few words here and there, crumbs from the tables others feast at. It is by far the biggest role of her fledging career, and her first public appearance in it. And quite frankly, ladies and gentlemen, quite frankly, it overwhelmed her. I wanted to cancel, to refund your ticket money, but she is what in our trade is called a trouper. She says she wants to continue, to be given another chance. But this isn't amateur night. You have paid good money to see a professional entertainment. So I am going to leave the decision to you, the audience, the people who pay our wages. Should I cancel? Or should she be given another chance?'

Apart from the odd dissenting voice, people who'd already had their money's worth by being given something else to grumble about, the answer was as he'd expected it to be. And they were just as vocal with it as they had been when complaining, the tone even carrying criticism of Titus for suggesting otherwise.

He looked at Nancy and indicated she should join him.

'Thank them,' Jack said, and gave her a gentle push in that direction.

She stood next to Titus and bobbed a curtsy, out of a vague notion that it was a theatrical sort of thing to do.

'Thank you,' she said into a silence.

'We're with you, love! Don't worry,' someone shouted from it.

That set them off again, the voices this time in her corner, behind the underdog. Which was what Titus, who knew his British public, had hoped and thought would happen.

And Nancy gazed into the clamouring dark of the auditorium and caught her breath. It was like coming in out of the cold to the welcoming warmth of family and friends. It was like the imaginary world she had lived in and yearned for as a child, and all her dreaming since. It was like coming home, after all these years.

'Thank you,' she said again, and the words lost in that clamour, she blew a kiss.

When she picked up the scene again with Jack, she took with her what the audience had given her. That, and Titus's version of how she came to be there, releasing her from having to pretend she was a principal actress, that she was Lizzie Peters, changed things for her. It allowed her to grow.

And she was still doing that at the end of their week there, still keeping Dolly on her toes. But she knew she was getting there, she could feel it. And in her own way, as herself, not pretending to be somebody else. Not imitating Lizzie Peters, with her Royal Academy assurance and polish, not even as Genevieve Clifford the actress, but as Nancy Dunn.

Chapter 41

Reuben left the phone box in Wellesley Regis on the Hampshire coast, his eyes bright, and breathing as if he'd been running.

But he controlled himself before getting back into the Ford, sitting in the passenger seat, pretending to Frank that the pier theatre had no idea where the visiting company had moved on to.

'Oh, well,' Frank said, relieved. 'I suggest back to London then, guv'nor, and wait for him there. As Nancy Dunn said, he has to go back. That's where it is for an actor.'

Reuben laughed. 'Had you there for a minute, didn't I. No, I got the address straight off. Said me and the wife were touring, just like the others, and that was it. But unlike the others, Frankie, my son, we've finally caught up with him. He's opening there tonight. *Tonight*. In Wiltshire,' he said, looking at the road atlas.

'Where the bleedin' hell's Wiltshire?'

'The next county up, that's all. Place called Castle Malmesley. The Tivoli Theatre.'

'And how far's that?'

'Not far. There it is, look. Castle Malmesley,' Reuben said, stabbing a finger at the page. 'It's what – seventy, eighty miles? If that. We'll have something to eat here first, then I see that cinema in the town has matinees. We'll do that, then make our way to this

Wiltshire place. Don't want to advertise ourselves too much there. Then do the business and get back.'

'Look, Books—'

'Don't argue, Frank, please,' Reuben said quietly, as if asking it for both their sakes, which he was.

Because if you do, he thought, *I'll settle it here and now. Put one in your head here and dump you in the bleedin' sea.*

For he now knew about Frank. Knew that Frank, his right-hand man, someone he'd welcomed into his home as a friend, and who had been his best man at his wedding, had gone over to the Triads.

The knowledge, following on from Frank's mention of them and West End protection money, had come to him like a whisper, like someone marking his card in a club or on the street. And it had struck like a dagger to the heart.

But he was over his treachery now. The thing to do was to see it only as business. The Triads were taking over the country, a recent report in the *News of the World* had said, and Frank no doubt wanted to get in on the ground floor. He understood that, understood ambition. But not at his expense. Not while taking what he had.

So as much as he regretted it, Frank would have to go.

He intended doing him as well with the cleaver. Frank and Eddie. Known to do business together. Including, obviously, helping themselves to what belonged to the Chinese.

Some people never learn, he thought. *Not until it's too late.*

* * *

Nancy, leaving the last of Wellesley Regis behind out of the bus window, remembered how pleased she'd been to learn that the next date was on the Hampshire coast, on a pier. When they had left St Anne's it was summer, the day a parade of it, its brilliant sunshine made for the seaside and a pier.

A summer that turned to rain almost as soon as they had arrived there, and which went on raining almost every day of their week. The evening as well, on what, when they were on stage, sounded like a tin roof, to go with the raucous din of a flock of starlings that had made their home under the pier.

All of which, she'd told herself, had added to her vocal practice for getting heard at the back row of the stalls.

Not that there was anyone, for the entire week, sitting in the back row. The Marina had a seating capacity of over five hundred, and those who had braved the rain, and had seen that week's film at the town cinema, were all sitting in the front rows of the auditorium, in their damp rain hats and mackintoshes, with an air of 'this had better be good', after they'd come out in this weather.

But despite its posh name Wellesley Regis had a good fish and chip shop, and Boots lending library obligingly allowed temporary membership, and the cinema that had taken away a lot of their business ran matinees to help take up the afternoons in the rain. And she had had another week's experience on the stage, and with the play.

So she wasn't complaining, eating the last of the ice cream they'd all bought in the rain before leaving, on their to Wiltshire.

Chapter 42

When Eddie and Jack met they knew each other almost immediately. Both men had shared a war and had the medals to prove it.

Eddie, the stage manager at the Tivoli, had come in early to sort out furniture for the first afternoon run-through. Before that, Titus wanted Nancy and Jack to rehearse some new business he'd come up with for a pivotal scene. So while he and the rest of the company were settling into their digs, Nancy and Jack had turned up at the theatre.

Eddie, the son of a Mozambique father and a Liverpudlian mother, was fresh from the Liverpool Playhouse, with an accent that reminded Jack of Dublin, and with the wit of that city and his hometown. He had served during the war as a rear gunner on Lancaster bombers, immediately winning Jack's respect. A nervous flyer, he was in awe of someone who did it while being lit up in a plastic bubble and fired at from below and in the air.

Eddie was on his own, his ASM off sick, but when Jack and Nancy arrived at the theatre the furniture for the business they were to rehearse was in position. And after a brew-up in the props room, and much talk, with an Irishman and a Liverpudlian, the army and RAF, doing most of it, they made a start.

While outside in the street, only yards from the Tivoli's main entrance, Reuben and Frank were sitting, waiting, in the Ford.

They had arrived as Jack and Nancy were entering through the door Eddie had left unlocked. Reuben saw Jack but not Nancy, who'd gone in first, after Jack had held it open for her.

'That's him. That's the actor!' Reuben had said, sitting up, rigid with excitement.

'We wait, don't we, Books?' Frank said, Reuben about to get out of the car. 'It's too early for him to stay there. Then we follow him to his digs, get the lay of the land before hitting him later. Yeah?'

'Yeah. Yeah, right. I wasn't thinking.'

'Not surprising. Him turning up like that,' Frank said, as if criticising Jack.

Reuben lasted nearly an hour before saying, 'He may have left by another door. We don't know where the stage door is. He might have left by that. I'm going to take a look.'

Frank nodded, knowing there was no point in doing anything else, the way Reuben was.

He watched him walk down to the entrance, peer in through the door, and then disappear through it.

There was no one around, and Reuben found he hadn't expected there to be. It was fate, he told himself, fate that walked with him into the auditorium, following the sound of voices, and found the actor waiting for him there.

He was on stage with a woman, and when Reuben saw her face he saw someone who couldn't be there. And what was left of his reason turned her into someone else.

Someone whose presence he had started to feel lately, sometimes startling him into swinging round, as if expecting, his scalp lifting, to see her there, looking at him. Someone who, a few days ago, when driving through Dulwich, he thought he had seen, was certain he had seen, coming out of a shoe shop. She could never pass a shoe shop.

Someone he knew then who had followed him there. It was Mary, the girlfriend who knew too much; he saw Mary looking at him as she had that night.

He was shouting in his head, but out of his mouth came only sound. *You're dead! You're dead!* he told her over and over, as if to force her back to where he had last seen her, in the depths of Epping Forest, with the rustling of what might have been anything among the trees, and in the light of a moon between clouds, earth from his spade falling on her upturned face, and her eyes open still.

He lifted the Colt and Jack, an old instinct kicking in, pushed Nancy the few feet into the wings that side as he fired, then fired again, and again, and again at whatever was in his head, the sour sweetness of the shots on the air.

'He found us,' Nancy got out shakily.

'He did that all right. Come on,' Jack said, pulling her by the hand past the prompt desk, out into where magic and illusion turned into rigging ropes, wooden scenery frames, canvas flats, spots and lighting bars, paint, wires and cables.

They ran down the first corridor they saw, wires hanging down a wall as if waiting for an electrician, then had to run back when they met a brick wall with half the plaster missing and graffiti scribbled on the rest.

They took another corridor, and Jack, looking back, saw Reuben walking after them, not hurrying, simply walking after them, and firing again.

With nowhere to hide, contained in a narrow corridor, all they could do was to run.

It's as if he's out for a day's sport, Jack thought. *Walking a grouse moor.*

'We'll just keep going, just keep going,' he told Nancy. He was hoping to find the stage door, or if not then somewhere to hide and jump him as he walked past.

'Eddie!' he yelled. 'Where the bloody hell is he?'

'Where are we going?'

'The stage door. We can get out that way.'

'Where's that?'

'How the devil would I know! I've never been here before,' he said, turning into another corridor.

'No, of course not. I'm sorry, I—'

'That's all right, that's all right, I understand. Don't worry, we'll get out of here. And at least we know he's no marksman,' he added, reassuring himself as well as her, while knowing he didn't have to be in confined spaces like those. Just keep firing in the right direction and the bullets would find them.

It sounded to him like a revolver, which meant five or six shots, but he could be topping up as he went. He wondered about Eddie, wondered if he had shown his face and been shot. Wondered if he had brought death into the building with him.

'Why don't we hide in one of these,' Nancy said breathlessly in a corridor of workrooms. 'Wardrobe,' she said, reading the name on the door. 'We could hide among the costumes.' She laughed shakily at it, and then swung her head round at the sound of Reuben shouting, out of sight but coming nearer.

'No. No, rooms are traps. Come on, keep going,' he said, and ducked his head at the crack of two or maybe three shots.

He thought of the last time someone had shot at him, and wondered how Abelie was. Abelie, the scent of honeysuckle and the warm south in his arms, adding his song to hers, knowing the thought of her for what it was, his mind giving him a break from a situation that he knew was going to end badly. And end soon.

They turned into a corridor off the one they were on, and rounding a bend in it found themselves back in the prompt corner.

They ran straight across the stage into the opposite wing and saw there that they could run no further, that there was a door out to backstage that side and it was blocked.

While at the rear of the building Eddie, returning through the stage door after buying cigarettes, and hearing the shots, thought someone was messing with the sound effects machine.

Then on his way to the prompt corner and the machine, he came to an abrupt halt at the sight of Reuben in the wing corridor calmly feeding bullets into his gun.

There were two phones in the building, but by the time he got to one it may be too late. It may already be too late. The gunman may be looking for a third victim.

Anxious not to be it, Eddie waited out of sight one end of a broken bathroom flat until Reuben had disappeared round the bend into the wing.

Then he went after him, not at all sure what he intended doing, but feeling that he ought to do something.

He picked up a claw hammer from the tool bench on the way into the wing.

Reuben had paused on the stage, just outside the wing, his gaze carefully searching the auditorium, with the same calmness as when he'd reloaded.

Eddie was relieved to see no dead actors on the stage. But if they had hidden in the opposite wing then they had a problem. In breach of fire regulations, he had stored furniture there for the run-through later, along with other bits and pieces, piled in front of the little-used door leading to the offices.

He then caught movement there, and knew that the gunman had also seen it, and had started to walk slowly and steadily in that direction, the gun held out in front of him.

'They're in here, they're in here,' Eddie whispered to him, standing in the gloom with the hammer poised. And then flattened himself against the wall as Reuben turned and fired in his direction, fired without taking proper aim, as if he were of no importance.

In the other wing Jack was frantically pulling furniture away from the door while Nancy kept watch. She saw Reuben fire into the prompt corner. Firing at nothing, she thought, or at ghosts, and found it in herself to feel sorry for him.

She didn't stop to think about it. She just did it. She stepped out onto the stage.

'Uncle Reuben,' she said, walking towards him. 'It's me, Nancy.'

Reuben came to a halt, staring at her. His eyes looked wounded, whatever was in his head at bay in them, and she instinctively reached a hand out to him.

And without a change of expression, as if simply doing what he'd been told to do, he lifted the Colt to her head.

'No…!' Jack screamed with rage and rushed at him, his fingers stiffened into weapons that had killed.

Reuben, confused, aimed the gun at Jack, and then back to Nancy. Eddie, seeing then where Reuben was standing, dropped the hammer he was about to run out with, and grabbed the lever on the wall opposite the prompt desk. Springing the spur on the top of it, he pulled down hard.

Reuben disappeared. And Jack almost followed him, teetering on the edge of a drop where the floor had been, two leaves of a trapdoor open on the still, crumpled figure of Reuben below.

Eddie came out of the wing grinning, a stage manager after pulling off a bit of spectacle.

'Panto time!' he said.

Jack, for once, was lost for words.

'Was that you, Eddie?' Nancy said faintly, her eyes still taking it in.

'Aye, it was, Genny, yes. And I almost missed the cue. Out cold,' he said, peering down at Reuben. 'Not surprising. That lift floor's solid pine.'

Jack found his voice. 'I thought you might be dead, man. I thought he might have shot you. Never have I been so glad to see the RAF.'

Eddie grinned at it. 'Didn't have my number on it, Jack. I was out buying fags.'

'Didn't have our number on it, either, thanks to you.'

'Yes, thank you, Eddie,' Nancy said, with a laugh that recognised how lucky they'd been.

Eddie waved it away. 'Who is the mad fella? Anybody we know?'

'It's a long story,' Jack said. 'One I'll tell when I buy the drinks later.'

'You heard that now, Genny. You're my witness. Well, whoever he is, we'd better get down there before he comes to. If he's coming to, that is. This way.'

Eddie led them back into the wings and down a flight of wooden stairs one side of the trapdoor lever.

'Is he dead?' Nancy asked.

'No,' Jack said, 'I don't think so.'

'I thought we were going to be,' she said.

'I'll let you into a secret, Genny,' Jack said. 'So did I. Where's the gun?'

'Here. It bounced.' Eddie picked it up. 'Looks like a toy.'

'It's a Colt thirty-eight. Won't stop an elephant, but we're not elephants,' Jack said, emptying the chamber of the remaining bullets.

Eddie saw Nancy looking around and said, 'This is our trap room, Genny. Called Hell. We use the lift there for taking stuff up, equipment, props, flats, and actors – up and down. We don't have a revolving stage but we have that. We used it at Christmas for our panto, *Sleeping Beauty*. Aurora, the Enchantress, appears from nowhere in a puff of coloured smoke. The kids loved it.'

'I bet,' she said.

'I think you know him,' Eddie said then. 'I mean, know him well.'

'Well, as I say, Eddie—' Jack started.

'He was my godfather,' Nancy said.

'Ah, I see,' Eddie said with vague sympathy.

'He was a – no. No, I'm not going to say that. I'm not going to say he was a good man, even if he's dead. He wasn't. He was a murderer. He was evil,' she said, and burst into tears.

Jack went to her and held her.

'Shock,' he mouthed to Eddie over her shoulder, as if embarrassed by it.

Eddie nodded. 'Yeah, right,' he said quietly. 'I'll – er – I'll go and phone.'

* * *

A short while after that, Frank, sitting with another cigarette in the Ford, heard its bell first, then watched a black Wolseley police car pull up in front of the theatre, followed by an ambulance.

He drove carefully through the town, a respectable citizen at the wheel, while considering where to lie low until whatever was coming, whatever Reuben had started, was over.

Chapter 43

Titus made the most of the incident in time for the first of the two local newspapers on Tuesday, throwing in a film star to go with a London gangster attempting to murder the play's leading man. Nancy, even as Genevieve Clifford, was kept out of it.

The paper came out at lunchtime. Not long after that, the booking office started to take reservations. And shortly after curtain up that evening, Eddie put the House Full sign out. As he did for the rest of their run there.

And when national newspapers picked up the story at the end of that week, Titus waited for transfer offers from West End managements, which never came, the play not being a farce or whodunit, as Dolly said.

But it gave them wider publicity, which they rode over the last three dates.

A vicar added to it by denouncing them from a pulpit in rural Oxfordshire, and a Nonconformist editorial in a local paper in Buckinghamshire also helped by thundering about where the inherent immorality of the stage leads, with its mix of film stars, jealous lovers, gangsters and guns, and, it wouldn't be at all surprised, it let it be known, dope smoking. The Full House boards went out in all three venues.

And the representatives of the local watch committees, guardians of their town's morals, insisted on tickets for opening nights to judge the play's content, and came away, perhaps, disappointed.

And at the end of those three weeks there was no longer any trace of Lizzie Peters or Genevieve Clifford. Out of them had now come Nancy Dunn as Miss Harris. Nancy Dunn, in a part she was steadily making her own, in a place she increasingly felt at home in, like nightly coming home.

The bus bearing *Love and Miss Harris* travelled from Wiltshire to Oxfordshire, and then Buckinghamshire to Hertfordshire, and the end of their tour, leaving behind a dying summer.

And leaving behind also the front-page news that Reuben had been declared unfit to stand trial for three murders, the evidence for them in the Colt, and an attempted murder, and had been committed indefinitely to a secure mental hospital.

When Henry Long read that, he felt able to phone Connie. Reuben's assets, including the house on the hill, seized as proceeds of crime, she was now happily living in sin with him in the flat above the Yellow Emperor, while waiting for her divorce to come through.

She busied herself making sure Henry stayed on the path of correctness, putting the shop on a more business-like footing, and starting a mail-order service that was already successful enough for Johnny Lee to be employed as general assistant. The shop had never been busier, nor Henry more content.

And sometimes, in the evenings, dance music could be heard coming from their home over the shop, and Connie singing, singing their song, soft and low.

The company's last date was in Bishop's Bridge in Hertfordshire. Where the Puritan conscience had stalked the seventeenth century, and, as Simon was able to tell them, the pointing finger of the town's Witchfinder General sent many an innocent local woman to the gallows. And where, during their week there, scandalous gossip and rumour, exchanged in the shops and in the streets, filled the seats each night.

And then Jack at the wheel of the Phantom led the bus for the last time out of a town, over the wooded hills and along the lanes of the Essex border country, down into Kent, to Ravenscourt Manor and Robin waiting.

Chapter 44

George and Robin were married in the afternoon in a registry office in Maidstone, carried there by Jack in the Rolls streaming white ribbons, and with Dolly and Titus as witnesses.

They walked out into a shower of confetti, their guests brought by the bus, emptied now of the tour, but still bearing its legend of love on the sides, and with Hector at the wheel in a suit, instead of his usual brown overalls.

Robin's sons were at the reception, and a younger brother, and the widowed friend George had shared a house with, and Robin's friends and neighbours. He had sold a small oil, from what he called the emergency fund in a suitcase under his bed, to buy a new, off-the-peg suit, shoes, and a couple of cases of decent champagne.

The painting was by Alfred Munnings, the horse painter, and when it went under the hammer at Christie's, it fetched considerably more than the amount he'd expected it to.

Leaving him with a rather large surplus, most of which he tried to give to Titus, in the form of funding another tour of the play next year. In this he was abetted by his brand-new wife, George, simply because she had had such fun on tour, and wanted to share it with Robin.

'And I've got quite a lot of my trust money left,' she added, both of them smiling at him expectantly, like children sure of adult approval for a jolly good idea.

And although this particular adult was Titus, who had little time for what others called reality, he had to refer to it in this instance, because there was simply no ignoring it.

'Tour where, my dears?' he said, breaking it gently. 'We've done the south of England. And all tours go out from Manchester in the north, and Swansea in Wales. And Scotland also tours its own plays.'

'Well, George could just write another play,' Robin said airily. 'She's good at that sort of thing.'

'My dear Robin,' George said. 'It took me nearly thirty years to write this one.'

'Oh, well, never mind. Just a thought,' Robin said, and then pointed an accusing finger at Titus's glass. 'Titus – your glass is empty, sir! Allow me.'

They were in the kitchen, where a good deal of the reception seemed to have gravitated, used food plates piled in the sink, bottles of wine and beer, empty and full, on the long table in the centre of the room, and a large barrel of Foxwhelp cider, a gift on this day from a neighbour.

Jack sought a quieter place, and, carrying a bottle of wine and two glasses, suggested the library to Nancy, because, he said, he wanted to talk to her about her acting.

Sitting with her in that room on a worn leather Chesterfield, space made for the wine among the books on a low table in front of them, he said how well she had handled the part, how far she had come in it.

'And you have,' he said then, as if noticing them for the first time, and looking into them, 'marvellously expressive eyes.'

'Oh, yes,' she said, guessing where this was heading, and wondering if she was going to head there with it.

'The camera will love them. The camera loves eyes. *Loves* them, Nancy. And yours will one day titillate males in the back rows of cinemas from – from here to there,' he said, waving vaguely, and she realised he was drunk, or very near it.

'The eyes, Nancy, have it – always!' he insisted. 'There is no hiding in them. Who we are is in there, and always will be. And there is no hiding from it. Yours, my dear Nancy, Nancy *a ghrá*, sweet colleen, are not only pretty, your heart is in them, and shines there.'

'Oh, the blarney,' she said.

He held up a hand in protest. 'No, no. I speak only of what I see. And the camera, the camera, Nancy, when you have your day in front of it, will love them. Love them and you. It will bring out who you are, bring out the urchin charm of Nancy Dunn, and run with her. You'll see.' His hand indicated the spread of her name in lights.

She waited, wanting to hear more of this.

'Nancy – Nancy, I don't think I've ever said this to you before. Ever! Correct me if I'm wrong, Nancy, correct me if I'm wrong. But *this*, I am sure, is the first time I have said it. The very first time. The very first time, Nancy, *a ghrá*,' he said softly, directing his green gaze at her.

'The very first time you've said what, Jack?'

'Hmm?' he said, abstracted, his mind suddenly elsewhere.

'You said it's the very first time you've said something. Said *what*?'

His thoughts, coming out of nowhere, were no longer of soft words and seduction. They were in a far less happy place. They had taken him back, reclaimed him.

But instead of shutting her out, he felt her nearness like an embrace, holding him while he talked. And when he started talking, almost without thinking, without meaning to, out it all came.

It wasn't at all what he envisaged happening in the library. His talk was of war, not love. He told her things he'd never told anyone else, all the memories he'd carried about with him, his voice sounding wearied with them.

He talked about the friends he'd lost, the friends he'd left behind, the things he'd done, had to do, and the things he'd seen, talked while she sat holding his hand, talked until the tears fell with the words.

Then he was silent, his head bowed as if spent by it. And she saw that he was near sleep.

She took his glass carefully from his hand, and settled him on the sofa with a cushion for his head, and took off his shoes. Then fetched her overcoat from her room as a blanket, and left him, deep in sleep, as if drained, closing the door quietly behind her.

* * *

The next morning the guests started to depart, including some of the cast, their luggage on the bus for a last ride on it to Maidstone railway station.

Jack and Nancy would be travelling back to London on it, with Dolly and Titus, staying with them until they had accommodation sorted out.

Wells was also leaving then, leaving the country eventually, even. 'That's me done here,' he'd said. 'I'm going back to the States next year. My cousin in New York will get me work. You should all come. The English do well there, he tells me.'

'Welsh,' Titus said.

'Irish,' Jack added.

'Call my second husband that,' Daphne said, 'and you'd get a history lesson.'

'Such a *small* island, and all that *bickering*,' Wells said, waving it fussily away.

Daphne laughed. She'd laughed a lot. She had crossed a desert of dryness, sweating and brittle with need sometimes, crossing it one foot in front of the other, and had now reached green fields, a place where she had found herself again.

She was retiring from acting and joining a friend who'd opened a drama school in Hove. And Wells, for now, was returning to his bedsit and shared landing bathroom in Streatham, and Simon to the family home in Warrington, to run up his parents' phone bill calling his London agent once a day.

It was, Titus thought, like the end of term, like the end of something.

The newly married couple weren't honeymooning, because they couldn't decide on anywhere interesting enough.

But Robin had got something arranged to mark the occasion, a surprise for his wife which arrived on the open back of a lorry at dawn the next day. A dawn flushed with birdsong and the mellow light of a late summer sun.

And George, dressed for a walk in the country, as Robin had suggested when waking her with tea, had walked out into it to find the skin of a hot air balloon stretched out on the lawns.

Hector was still sleeping, but everybody else was there, Jack and Nancy turning out to wave them off, and Dolly and Titus.

George smiled at Robin, with memories of another time in it, another hot air balloon striped like seaside rock on the lawns at dawn.

'What fun,' she said, and kissed him.

The pilot and two helpers busied themselves tying the balloon to the gas burners and wicker basket, and then inflating it using a large fan, small tides of cold air rippling through it.

The morning loud then with the roar of the burners breathing life into the balloon, heating the cold air, the basket pulled, stumbling, when it took shape, as if trying to hold it back from the sky.

The basket was pulled upright and steadied. The pilot, in flying jacket and deerstalker hat, boarded it with George and Robin, and the balloon drifted for a moment, as if blown, before lifting, taking off to cheers and waving.

Titus watched it rising, seeking the freedom of the sky like a bird, its brightness climbing higher and higher, taking his thoughts with it, soaring above the humdrum, the things that held them there. And in the light of that new day he saw another, distant dawn, its shining horizon a beacon of fate. Saw it instantly, on his way to it already in his mind, travelling there not in a hot air balloon, but on a number 9 bus.

Preview

Miss Harris in the New World
(Company of Fools, Book 2)

The Red Lion production of *Love and Miss Harris* is booked to tour America, opening in Manhattan.

On arrival the group find that it's not the Manhattan with the Great White Way of Broadway at its glittering heart, but the part between the Bowery and the East River, on the Lower East Side, a vaudeville venue owned by a local mobster. And when members of a rival gang decide to disrupt the play, the action shifts from the theatre's state to its auditorium…

Determined to fulfil the rest of their tour dates, the company heads west from New York. But try as they might to shake it off, trouble seems to follow them all the way.

Also available

The Cuckoos of Batch Magna
(Batch Magna, Book 1)

When Sir Humphrey Strange, 8th Baronet and squire of Batch Magna, departs this world for the Upper House, what's left of his estate passes, through the ancient law of entailment, to distant relative Humph, an amiable, overweight short-order cook from the Bronx.

Sir Humphrey Franklin T. Strange, 9th Baronet and squire of Batch Magna, as Humph now most remarkably finds himself to be, is persuaded by his Uncle Frank, a small-time Wall Street broker, to make a killing by turning the sleepy backwater into a theme-park image of rural England, a playground for the world's rich.

But while the village pub and shop put out the Stars and Stripes in welcome, the tenants of the estate's dilapidated houseboats tear up their notices to quit, and led by pulp-crime writer Phineas Cook and the one-eyed Lt-Commander James Cunningham, they run up the Union Jack and prepare to engage.

OUT NOW

About the Company of Fools series

A collection of theatrical misfits go on tour, in this nostalgic trip back in time – sure to delight fans of P.G. Wodehouse and Jerome K. Jerome.

Their home theatre in the East End of London having been bombed during the war, The Red Lion Touring Company embarks on a tour of Britain to take a play written by their new benefactress into the provinces.

This charming series transports the reader to a lost post-war world of touring rep theatre and once-grand people who have fallen on harder times, smoggy streets, and shared bonhomie over a steaming kettle.

Titles in the series:

Love and Miss Harris

Miss Harris in the New World

Also by Peter Maughan – The Batch Magna series:

The Cuckoos of Batch Magna

Sir Humphrey of Batch Hall

The Batch Magna Caper

Clouds in a Summer Sky

The Ghost of Artemus Strange

About the Author

Peter Maughan's early ambition to be a landscape painter ran into a lack of talent – or enough of it to paint to his satisfaction what he saw. He worked on building sites, in wholesale markets, on fairground rides and in a circus. And travelled the West Country, roaming with the freedom of youth, picking fruit, and whatever other work he could get, sleeping wherever he could, before moving on to wherever the next road took him. A journeying out of which came his non-fiction work *Under the Apple Boughs,* when he came to see that he had met on his wanderings the last of a village England. After travelling to Jersey in the Channel Islands to pick potatoes, he found work afterwards in a film studio in its capital, walk-ons and bit parts in the pilot films that were made there, and as a contributing script writer. He studied at the Actor's Workshop in London, and worked as an actor in the UK and Ireland (in the heyday of Ardmore Studios). He founded and ran a fringe theatre in Barnes, London, and living on a converted Thames sailing barge among a small colony of houseboats on the River Medway, wrote pilot film scripts as a freelance deep in the green shades of rural Kent. An idyllic, heedless time in that other world of the river, which later, when he had collected enough rejection letters learning his craft as a novelist, he transported to a river valley in the Welsh Marches, and turned into the Batch Magna novels.

Peter is married and lives currently in Wales.

Note from the Publisher

If you enjoyed this book, we are delighted to share also *The Famous Cricket Match*, a short story by Peter Maughan in his Batch Magna series...

To get your **free copy of *The Famous Cricket Match***, as well as receive updates on further releases by Peter Maughan, sign up at farragobooks.com/batch-magna-signup